The Bridge

of

San Luis Rey

Books by Thornton Wilder

Novels
The Cabala
The Bridge of San Luis Rey
The Woman of Andros
Heaven's My Destination
The Ides of March
The Eighth Day
Theophilus North

Collections of Short Plays
The Angel That Troubled the Waters
The Long Christmas Dinner & Other Plays in One Act

Plays
Our Town
The Merchant of Yonkers
The Skin of Our Teeth
The Matchmaker
The Alcestiad

Essays
American Characteristics & Other Essays
The Journals of Thornton Wilder, 1939–1961

Thornton Wilder

The Bridge
of
San Luis Rey

PERENNIAL CLASSICS

First Perennial Library edition published 1986.

First Perennial Classics edition published 1998.
Perennial Classics are published by Perennial, an imprint of Harper-Collins Publishers.

Library of Congress Cataloging-in-Publication Data

Wilder, Thornton.
 The bridge of San Luis Rey / Thornton Wilder.
 p. cm.—(Perennial classics)
 ISBN 0-06-008887-7
 1. Bridges—Accidents—Fiction. 2. Accident victims—Fiction.
3. Peru—Fiction. I. Title. II. Perennial classic.

PS3545.I345B7 2003
812'.52—dc21

2002044963

07 WB/RRD 20 19 18 17 16 15 14 13

To My Mother

Contents

Foreword

—⟋⟍—

Thornton Wilder's Bridge of San Luis Rey *is as close to perfect a* moral fable as we are ever likely to get in American literature. Written near the end of the Roaring Twenties by a man barely out of his own twenties, it nonetheless feels, in its exquisite universality and ease of timeless application, ancient, classical, almost biblical. When we read the novel today, seventy-five years after its first publication, we nod in admiration, and we wonder at its uncanny ability to describe ourselves to ourselves in terms that are both essential to our species and particular to our times. One merely has to consider the central question raised by the novel, which, according to Wilder himself, was simply: "Is there a direction and meaning in lives beyond the individual's own will?" It is perhaps the largest and most profoundly personal philosophical inquiry that we can undertake. It is the question that defines us as human beings.

The novel begins precisely at noon on July 20, 1714, when a bridge on the Royal Road between Lima and Cuzco, "the finest bridge in all Peru," inexplicably collapses, and five people who happen at that moment to be crossing the bridge plummet to their deaths. "The bridge seemed to be among the things that

last forever; it was unthinkable that it should break." A devout, metaphysically anxious Franciscan missionary to the natives, a man named Brother Juniper, witnesses the collapse of the bridge and almost at once asks of the event, "Why did this happen to *those* five?" He is convinced that the accident cannot be other than "a sheer Act of God," and believes, therefore, that a scrupulously scientific examination of those five lives will reveal why they, and no one else among the thousands who might just as easily have been crossing to or from Lima at that moment, were killed. He decides to ferret out the facts of those lives: "He thought he saw in the same accident the wicked visited by destruction and the good called early to Heaven. He thought he saw pride and wealth confounded as an object lesson to the world, and he thought he saw humility crowned and rewarded for the edification of the city." Brother Juniper's pursuit of "the facts of those lives" will be a devout Christian's scientific investigation into the will of God undertaken for the strict purpose of proving to his converts ("poor, obstinate converts, so slow to believe that their pains were inserted into their own lives for their own good") that our destinies are controlled by God and that, therefore, regardless of how skewed toward randomness and chaos and suffering all things seem, everything—even the apparently accidental collapse of a bridge—has a divine purpose.

As his investigation proceeds, we eventually learn, of course, that those five lives were not at all what they at first seemed to have been. They are a complex, engaging, all-too-human mix of characters who, by virtue of there being five, imply an entire community, perhaps even a species—one of the many reasons we can read the novel today and believe that it's about us. We're told first of the aged crone, the Marquesa de Montemayor, a widowed, lonely woman permanently alienated from her beloved daughter, Clara, who has fled her mother's suffocating love to far-off Spain and married a count. The Marquesa compulsively courts her daughter's favor with a series of voluminous,

high-style, literary letters that portray the writer as a manipulative, self-pitying narcissist, although in time we learn that there is more, much more, to her character than that. As, one hopes, would be the case for any of us: if our secret lives were sufficiently examined and known, we would not seem better or worse than first thought; only more complex and mysterious.

Falling to her death with the Marquesa is the old woman's maid and faithful companion, a convent-raised orphan girl named Pepita; she dies alongside a young man, Esteban, who, in despair over the death of his twin brother, has recently botched a suicide attempt and has reluctantly decided to begin his life anew by running off to sea. Also crossing the bridge that fateful noon was Uncle Pio, an "aged Harlequin," a literary man of the theater and retired adventurer who has devoted long years of his life to the tutelage and sponsorship of the great Peruvian actress Camila Perichole, now retired and living in rural seclusion. Accompanying Uncle Pio is a child, Jaime, the son of the famed actress, who has been given over to the old man to be taken back to Lima, there to be educated and protected by him just as she herself was years earlier. There are many memorable, gorgeously drawn, minor characters as well: the roustabout sea captain who saves Esteban from suicide; the sybaritic Viceroy of Peru, who makes Camila Perichole his mistress; the Abbess Madre María del Pilar, who rescues the orphans of Lima, including Pepita and Esteban and his twin brother, Manuel. But in the aftermath of the accident, it is the lives of the five who are killed that we, and Brother Juniper, come to know most intimately. Brother Juniper is our naïve, somewhat unreliable stand-in, and theirs are the fates that he and we must closely examine and contemplate. His investigation is ours. His conclusions, however, will not be ours. They will be judged heretical, and he will suffer terribly for having come to them.

The underlying assumption of the novel is that any one of us could have been on that bridge when it collapsed and threw five

people into the abyss. According to Wilder, the plot, such as it is, was inspired "in its external action by a one-act play by Prosper Mérimée, which takes place in Latin America and one of whose characters is a courtesan. However," he goes on, "the central idea of the work, the justification for a number of human lives that comes up as a result of the sudden collapse of a bridge, stems from friendly arguments with my father, a strict Calvinist." It's an argument, if not always friendly, that most of us have had at one time or another, if not with a Calvinist father or Jesuitical friend, then with ourselves. And we have learned that such an argument usually leads us to either a stubborn affirmation of belief or a rote recitation of material fact.

But as Brother Juniper notes, "The discrepancy between faith and the facts is greater than is generally assumed." The abyss that lies between the two is thickly layered with the mystery of the meaning of human existence, and if we are to penetrate those layers of mystery, which is, after all, the ultimate aim of every serious novelist, then we must, as Wilder says in an interview, "pose the question correctly and clearly." Surely, this argues that before we can ask what is the *meaning* of human existence, we must ask what is its *nature*. As with all great moral fables, this is precisely what is asked, and answered, by *The Bridge of San Luis Rey*. And if with this novel we do not penetrate to the very bottom of the abyss, to the final, defining mystery, we descend very near to it.

For thousands of years, readers in search of answers to such ultimate questions have turned to the moral fable. Its form and structure, rhetorical tropes, and stylistic conventions combine naturally and efficiently to dramatize the questions and propose answers that, in philosophical terms, must be not merely plausible but, in terms of our personal experience in the world, verifiable as well. *The Bridge of San Luis Rey* is both typical of the form and exemplary. In modern times, it's a form that more often has attracted poets than fiction writers, and among the

novelists only Nathaniel Hawthorne and Jorge Luis Borges have written moral fables that come up to this novel's artistic and philosophical standards.

There is something about the antique tone and atmosphere of these works that allows one to achieve almost immediate liftoff from one's mundane, day-to-day life and travel to a world of long ago and far away, where one can more easily consider ultimate matters. It's perhaps a necessary element of fable. We begin in the real, factual world, but only in order to leave it. The first sentence of *The Bridge of San Luis Rey* tells us simply the historical fact that "On Friday noon, July the twentieth, 1714, the finest bridge in all Peru broke and precipitated five travelers into the gulf below." But by the time we have finished the entire paragraph, we have been transported to colonial Peru, to the Andes, to the provincial capital of Lima, where the ashes of the Inquisition and the Spanish Conquest still smolder—for his readers, an exotic, utterly unfamiliar world and one that Wilder himself would not visit until 1941.

In certain ways, the prose seems antique, although not in the least antiquated. It reads almost as if freshly translated from an eighteenth-century Spanish chronicle composed by a brilliantly lucid stylist. Wilder's sentences are elegant, but never self-admiring, exquisitely balanced, yet not overformal, and complex without being elaborate. They are closer in construction and diction to Hawthorne's sentences than to those of Wilder's famous contemporaries, Hemingway, Fitzgerald, Faulkner, and Dos Passos. Appropriate to the form, it's an aphoristic style, resembling that of wisdom-literature, as in, "Now he discovered that secret from which one never recovers, that even in the most perfect love one person loves less profoundly than the other. There may be two equally good, equally gifted, equally beautiful, but there can never be two that love one another equally well." Also typical of the form, but executed here with mild irony and aplomb, Wilder indulges in old-fashioned catalogues

("He possessed the six attributes of the adventurer—a memory for names and faces, with the aptitude for altering his own; the gift of tongues; inexhaustible invention; secrecy; the talent for falling into conversation with strangers; and that freedom from conscience that springs from a contempt for the dozing rich he preyed upon"), broad symbols and flattened emblems, symmetries, parallelisms, and interlocking triangular relationships, reminding one at times of certain postmodernist writers like Milan Kundera and Umberto Eco. Though Wilder is in no way a "writer's writer," *The Bridge of San Luis Rey* can be read as a writer's manual of style.

The novel lives on, however, generation after generation, not for the excellence of its style or for the simplicity and efficiency of its construction or for the warm vividness of its characters. It lives on because it celebrates our conflicted, contradictory, eternal human nature, our essential *humanity*. We are the only species that does not know its own nature naturally and with each new generation has to be shown it anew. It is interesting, therefore, and possibly useful to consider this novel in the long and (at the time of this writing) still darkening shadow of the terrorist attacks on New York City and Washington, D.C., on September 11, 2001.

Our relation to those terrible events is not unlike Brother Juniper's relation to the collapse of the bridge. On that day in September and over the months that followed, we all, thanks to the miracle of modern video technology, became witnesses to an event that defies our moral understanding and tempts us to try puzzling out the mind of God, hoping thereby to justify the ways of God to man. This was Brother Juniper's obsession and his heresy. For many of us, it has become ours, too. And it was not merely appropriate, it was a necessary admonition, that, at the memorial service in New York for British victims of the attack on the World Trade Center, British Prime Minister Tony Blair chose to read the closing sentences of *The Bridge of San*

Luis Rey: "But soon we shall die and all memory of those five will have left the earth, and we ourselves shall be loved for a while and forgotten. But the love will have been enough; all those impulses of love return to the love that made them. Even memory is not necessary for love. There is a land of the living and a land of the dead and the bridge is love, the only survival, the only meaning."

—Russell Banks
Saratoga Springs, New York

The Bridge

of

San Luis Rey

Part One

Perhaps an Accident

—⁓—

On Friday noon, July the twentieth, 1714, the finest bridge in all
Peru broke and precipitated five travelers into the gulf below.
This bridge was on the highroad between Lima and Cuzco and
hundreds of persons passed over it every day. It had been woven
of osier by the Incas more than a century before and visitors to
the city were always led out to see it. It was a mere ladder of thin
slats swung out over the gorge, with handrails of dried vine.
Horses and coaches and chairs had to go down hundreds of feet
below and pass over the narrow torrent on rafts, but no one, not
even the Viceroy, not even the Archbishop of Lima, had
descended with the baggage rather than cross by the famous
bridge of San Luis Rey. St. Louis of France himself protected it,
by his name and by the little mud church on the further side.
The bridge seemed to be among the things that last forever; it
was unthinkable that it should break. The moment a Peruvian
heard of the accident he signed himself and made a mental cal-
culation as to how recently he had crossed by it and how soon he
had intended crossing by it again. People wandered about in a
trance-like state, muttering; they had the hallucination of seeing
themselves falling into a gulf.

There was a great service in the Cathedral. The bodies of the victims were approximately collected and approximately separated from one another, and there was great searching of hearts in the beautiful city of Lima. Servant girls returned bracelets which they had stolen from their mistresses, and usurers harangued their wives angrily, in defense of usury. Yet it was rather strange that this event should have so impressed the Limeans, for in that country those catastrophes which lawyers shockingly call the "acts of God" were more than usually frequent. Tidal waves were continually washing away cities; earthquakes arrived every week and towers fell upon good men and women all the time. Diseases were forever flitting in and out of the provinces and old age carried away some of the most admirable citizens. That is why it was so surprising that the Peruvians should have been especially touched by the rent in the bridge of San Luis Rey.

Everyone was very deeply impressed, but only one person did anything about it, and that was Brother Juniper. By a series of coincidences so extraordinary that one almost suspects the presence of some Intention, this little red-haired Franciscan from Northern Italy happened to be in Peru converting the Indians and happened to witness the accident.

It was a very hot noon, that fatal noon, and coming around the shoulder of a hill Brother Juniper stopped to wipe his forehead and to gaze upon the screen of snowy peaks in the distance, then into the gorge below him filled with the dark plumage of green trees and green birds and traversed by its ladder of osier. Joy was in him; things were not going badly. He had opened several little abandoned churches and the Indians were crawling in to early Mass and groaning at the moment of miracle as though their hearts would break. Perhaps it was the pure air from the snows before him; perhaps it was the memory that brushed him for a moment of the poem that bade him raise his eyes to the helpful hills. At all events he felt at peace. Then his

glance fell upon the bridge, and at that moment a twanging noise filled the air, as when the string of some musical instrument snaps in a disused room, and he saw the bridge divide and fling five gesticulating ants into the valley below.

Anyone else would have said to himself with secret joy: "Within ten minutes myself . . . !" But it was another thought that visited Brother Juniper: "Why did this happen to _those_ five?" If there were any plan in the universe at all, if there were any pattern in a human life, surely it could be discovered mysteriously latent in those lives so suddenly cut off. Either we live by accident and die by accident, or we live by plan and die by plan. And on that instant Brother Juniper made the resolve to inquire into the secret lives of those five persons, that moment falling through the air, and to surprise the reason of their taking off.

It seemed to Brother Juniper that it was high time for theology to take its place among the exact sciences and he had long intended putting it there. What he had lacked hitherto was a laboratory. Oh, there had never been any lack of specimens; any number of his charges had met calamity,—spiders had stung them; their lungs had been touched; their houses had burned down and things had happened to their children from which one averts the mind. But these occasions of human woe had never been quite fit for scientific examination. They had lacked what our good savants were later to call _proper control_. The accident had been dependent upon human error, for example, or had contained elements of probability. But this collapse of the bridge of San Luis Rey was a sheer Act of God. It afforded a perfect laboratory. Here at last one could surprise His intentions in a pure state.

You and I can see that coming from anyone but Brother Juniper this plan would be the flower of a perfect skepticism. It resembled the effort of those presumptuous souls who wanted to walk on the pavements of Heaven and built the Tower of

Babel to get there. But to our Franciscan there was no element of doubt in the experiment. He knew the answer. He merely wanted to prove it, historically, mathematically, to his converts,—poor obstinate converts, so slow to believe that their pains were inserted into their lives for their own good. People were always asking for good sound proofs; doubt springs eternal in the human breast, even in countries where the Inquisition can read your very thoughts in your eyes.

This was not the first time that Brother Juniper had tried to resort to such methods. Often on the long trips he had to make (scurrying from parish to parish, his robe tucked up about his knees, for haste) he would fall to dreaming of experiments that justify the ways of God to man. For instance, a complete record of the Prayers for Rain and their results. Often he had stood on the steps of one of his little churches, his flock kneeling before him on the baked street. Often he had stretched his arms to the sky and declaimed the splendid ritual. Not often, but several times, he had felt the virtue enter him and seen the little cloud forming on the horizon. But there were many times when weeks went by . . . but why think of them? It was not himself he was trying to convince that rain and drought were wisely apportioned.

Thus it was that the determination rose within him at the moment of the accident. It prompted him to busy himself for six years, knocking at all the doors in Lima, asking thousands of questions, filling scores of notebooks, in his effort at establishing the fact that each of the five lost lives was a perfect whole. Everyone knew that he was working on some sort of memorial of the accident and everyone was very helpful and misleading. A few even knew the principal aim of his activity and there were patrons in high places.

The result of all this diligence was an enormous book, which as we shall see later, was publicly burned on a beautiful Spring morning in the great square. But there was a secret copy and after a great many years and without much notice it found its

way to the library of the University of San Marco. There it lies
between two great wooden covers collecting dust in a cupboard.
It deals with one after another of the victims of the accident,
cataloguing thousands of little facts and anecdotes and testi-
monies, and concluding with a dignified passage describing why
God had settled upon that person and upon that day for His
demonstration of wisdom. Yet for all his diligence Brother
Juniper never knew the central passion of Doña María's life; nor
of Uncle Pio's, not even of Esteban's. And I, who claim to know
so much more, isn't it possible that even I have missed the very
spring within the spring?

Some say that we shall never know and that to the gods we
are like the flies that the boys kill on a summer day, and some
say, on the contrary, that the very sparrows do not lose a feather
that has not been brushed away by the finger of God.

Part Two

The Marquesa de Montemayor

—ɯ—

Any Spanish schoolboy is required to know today more about Doña
María, Marquesa de Montemayor, than Brother Juniper was to
discover in years of research. Within a century of her death her
letters had become one of the monuments of Spanish literature
and her life and times have ever since been the object of long
studies. But her biographers have erred in one direction as
greatly as the Franciscan did in another; they have tried to invest
her with a host of graces, to read back into her life and person
some of the beauties that abound in her letters, whereas all real
knowledge of this wonderful woman must proceed from the act
of humiliating her and of divesting her of all beauties save one.

She was the daughter of a cloth-merchant who had acquired
the money and the hatred of the Limeans within a stone's-throw
of the Plaza. Her childhood was unhappy: she was ugly; she stut-
tered; her mother persecuted her with sarcasms in an effort to
arouse some social charms and forced her to go about the town
in a veritable harness of jewels. She lived alone and she thought
alone. Many suitors presented themselves, but as long as she
could she fought against the convention of her time and was
determined to remain single. There were hysterical scenes with

her mother, recriminations, screams and slamming of doors. At last at twenty-six she found herself penned into marriage with a supercilious and ruined nobleman and the Cathedral of Lima fairly buzzed with the sneers of her guests. Still she lived alone and thought alone, and when an exquisite daughter was born to her she fastened upon her an idolatrous love. But little Clara took after her father; she was cold and intellectual. At the age of eight she was calmly correcting her mother's speech and presently regarding her with astonishment and repulsion. The frightened mother became meek and obsequious but she could not prevent herself from persecuting Doña Clara with nervous attention and a fatiguing love. Again there were hysterical recriminations, screams and slamming of doors. From the offers of marriage that fell to her, Doña Clara deliberately chose the one that required her removal to Spain. So to Spain she went, to that land from which it takes six months to receive an answer to one's letter. The leave-taking before so long a voyage became in Peru one of the formal services of the Church. The ship was blessed and as the space widened between the vessel and the beach both companies knelt and sang a hymn that never failed to sound weak and timid in all that open air. Doña Clara sailed with most admirable composure, leaving her mother to gaze after the bright ship, her hand pressing now her heart and now her mouth. Blurred and streaked became her view of the serene Pacific and the enormous clouds of pearl that hang forever motionless above it.

Left alone in Lima the Marquesa's life grew more and more inward. She became increasingly negligent in her dress and like all lonely people she talked to herself audibly. All her existence lay in the burning center of her mind. On that stage were performed endless dialogues with her daughter, impossible reconciliations, scenes eternally recommenced of remorse and forgiveness. On the street you beheld an old woman, her red wig fallen a little over one ear, her left cheek angry with a leprous

affection, her right with a complementary adjustment of rouge. Her chin was never dry; her lips were never still. Lima was a city of eccentrics, but even there she became its jest as she drove through the streets or shuffled up the steps of its churches. She was thought to be continuously drunk. Worse things were said of her and petitions were afloat that she be locked up. She had been denounced three times before the Inquisition. It is not impossible that she might have been burned had her son-in-law been less influential in Spain and had she not somehow collected a few friends about the viceregal court who suffered her for her oddity and her wide reading.

The distressing character of the relations between mother and daughter were further embittered by misunderstandings over money. The Condesa received a handsome allowance from her mother and frequent gifts. Doña Clara soon became the outstanding woman of intelligence at the Spanish court. All the wealth of Peru would have been insufficient to maintain her in the grandiose style she fancied for herself. Strangely enough her extravagance proceeded from one of the best traits in her nature: she regarded her friends, her servants and all the interesting people in the capital as her children. In fact there seemed only one person in the world towards whom she did not expend herself in kind offices. Among her *protégés* was the cartographer De Blasiis (whose *Maps of the New World* was dedicated to the Marquesa de Montemayor amid the roars of the courtiers at Lima who read that she was the *"admiration of her city and a rising sun in the West"*); another was the scientist Azuarius whose treatise on the laws of hydraulics was suppressed by the Inquisition as being too exciting. For a decade the Condesa literally sustained all the arts and sciences of Spain; it was not her fault that nothing memorable was produced in that time.

About four years after Doña Clara's departure Doña María received her permission to visit Europe. On both sides the visit was anticipated with resolutions well nourished on self-reproach:

the one to be patient, the other to be undemonstrative. Both failed. Each tortured the other and was on the point of losing her mind under the alternations of self-rebuke and the outbursts of passion. At length one day Doña María rose before dawn, daring no more than to kiss the door behind which her daughter was sleeping, took ship and returned to America. Henceforth letter-writing had to take the place of all the affection that could not be lived.

Hers were the letters that in an astonishing world have become the text-book of schoolboys and the ant-hill of the grammarians. Doña María would have invented her genius had she not been born with it, so necessary was it to her love that she attract the attention, perhaps the admiration, of her distant child. She forced herself to go out into society in order to cull its ridicules; she taught her eye to observe; she read the master-pieces of her language to discover its effects; she insinuated her-self into the company of those who were celebrated for their conversation. Night after night in her baroque palace she wrote and rewrote the incredible pages, forcing from her despairing mind those miracles of wit and grace, those distilled chronicles of the viceregal court. We know now that her daughter barely glanced at the letters and that it is to the son-in-law that we owe their preservation.

The Marquesa would have been astonished to learn that her letters were immortal. Yet many critics have accused her of keeping one eye on posterity and point to a number of letters that have all the air of being bravura pieces. To them it seems impossible that Doña María should have put herself to the same pains to dazzle her daughter that most artists expend on dazzling the public. Like her son-in-law they misunderstood her: the Conde delighted in her letters, but he thought that when he had enjoyed the style he had extracted all their richness and intention, missing (as most readers do) the whole purport of literature, which is the notation of the heart. Style is but the faintly

contemptible vessel in which the bitter liquid is recommended to the world. The Marquesa would even have been astonished to learn that her letters were very good, for such authors live always in the noble weather of their own minds and those productions which seem remarkable to us are little better than a day's routine to them.

This was the old woman who hour by hour would sit upon her balcony, her odd straw hat casting a purple shadow across her lined and yellow face. How often as she turned her pages with her gemmed hands, she would ask herself, almost with amusement, whether the constant pain at her heart had an organic seat. She wondered whether a subtle doctor cutting through to that battered throne could at last discover a sign and lifting his face to the amphitheater cry out to his students: "This woman has suffered, and her suffering has left its mark upon the structure of her heart." This idea had so often visited her that one day she wrote it into a letter and her daughter scolded her for an introspective and for making a cult of sorrow.

The knowledge that she would never be loved in return acted upon her ideas as a tide acts upon cliffs. Her religious beliefs went first, for all she could ask of a god, or of immortality, was the gift of a place where daughters love their mothers; the other attributes of Heaven you could have for a song. Next she lost her belief in the sincerity of those about her. She secretly refused to believe that anyone (herself excepted) loved anyone. All families lived in a wasteful atmosphere of custom and kissed one another with secret indifference. She saw that the people of this world moved about in an armor of egotism, drunk with self-gazing, athirst for compliments, hearing little of what was said to them, unmoved by the accidents that befell their closest friends, in dread of all appeals that might interrupt their long communion with their own desires. These were the sons and daughters of Adam from Cathay to Peru. And when on the balcony her thoughts reached this turn, her mouth would contract with

shame for she knew that she too sinned and that though her love for her daughter was vast enough to include all the colors of love, it was not without a shade of tyranny: she loved her daughter not for her daughter's sake, but for her own. She longed to free herself from this ignoble bond; but the passion was too fierce to cope with. And then on that green balcony a strange warfare would shake the hideous old lady, a singularly futile struggle against a temptation to which she would never have the opportunity of succumbing. How could she rule her daughter when her daughter saw to it that four thousand miles lay between them? Nevertheless Doña María wrestled with the ghost of her temptation and was worsted on every occasion. She wanted her daughter for herself; she wanted to hear her say: "You are the best of all possible mothers"; she longed to hear her whisper: "Forgive me."

About two years after her return from Spain there took place a series of inconspicuous events that had a great deal to tell about the inner life of the Marquesa. Only the faintest allusion to them occurs in the Correspondence, but as that is found in Letter XXII which contains other signs I shall do my best to give a translation and commentary of the first part of the letter:

"*Are there no doctors in Spain? Where are those good men from Flanders that used to help you so? Oh, my treasure, how can we punish you enough for letting your cold endure so many weeks? Don Vicente, I implore you to make my child see reason. Angels of Heaven, I implore you to make my child see reason. Now that you are better, I beg of you, resolve that when the first warning of a cold comes you will steam yourself well and go to bed. Here in Peru I am helpless; I can do nothing. Do not be self-willed, my beloved. God bless you. I am enclosing in today's packet the gum of some tree which the sisters of San Tomás peddle from door to door. Whether it be of much use I know not. It can do no harm. I am told that in the convent the silly sisters inhale it so diligently that one cannot smell the incense at Mass. Whether it be worth anything I know not; try it.*

"Rest easy, my love, I am sending His Most Catholic Majesty the perfect gold chain." (Her daughter had written her: *"The chain arrived in good condition and I wore it at the christening of the Infante. His Most Catholic Majesty was gracious enough to admire it and when I told Him that you had given it me He sent you His compliments upon your taste. Do not fail to send Him one as like it as possible; send it at once, by way of the Chamberlain."*) *"He need never know that in order to obtain it I had to walk into a picture. Do you remember that in the sacristy of San Martin there is a portrait by Velasquez of the Viceroy who founded the monastery and of his wife and brat? and that his wife is wearing a gold chain? I resolved that only that chain would do. So one midnight I slipped into the sacristy, climbed upon the robing-table like a girl of twelve and walked in. The canvas resisted for a moment, but the painter himself came forward to lift me through the pigment. I told him that the most beautiful girl in Spain wished to present the finest gold chain that could be found to the most gracious king in the world. It was as simple as that, and there we stood talking, we four, in the gray and silvery air that makes a Velasquez. Now I keep thinking about a more golden light; I keep looking at the Palace: I must pass the evening in a Titian. Would the Viceroy let me?*

"But His Excellency has the gout again. I say 'again' because the flattery of the court insists that there are times when he is free of it. This being Saint Mark's day His Excellency started out to visit the University where twenty-two new doctors were being brought into the world. He had hardly been carried from his divan to his coach when he screamed and refused to go any farther. He was carried back to his bed where he broke a most delicious cigar and sent for the Perichole. And while we listened to long doctrinal addresses, more or less in Latin, he heard all about us, more or less in Spanish, from the reddest and cruelest lips in town." (Doña María permitted herself this passage, although she had just read in her daughter's last letter: *"How many times must I tell you to be more cautious in the things you say in your letters? They often show signs*

of having been opened on the journey. Nothing could be more ill-judged than your remarks on the you-know-what-I-mean at Cuzco. Such remarks are not funny, even though Vicente did compliment you upon them in his postscript, and they might get us into a great deal of trouble with Certain Persons here in Spain. I continue to be astonished that your indiscretions have not long since led to your being ordered to retire to your farm.")

"There was a great press at the Exercises and two women fell from the balcony, but God in His goodness saw that they fell on Doña Merced. All three are badly hurt, but will be thinking of other things within a year. The President was speaking at the moment of the accident and being short-sighted could not imagine what the disturbance of cries and talk and falling bodies could be about. It was very pleasant to see him bowing, under the impression that he was being applauded.

"Speaking of the Perichole, and of applause, you should know that Pepita and I decided to go to the Comedia this evening. The public still idolizes its Perichole; it even forgives her her years. We are told that she saves what she can, every morning, by passing alternate pencils of ice and fire across her cheeks." (Translation falls especially short of this conceit which carries the whole flamboyance of the Spanish language. It was intended as an obsequious flattery of the Condesa, and was untrue. The great actress was twenty-eight at this time; her cheeks had the smoothness and polish of dark yellow marble and would certainly have retained that quality for many years. Apart from the cosmetics required by her performances the only treatment Camila Perichole afforded her face was to throw cold water at it twice a day, like a peasant woman at a horse trough.) *"That curious man they call Uncle Pio is by her all the time. Don Rubio says that he cannot make out whether Uncle Pio is her father, her lover, or her son. The Perichole gave a wonderful performance. Scold me all you like for a provincial ninny, you have no such actresses in Spain."* And so on.

It is on this visit to the theater that further matter hangs. She decided to go to the Comedia where the Perichole was playing Doña Leonor in Moreto's *Trampa Adelante;* perhaps some material could be derived from the visit for her daughter's next letter. She took with her Pepita, a little girl about whom later we shall learn much. Doña María had borrowed her from the orphanage connected with the Convent of Santa María Rosa de las Rosas to be her companion. The Marquesa sat in her box gazing with flagging attention at the brilliant stage. Between the acts it was the Perichole's custom to lay aside the courtly rôle and appear before the curtain to sing a few topical songs. The malicious actress had seen the Marquesa arrive and presently began improvising couplets alluding to her appearance, her avarice, her drunkenness, and even to her daughter's flight from her. The attention of the house was subtly directed to the old woman and a rising murmur of contempt accompanied the laughter of the audience. But the Marquesa, deeply moved by the first two acts of the comedy, scarcely saw the singer and sat staring before her, thinking about Spain. Camila Perichole became bolder and the air was electric with the hatred and glee of the crowd. At last Pepita plucked the Marquesa's sleeve and whispered to her that they should go. As they left the box the house arose and burst into a roar of triumph; the Perichole flung herself into a frenzied dance, for she saw the manager at the back of the hall and knew that her salary had been increased. But the Marquesa remained unaware of what had taken place; in fact she was quite pleased, for during the visit she had contrived a few felicitous phrases, phrases (who knows) that might bring a smile to her daughter's face and might make her murmur: "Really, my mother is charming."

In due time the report reached the Viceroy's ears that one of his aristocrats had been openly baited in the theater. He summoned the Perichole to the Palace and ordered her to call upon

the Marquesa and to apologize. The trip was to be made barefoot and in a black dress. Camila argued and fought, but all she gained was a pair of shoes.

The Viceroy had three reasons for insisting. In the first place the singer had taken liberties with his court. Don Andrés had contrived to make exile endurable by building up a ceremonial so complicated that it could be remembered only by a society that had nothing else to think about. He nursed his little aristocracy and its minute distinctions and any insult paid to a Marquesa was an insult to His Person. In the second place, Doña María's son-in-law was an increasingly important personage in Spain, laden with possibilities of injury to the Viceroy, nay with the possibility of supplanting him. The Conde Vicente d'Abuirre must not be vexed, even through his half-wit mother-in-law. Finally, the Viceroy was delighted to humble the actress. He suspected that she was deceiving him with a matador, perhaps with an actor,—between the flattery of the court and the inertia of gout he could not quite make out who it was; at all events, it was clear that the singer was beginning to forget that he was one of the first men in the world.

The Marquesa, beside not having heard the scurrilous songs, was in other ways unprepared for the actress's visit. You should know that after the departure of her daughter, Doña María had lighted upon a certain consolation: she had taken to drinking. Everyone drank *chicha* in Peru and there was no particular disgrace in being found unconscious on a feast day. Doña María had begun to discover that her feverish monologues had a way of keeping her awake all night. Once she took a delicate fluted glassful of *chicha* on retiring. Oblivion was so sweet that presently she stole larger amounts and tried dissimulating their effects from Pepita; she hinted that she was not well, and represented herself as going into a decline. At last she resigned all pretense. The boats that carried her letter to Spain did not leave

oftener than once a month. During the week that preceded the making of the packet she observed a strict regimen and cultivated the city assiduously for material. At last on the eve of the post she wrote the letter, making up the bundle towards dawn and leaving it for Pepita to deliver to the agent. Then as the sun rose she would shut herself up in her room with some flagons and drift through the next few weeks without the burden of consciousness. Finally she would emerge from her happiness and prepare to go into a state of "training" in preparation for the writing of another letter.

Thus on the night following the scandal in the theater she wrote Letter XXII and retired to bed with a carafe. All next day Pepita moved about the room, glancing anxiously at the figure on the bed. The next afternoon Pepita brought her needlework into the room. The Marquesa lay staring at the ceiling with wide-open eyes, talking to herself. Towards dusk Pepita was called to the door and informed that the Perichole had come to see the mistress. Pepita remembered the theater very well and sent back word angrily that the mistress refused to see her. The man carried the message to the street door, but returned awestruck with the news that the Señora Perichole was armed with a letter from the Viceroy presenting her to the lady. Pepita tiptoed to the bed and started talking to the Marquesa. The glazed eyes moved to the girl's face. Pepita shook her gently. With great effort Doña María tried to fix her mind on what was being said to her. Twice she lay back, refusing to seize the meaning, but at last, like a general calling together in a rain and by night the dispersed division of his army she assembled memory and attention and a few other faculties and painfully pressing her hand to her forehead she asked for a bowl of snow. When it was brought her, she long and drowsily pressed handfuls of it against her temples and cheeks; then rising she stood for a long time leaning against the bed and looking at her shoes. At last she

raised her head with decision, she called for her fur-trimmed cloak and a veil. She put them on and tottered into her handsomest reception room where the actress stood waiting for her.

Camila had intended to be perfunctory and if possible impudent, but now she was struck for the first time with the dignity of the old woman. The mercer's daughter could carry herself at times with all the distinction of the Montemayors and when she was drunk she wore the grandeur of Hecuba. For Camila the half-closed eyes had the air of weary authority and she began almost timidly:

"I come, señora, to make sure that you could not have misunderstood anything I said on the evening that Your Grace did me the honor to visit my theater."

"Misunderstood? Misunderstood?" said the Marquesa.

"Your Grace might have misunderstood and thought that my words were intended to be disrespectful to Your Grace."

"To me?"

"Your Grace is not offended at her humble servant? Your Grace is aware that a poor actress in my position may be carried beyond her intentions . . . that it is very difficult . . . that everything. . . ."

"How can I be offended, señora? All that I can remember is that you gave a beautiful performance. You are a great artist. You should be happy, happy. My handkerchief, Pepita. . . ."

The Marquesa brought out these words very rapidly and vaguely, but the Perichole was confounded. A piercing sense of shame filled her. She turned crimson. At last she was able to murmur:

"It was in the songs between the acts of the comedy. I was afraid Your Grace . . ."

"Yes, yes. I remember now. I left early. Pepita, we left early, did we not? But, señora, you are good enough to forgive my leaving early, yes, even in the middle of your admirable perfor-

mance. I forget why we left. Pepita . . . oh, some indisposition. . . ."

It was impossible that anyone in the theater could have missed the intention of the songs. Camila could only assume that the Marquesa, out of a sort of fantastic magnanimity, was playing the farce of not having noticed it. She was almost in tears: "But you are so good to overlook my childishness, señora,—I mean Your Grace. I did not know. I did not know your goodness. Señora, permit me to kiss your hand."

Doña María held out her hand astonished. She had not for a long time been addressed with such consideration. Her neighbors, her tradespeople, her servants—for even Pepita lived in awe of her,—her very daughter had never approached her thus. It induced a new mood in her; one that must very likely be called maudlin. She became loquacious:

"Offended, offended at you, my beautiful, . . . my gifted child? Who am I, a . . . an unwise and unloved old woman, to be offended at you? I felt, my daughter, as though I were—what says the poet?—*surprising through a cloud the conversation of the angels.* Your voice kept finding new wonders in our Moreto. When you said:

> *Don Juan, si mi amor estimas,*
> *Y la fe segura es necia,*
> *Enojarte mis temores*
> *Es no querarme discreta.*
> *¿Tan seguros. . . .*

and so on,—that was true! And what a gesture you made at the close of the First Day. There, with your hand so. Such a gesture as the Virgin made, saying to Gabriel: How is it possible that I shall have a child? No, no, you will begin to have resentment at me, for I am going to tell you about a gesture that you may

remember to use some day. Yes, it would fit well into that scene where you forgive your Don Juan de Lara. Perhaps I should tell you that I saw it made one day by my daughter. My daughter is a very beautiful woman . . . everyone thinks. Did . . . did you know my Doña Clara, Señora?"

"Her Grace often did me the honor of visiting my theater. I knew the Condesa well by sight."

"Do not remain so, on one knee, my child.—Pepita, tell Jenarito to bring this lady some sweetcakes at once. Think, one day we fell out, I forget over what. Oh, there is nothing strange in that; all we mothers from time to time. . . . Look, can you come a little closer? You must not believe the town that says she was unkind to me. You are a great woman with a beautiful nature and you can see further than the crowd sees in these matters.—It is a pleasure to talk to you. What beautiful hair you have! What beautiful hair!—She had not a warm impulsive nature, I know that. But, oh, my child, she has such a store of intelligence and graciousness. Any misunderstandings between us are so plainly my fault; is it not wonderful that she is so quick to forgive me? This day there fell one of those little moments. We both said hasty things and went off to our rooms. Then each turned back to be forgiven. Finally only a door separated us and there we were pulling it in contrary ways. But at last she . . . took my . . . face . . . thus, in her two white hands. So! Look!"

The Marquesa almost fell out of her chair as she leaned forward, her face streaming with happy tears, and made the beatific gesture. I should say the mythical gesture, for the incident was but a recurring dream.

"I am glad you are here," she continued, "for now you have heard from my own lips that she is not unkind to me, as some people say. Listen, señora, the fault was mine. Look at me. Look at me. There was some mistake that made me the mother of so beautiful a girl. I am difficult. I am trying. You and she are great women. No, do not stop me: you are rare women, and I am only

a nervous . . . a foolish . . . a stupid woman. Let me kiss your feet. I am impossible. I am impossible. I am impossible."

Here indeed the old woman did fall out of her chair and was gathered up by Pepita and led back to her bed. The Perichole walked home in consternation and sat for a long time gazing into her eyes in the mirror, her palms pressed against her cheeks.

But the person who saw most of the difficult hours of the Marquesa was her little companion, Pepita. Pepita was an orphan and had been brought up by that strange genius of Lima, the Abbess Madre María del Pilar. The only occasion upon which the two great women of Peru (as the perspective of history was to reveal them) met face to face was on the day when Doña María called upon the directress of the Convent of Santa María Rosa de las Rosas and asked if she might borrow some bright girl from the orphanage to be her companion. The Abbess gazed hard at the grotesque old woman. Even the wisest people in the world are not perfectly wise and Madre María del Pilar who was able to divine the poor human heart behind all the masks of folly and defiance, had always refused to concede one to the Marquesa de Montemayor. She asked her a great many questions and then paused to think. She wanted to give Pepita the worldly experience of living in the palace. She also wanted to bend the old woman to her own interests. And she was filled with a somber indignation, for she knew she was gazing at one of the richest women in Peru, and the blindest.

She was one of those persons who have allowed their lives to be gnawed away because they have fallen in love with an idea several centuries before its appointed appearance in the history of civilization. She hurled herself against the obstinacy of her time in her desire to attach a little dignity to women. At midnight when she had finished adding up the accounts of the House she would fall into insane vision of an age when women could be organized to protect women, women travelling, women as servants, women when they are old or ill, the women

she had discovered in the mines of Potosí, or in the workrooms of the cloth-merchants, the girls she had collected out of doorways on rainy nights. But always the next morning she had to face the fact that the women in Peru, even her nuns, went through life with two notions: one, that all the misfortunes that might befall them were merely due to the fact that they were not sufficiently attractive to bind some man to their maintenance and, two, that all the misery in the world was worth his caress. She had never known any country but the environs of Lima and she assumed that all its corruption was the normal state of mankind. Looking back from our century we can see the whole folly of her hope. Twenty such women would have failed to make any impression on that age. Yet she continued diligently in her task. She resembled the swallow in the fable who once every thousand years transferred a grain of wheat, in the hope of rearing a mountain to reach the moon. Such persons are raised up in every age; they obstinately insist on transporting their grains of wheat and they derive a certain exhilaration from the sneers of the bystanders. "How queerly they dress!" we cry. "How queerly they dress!"

Her plain red face had great kindliness, and more idealism than kindliness, and more generalship than idealism. All her work, her hospitals, her orphanage, her convent, her sudden journeys of rescue, depended upon money. No one harbored a fairer admiration for mere goodness, but she had been obliged to watch herself sacrificing her kindliness, almost her idealism, to generalship, so dreadful were the struggles to obtain her subsidies from her superiors in the church. The Archbishop of Lima, whom we shall know later in a more graceful connection, hated her with what he called a Vatinian hate and counted the cessation of her visits among the compensations for dying.

Lately she had felt not only the breath of old age against her cheek, but a graver warning. A chill of terror went through her, not for herself, but for her work. Who was there in Peru to value

the things she had valued? And rising one day at dawn she had made a rapid journey through her hospital and convent and orphanage, looking for a soul she might train to be her successor. She hurried from empty face to empty face, occasionally pausing more from hope than conviction. In the courtyard she came upon a company of girls at work over the linen and her eyes fell at once upon a girl of twelve who was directing the others at the trough and at the same time recounting to them with great dramatic fire the less probable miracles in the life of Saint Rose of Lima. So it was that the search ended with Pepita. The education for greatness is difficult enough at any time, but amid the sensibilities and jealousies of a convent it must be conducted with fantastic indirection. Pepita was assigned to the most disliked tasks in the House, but she came to understand all the aspects of its administration. She accompanied the Abbess on her journeys, even though it was in the capacity of custodian of the eggs and vegetables. And everywhere, by surprise, hours would open up in which the Directress suddenly appeared and talked to her at great length, not only on religious experience, but on how to manage women and how to plan contagious wards and how to beg for money. It was a step in this education for greatness that led to Pepita's arriving one day and entering upon the crazy duties of being Doña María's companion. For the first two years she merely came for occasional afternoons, but finally she came to the palace to live. She never had been taught to expect happiness, and the inconveniences, not to say terrors, of her new position did not seem to her excessive for a girl of fourteen. She did not suspect that the Abbess, even there, was hovering above the house, herself estimating the stresses and watching for the moment when a burden harms and not strengthens.

A few of Pepita's trials were physical: for example, the servants in the house took advantage of Doña María's indisposition; they opened up the bedrooms of the palace to their relatives; they stole freely. Alone Pepita stood out against them

and suffered a persecution of small discomforts and practical jokes. Her mind, similarly, had its distresses: when she accompanied Doña María on her errands in the city, the older woman would be seized with the desire to dash into a church, for what she had lost of religion as faith she had replaced with religion as magic. "Stay here in the sunlight, my dear child; I shall not be long," she would say. Doña María would then forget herself in a reverie before the altar and leave the church by another door. Pepita had been brought up by Madre María del Pilar to an almost morbid obedience and when after many hours she ventured into the church and made sure that her mistress was no longer there, still she returned to the street-corner and waited while the shadows fell gradually across the square. Thus waiting in public she suffered all the torture of a little girl's self-consciousness. She still wore the uniform of the orphanage (which a minute's thoughtfulness on the part of Doña María could have altered) and she suffered hallucinations wherein men seemed to be staring at her and whispering—nor were these always hallucinations. No less her heart suffered, for on some days Doña María would suddenly become aware of her and would talk to her cordially and humorously, would let appear for a few hours all the exquisite sensibility of the Letters; then, on the morrow she would withdraw into herself again and, while never harsh, would become impersonal and unseeing. The beginnings of hope and affection that Pepita had such need to expend would be wounded. She tiptoed about the palace, silent, bewildered, clinging only to her sense of duty and her loyalty to her "mother in the Lord," Madre María del Pilar, who had sent her there.

Finally a new fact appeared that was to have considerable effect on the lives of both the Marquesa and her companion: *"My dear mother,"* wrote the Condesa, *"the weather has been most exhausting and the fact that the orchards and gardens are in bloom only*

makes it the more trying. I could endure flowers if only they had no perfume. I shall therefore ask your permission to write you at less length than usual. If Vicente returns before the post leaves he will be delighted to finish out the leaf and supply you with those tiresome details about myself which you seem to enjoy so. I shall not go to Grignan in Provence as I expected this Fall, as my child will be born in early October."

What child? The Marquesa leaned against the wall. Doña Clara had foreseen the exhausting importunities that this news would waken in her mother and had sought to mitigate them by the casualness of her announcement. The ruse did not succeed. The famous Letter XLII was the answer.

Now at length the Marquesa had something to be anxious about: her daughter was to become a mother. This event, which merely bored Doña Clara, discovered a whole new scale of emotions in the Marquesa. She became a mine of medical knowledge and suggestion. She combed the city for wise old women and poured into her letters the whole folkwisdom of the New World. She fell into the most abominable superstition. She practiced a degrading system of taboos for her child's protection. She refused to allow a knot in the house. The maids were forbidden to tie up their hair and she concealed upon her person ridiculous symbols of a happy delivery. On the stairs the even steps were marked with red chalk and a maid who accidentally stepped upon an even step was driven from the house with tears and screams. Doña Clara was in the hands of malignant Nature who reserves the right to inflict upon her children the most terrifying jests. There was an etiquette of propitiation which generations of peasant women had found comforting. So vast an army of witnesses surely implied that there was some truth in it. At least it could do no harm, and Perhaps it did good. But the Marquesa did not only satisfy the rites of paganism; she studied the prescriptions of Christianity as well. She arose in the dark and stumbled through the streets to the earliest Masses. She hysterically

hugged the altar-rails trying to rend from the gaudy statuettes a sign, only a sign, the ghost of a smile, the furtive nod of a waxen head. Would all be well? Sweet, sweet Mother, would all be well?

At times, after a day's frantic resort to such invocations, a revulsion would sweep over her. Nature is deaf. God is indifferent. Nothing in man's power can alter the course of law. Then on some street-corner she would stop, dizzy with despair, and leaning against a wall would long to be taken from a world that had no plan in it. But soon a belief in the great Perhaps would surge up from the depths of her nature and she would fairly run home to renew the candles above her daughter's bed.

At last the time came to satisfy the supreme rite of Peruvian households looking forward to this event: she made the pilgrimage to the shrine of Santa María de Cluxambuqua. If there resided any efficacy in devotion at all, surely it lay in a visit to this great shrine. The ground had been holy through three religions; even before the Incan civilization distraught human beings had hugged the rocks and lashed themselves with whips to wring their will from the skies. Thither the Marquesa was carried in her chair, crossing the bridge of San Luis Rey and ascending up into the hills toward the city of large-girdled women, a tranquil town, slow-moving and slow-smiling; a city of crystal air, cold as the springs that fed its many fountains; a city of bells, soft and musical, and tuned to carry on with one another the happiest quarrels. If anything turned out for disappointment in the town of Cluxambuqua the grief was somehow assimilated by the overwhelming immanence of the Andes and by the weather of quiet joy that flowed in and about the side-streets. No sooner did the Marquesa see from a distance the white walls of this town perched on the knees of the highest peaks than her fingers ceased turning the beads and the busy prayers of her fright were cut short on her lips.

She did not even alight at the inn, but leaving Pepita to arrange for their stay she went on to the church and knelt for a

long time patting her hands softly together. She was listening to the new tide of resignation that was rising within her. Perhaps she would learn in time to permit both her daughter and her gods to govern their own affairs. She was not annoyed by the whispering of the old women in padded garments who sold candles and medals and talked about money from dawn to dark. She was not even distracted by an officious sacristan who tried to collect a fee for something or other and who, from spite, made her change her place under the pretext of repairing a tile on the floor. Presently she went out into the sunshine and sat on the steps of the fountain. She watched the little processions of invalids slowly revolving about the gardens. She watched three hawks plunging about the sky. The children who had been playing by the fountain stared at her for a moment, and went away alarmed, but a llama (a lady with a long neck and sweet shallow eyes, burdened down by a fur cape too heavy for her and picking her way delicately down an interminable staircase) came over and offered her a velvet cleft nose to stroke. The llama is deeply interested in the men about her, is even fond of pretending that she too is one of them and of inserting her head into their conversations as though in a moment she would lift her voice and contribute a wan and helpful comment. Soon Doña María was surrounded by a number of these sisters who seemed on the point of asking her why she clapped her hands so and how much her veiling cost a yard.

Doña María had arranged that any letters arriving from Spain should be brought to her at once by a special messenger. She had travelled slowly from Lima and even now as she sat in the square a boy from her farm ran up and put into her hand a large packet wrapped in parchment and dangling some nuggets of sealing-wax. Slowly she undid the wrappings. With measured stoic gestures she read first an affectionate and jocose note from her son-in-law; then her daughter's letter. It was full of wounding remarks rather brilliantly said, perhaps said for the sheer virtuos-

ity of giving pain neatly. Each of its phrases found its way through the eyes of the Marquesa, then, carefully wrapped in understanding and forgiveness it sank into her heart. At last she arose, gently dispersed the sympathetic llamas, and with a grave face returned to the shrine.

While Doña María was passing the late afternoon in the Church and in the Square, Pepita was left to prepare their lodging. She showed the porters where to lay down the great wicker hampers and set about unpacking the altar, the brazier, the tapestries and the portraits of Doña Clara. She descended into the kitchen and gave the cook exact instructions as to the preparations of a certain porridge upon which the Marquesa principally subsisted. Then she returned to the rooms and waited. She resolved to write a letter to the Abbess. She hung for a long time over the quill, staring into the distance with trembling lip. She saw the face of Madre María del Pilar, so red and scrubbed, and the wonderful black eyes. She heard her voice as at the close of supper (the orphans sitting with lowered eyes and folded hands) she commented on the events of the day, or as, by candlelight, she stood among the beds of the hospital and announced the theme for meditation during the night. But most clearly of all Pepita remembered the sudden interviews when the Abbess (not daring to wait until the girl was older) had discussed with her the duties of her office. She had talked to Pepita as to an equal. Such speech is troubling and wonderful to an intelligent child and Madre María del Pilar had abused it. She had expanded Pepita's vision of how she should feel and act beyond the measure of her years. And she had unthinkingly turned upon Pepita the full blaze of her personality, as Jupiter had turned his upon Semele. Pepita was frightened by her sense of insufficiency; she hid it and wept. And then the Abbess had cast the child into the discipline of this long solitude, where Pepita struggled, refusing to let herself believe that she had been abandoned. And now from this strange inn in these strange mountains, where the altitude was

making her lightheaded, Pepita longed for the dear presence, the only real thing in her life.

She wrote a letter, all inkstains and incoherence. Then she went downstairs to see about fresh charcoal and to taste the porridge.

The Marquesa came in and sat down at the table. "I can do no more. What will be, will be," she whispered. She unbound from her neck the amulets of her superstition and dropped them into the glowing brazier. She had a strange sense of having antagonized God by too much prayer and so addressed Him now obliquely. "After all it is in the hands of another. I no longer claim the least influence. What will be, will be." She sat for a long time, her palms against her cheeks, making a blank of her mind. Her eyes fell on Pepita's letter. She opened it mechanically and started to read. She had read a full half of it before her attention was aware of the meaning of the words: "*. . . but all this is nothing if you like me and wish me to stay with her. I oughtn't to tell you but every now and then the bad chambermaids lock me up in rooms and steal things and perhaps My Lady will think that I steal them. I hope not. I hope you are well and not having any trouble in the hospital or anywhere. Though I never see you I think of you all the time and I remember what you told me, my dear mother in God. I want to do only what you want, but if you could let me come back for a few days to the convent, but not if you do not wish it. But I am so much alone and not talking to anyone, and everything. Sometimes I do not know whether you have forgotten me and if you could find a minute to write me a little letter or something, I could keep it, but I know how busy you are. . . .*"

Doña María read no further. She folded the letter and put it aside. For a moment she was filled with envy: she longed to command another's soul as completely as this nun was able to do. Most of all she longed to be back in this simplicity of love, to throw off the burden of pride and vanity that hers had always carried. To quiet the tumult in her mind she picked up a book of

devotion and tried to fix her attention upon the words. But after a moment she suddenly felt the need to reread the whole letter, to surprise, if possible, the secret of so much felicity.

Pepita returned bringing the supper in her hands, followed by a maid. Doña María watched her over the top of her book as she would have watched a visitor from Heaven. Pepita tiptoed about the room laying the table and whispering directions to her assistant.

"Your supper is ready, My Lady," she said at last.

"But, my child, you are going to eat with me?" In Lima Pepita generally sat down at the table with her mistress.

"I thought you would be tired, My Lady. I had my supper downstairs."

"She does not wish to eat with me," thought the Marquesa. "She knows me and has rejected me."

"Would you like me to read aloud to you while you are eating, My Lady?" asked Pepita, who felt that she had made a mistake.

"No. You may go to bed, if you choose."

"Thank you, My Lady."

Doña María had risen and approached the table. With one hand on the back of the chair she said haltingly: "My dear child, I am sending off a letter to Lima in the morning. If you have one you can enclose it with mine."

"No, I have none," said Pepita. She added hastily: "I must go downstairs and get you the new charcoal."

"But, my dear, you have one for . . . Madre María del Pilar. Wouldn't you . . . ?"

Pepita pretended to be busy over the brazier. "No, I'm not going to send it," she said. She was aware during the long pause that followed that the Marquesa was staring at her in stupefaction. "I've changed my mind."

"I know she would like a letter from you, Pepita. It would make her very happy. I know."

Pepita was reddening. She said loudly: "The innkeeper said

that there would be some new charcoal ready for you at dark. I'll tell them to bring it up now." She glanced hastily at the old woman and saw that she had not ceased from staring at her with great sad inquiring eyes. Pepita felt that these were not things one talked about, but the strange woman seemed to be feeling the matter so strongly that Pepita was willing to concede one more answer: "No, it was a bad letter. It wasn't a good letter."

Doña María fairly gasped. "Why, my dear Pepita, I think it was very beautiful. Believe me, I know. No, no; what could have made it a bad letter?"

Pepita frowned, hunting for a word that would close the matter.

"It wasn't . . . it wasn't . . . brave," she said. And then she would say no more. She carried the letter off into her own room and could be heard tearing it up. Then she got into bed and lay staring into the darkness, still uncomfortable at having talked in such a fashion. And Doña María sat down to her dish amazed.

She had never brought courage to either life or love. Her eyes ransacked her heart. She thought of the amulets and of her beads, her drunkenness . . . she thought of her daughter. She remembered the long relationship, crowded with the wreckage of exhumed conversations, of fancied slights, of inopportune confidences, of charges of neglect and exclusion (but she must have been mad that day; she remembered beating upon the table). "But it's not my fault," she cried. "It's not my fault that I was so. It was circumstance. It was the way I was brought up. Tomorrow I begin a new life. Wait and see, oh my child." At last she cleared away the table and sitting down wrote what she called her first letter, her first stumbling misspelled letter in courage. She remembered with shame that in the previous one she had piteously asked her daughter how much she loved her, and had greedily quoted the few and hesitant endearments that Doña Clara had lately ventured to her. Doña María could not recall those pages, but she could write some new ones, free and

generous. No one else has regarded them as stumbling. It is the famous Letter LVI, known to the Encyclopedists as her Second Corinthians because of its immortal paragraph about love: "Of the thousands of persons we meet in a lifetime, my child . . ." and so on. It was almost dawn when she finished the letter. She opened the door upon her balcony and looked at the great tiers of stars that glittered above the Andes. Throughout the hours of the night, though there had been few to hear it, the whole sky had been loud with the singing of these constellations. Then she took a candle into the next room and looked at Pepita as she slept, and pushed back the damp hair from the girl's face. "Let me live now," she whispered. "Let me begin again."

Two days later they started back to Lima, and while crossing the bridge of San Luis Rey the accident which we know befell them.

Part Three

Esteban

One morning twin boys were discovered in the foundlings' basket
before the door of the Convent of Santa María Rosa de las
Rosas. Names were found for them almost before the arrival of
the wet-nurse, but the names were not as useful to them as our
names are to most of us, for no one ever succeeded in telling the
boys apart. There was no way of knowing who their parents
were, but Limean gossips, noticing as the boys grew older how
straight they held themselves and how silent and somber they
were, declared them to be Castilian and laid them in turn at all
sorts of crested doorways. The person in the world who came
nearest to being their guardian was the Abbess of the Convent.
Madre María del Pilar had come to hate all men, but she grew
fond of Manuel and Esteban. In the late afternoon she would
call them into her office, send for some cakes from the kitchen,
and tell them stories about the Cid and Judas Maccabeus and the
thirty-six misfortunes of Harlequin. She grew to love them so,
that she would catch herself gazing deep into their black and
frowning eyes, looking for those traits that would appear when
they grew to be men, all that ugliness, all that soullessness that
made hideous the world she worked in. They grew up about the

convent until they were a little past the age when their presence began to be a slight distraction to the dedicated sisters. From thence they became vaguely attached to all the sacristies in town: they trimmed all the cloister hedges; they polished every possible crucifix; they passed a damp cloth once a year over most of the ecclesiastical ceilings. All Lima knew them well. When the priest rushed through the streets carrying his precious burden into a sickroom either Esteban or Manuel was to be seen striding behind him, swinging a censor. As they grew older, however, they showed no desire for the clerical life. They gradually assumed the profession of the scribe. There were few printing presses in the New World and the boys soon made a fair living transcribing comedies for the theater, ballads for the crowds, and advertisements for the merchants. Above all they were the copyists of the choir masters and made endless parts of the motets of Morales and Vittoria.

Because they had no family, because they were twins, and because they were brought up by women, they were silent. There was in them a curious shame in regard to their resemblance. They had to live in a world where it was the subject of continual comment and joking. It was never funny to them and they suffered the eternal pleasantries with stolid patience. From the years when they first learned to speak they invented a secret language for themselves, one that was scarcely dependent on the Spanish for its vocabulary, or even for its syntax. They resorted to it only when they were alone, or at great intervals in moments of stress whispered it in the presence of others. The Archbishop of Lima was something of a philologist; he dabbled in dialects; he had even evolved quite a brilliant table for the vowel and consonant changes from Latin into Spanish and from Spanish into Indian-Spanish. He was storing up notebooks of quaint lore against an amusing old age he planned to offer himself back on his estates outside Segovia. So when he heard one day about the

secret language of the twin brothers, he trimmed some quills and sent for them. The boys stood humiliated upon the rich carpets of his study while he tried to extract from them their *bread* and *tree* and their *I see* and *I saw*. They did not know why the experience was so horrible to them. They bled. Long shocked silences followed each of the Archbishop's questions, until finally one or the other mumbled an answer. The priest thought for a while that they were merely in awe before his rank and before the luxury of his apartment, but at last, much perplexed, he divined the presence of some deeper reluctance and sadly let them go.

This language was the symbol of their profound identity with one another, for just as resignation was a word insufficient to describe the spiritual change that came over the Marquesa de Montemayor on that night in the inn at Cluxambuqua, so *love* is inadequate to describe the tacit almost ashamed oneness of these brothers. What relationship is it in which few words are exchanged, and those only about the details of food, clothing and occupation; in which the two persons have a curious reluctance even to glance at one another; and in which there is a tacit arrangement not to appear together in the city and to go on the same errand by different streets? And yet side by side with this there existed a need of one another so terrible that it produced miracles as naturally as the charged air of a sultry day produces lightning. The brothers were scarcely aware of it themselves, but telepathy was a common occurrence in their lives, and when one returned home the other was always aware of it when his brother was still several streets away.

Suddenly they discovered that they were tired of writing. They went down to the sea and found an occupation in loading and unloading vessels, not ashamed of working side by side with Indians. They drove teams across the provinces. They picked fruit. They were ferrymen. And always they were silent. Their

somber faces took on from these labors a male and gypsy cast. Their hair was seldom cut and under the dark mat their eyes looked up suddenly surprised and a little sullen. All the world was remote and strange and hostile except one's brother.

But at last the first shadow fell across this unity and the shadow was cast by the love of women. They had returned to the city and resumed the copying of parts for the theater. One night the manager, foreseeing a thinning house, gave them a free admission. The boys did not like what they found there. Even speech was for them a debased form of silence; how much more futile is poetry which is a debased form of speech. All those allusions to honor, reputation, and the flame of love, all the metaphors about birds, Achilles and the jewels of Ceylon were fatiguing. In the presence of literature they had the same darkling intelligence that stirs for a time behind the eyes of a dog, but they sat on patiently, gazing at the bright candles and the rich clothes. Between the acts of the comedy the Perichole stepped out of her rôle, put on twelve petticoats and danced before the curtain. Esteban had some copying still to do, or pretended so, and went home early; but Manuel stayed on. The red stockings and shoes of the Perichole had made their impression.

Both brothers had fetched and carried their manuscripts up and down the dusty stairs behind the stage. There they had seen an irritable girl in a soiled bodice mending her stockings before a mirror while her stage director read aloud her lines for memorization. She had let fall upon the boys for a moment the detonation of her amazing eyes, immediately dissipated in her amused recognition that they were twins. Forthwith she had dragged them into the room and placed them side by side. Carefully, amusedly and remorselessly she had peered into every square inch of their faces, until finally laying one hand on Esteban's shoulder she had cried out: "This one is the younger!" That had been several years before and neither brother had thought of the episode again.

Henceforth all Manuel's errands seemed to lead him past the theater. Late at night he would drift about among the trees beneath her dressing-room window. It was not the first time that Manuel had been fascinated by a woman (both brothers had possessed women, and often, especially during their years at the waterfront; but simply, latinly), but it was the first time that his will and imagination had been thus overwhelmed. He had lost that privilege of simple nature, the dissociation of love and pleasure. Pleasure was no longer as simple as eating; it was being complicated by love. Now was beginning that crazy loss of one's self, that neglect of everything but one's dramatic thoughts about the beloved, that feverish inner life all turning upon the Perichole and which would so have astonished and disgusted her had she been permitted to divine it. This Manuel had not fallen in love through any imitation of literature. It was not of him, at all events, that the bitterest tongue in France had remarked only fifty years before: that many people would never have fallen in love if they had not heard about it. Manuel read little; he had only been once to the theater (where above all there reigns the legend that love is a devotion) and the Peruvian tavern-songs that he might have heard, unlike those of Spain, reflected very little of the romantic cult of an idealized woman. When he said over to himself that she was beautiful and rich and fatiguingly witty and the Viceroy's mistress, none of these attributes that made her less obtainable had the power to quench his curious and tender excitement. So he leaned against the trees in the dark, his knuckles between his teeth, and listened to his loud heart-beats.

But the life that Esteban was leading had been full enough for him. There was no room in his imagination for a new loyalty, not because his heart was less large than Manuel's, but because it was of a simpler texture. Now he discovered that secret from which one never quite recovers, that even in the most perfect love one person loves less profoundly than the other. There may

be two equally good, equally gifted, equally beautiful, but there may never be two that love one another equally well. So Esteban sat up in their room by a guttering candle, his knuckles between his teeth, and wondered why Manuel was so changed and why the whole meaning had gone out of their life.

One evening Manuel was stopped on the street by a small boy who announced to him that the Perichole wished him to call upon her at once. Manuel turned in his path and went to the theater. Straight, somber and impersonal, he entered the actress's room and stood waiting. Camila had a service to ask of Manuel and she thought a few preliminary blandishments were necessary, but she scarcely paused in combing a blond wig that was dressed upon the table before her.

"You write letters for people, don't you? I want you to write a letter for me, please. Please come in."

He came forward two steps.

"You never pay me the least visit either of you. That's not Spanish of you." (Meaning courteous.) "Which are you, Manuel or Esteban?"

"Manuel."

"It doesn't matter. You are both unfriendly. Neither of you ever comes to see me. Here I sit learning stupid lines all day and no one ever comes to see me but a lot of peddlers. It is because I am an actress, no?"

This was not very artful, but for Manuel it was unspeakably complicated. He merely stared at her from the shadows of his long hair and left her to improvise.

"I am going to engage you to write a letter for me, a very secret letter. But now I can see that you don't like me and that to ask you to write a letter would be as good as reading it aloud in all the wine-shops. What does that look mean, Manuel? Are you my friend?"

"Yes, señora."

"Go away. Send me Esteban. You do not even say *Yes, señora* as a friend would say it."

Long pause. Presently she raised her head: "Are you still there, Unfriendly?"

"Yes, señora . . . you can trust me to do anything for you . . . you can trust . . ."

"If I ask you to write one letter for me, or two letters, you promise never to mention to a human being what is in them, or even that you wrote them?"

"Yes, señora."

"What do you promise by?—by the Virgin Mary?"

"Yes, señora."

"And by the heart of Saint Rose of Lima?"

"Yes, señora."

"Name of the Name, Manuel, anyone would think you were as stupid as an ox. Manuel, I am very angry with you. You are not stupid. You don't look stupid. Please don't say just *Yes, señora* again. Don't be stupid or I'll send for Esteban. Is anything the matter with you?"

Here Manuel cast himself upon the Spanish language and exclaimed with unnecessary vigor: "I swear by the Virgin Mary and the heart of Saint Rose of Lima that all that has to do with the letter will be secret."

"Even from Esteban," prompted the Perichole.

"Even from Esteban."

"Well, that's better." She motioned him to sit down at a table where writing materials were already laid out. As she dictated she strode about the room, frowning, swinging her hips. With her arms akimbo, she hugged her shawl about her shoulders defiantly.

"*Camila Perichole kisses the hands of Your Excellency and says*—No, take another piece of paper and begin again. *The señora Micaela Villegas, artist, kisses the hands of Your Excellency*

and says that, being the victim of the envious and lying friends that Y.E.'s goodness permits about Him, she can no longer fight against the calumnies that Y.E. believes servant has always valued Y.E.'s friendship and has never committed, nor even thought, an offense against it, but she can no longer fight against the calumnies that Y.E. believes so readily. Señora Villegas, artist, called the Perichole, therefore returns herewith such of Y.E.'s gifts as have not been placed beyond recall, since without Y.E.'s confidence, Y.E.'s servant can take no pleasure in them."

Camila continued walking about the room for several minutes, consumed by her thoughts. Presently without so much as glancing at her secretary, she commanded: "Take another leaf. *Have you gone mad? Do not ever think of dedicating another bull to me again. It has caused a frightful war. Heaven protect you, my colt. Friday night, the same place, the same time. I may be a little late, for the fox is wide awake.* That will be all."

Manuel rose.

"You swear that you have made no errors?"

"Yes, I swear."

"There is your money."

Manuel took the money.

"I shall want you to write me more letters from time to time. My uncle Pio generally writes my letters; these I do not wish him to know about. Good night. Go with God."

"Go with God."

Manuel descended the stairs and stood for a long time among the trees, not thinking, not moving.

Esteban knew that his brother was continually brooding over the Perichole, but he never suspected that he saw her. From time to time during the next two months a small boy would approach him in great haste and ask whether he were Manuel or Esteban, and being informed that he was only Esteban, the boy would add that Manuel was wanted at the theater. Esteban assumed

that the call was for copyist's work and was therefore utterly unprepared for a visit that they received one night in their room.

It was almost midnight. Esteban had gone to bed, and lay gazing out from under the blanket at the candle beside which his brother was working. There was a light tap at the door and Manuel opened to admit a lady heavily veiled, out of breath and nervous. She threw back the scarf from her face and said hurriedly:

"Quick, ink and paper. You are Manuel, yes? You must do a letter for me at once."

For a moment her glance fell on the two bright eyes that glared at her from the edge of the cot. She murmured: "Eu . . . you must excuse me. I know it is late. It was necessary . . . I must come." Then turning to Manuel, she whispered into his ear: "Write this: *I, the Perichole, am not accustomed to wait at a rendez-vous.* Have you finished that? *You are only a cholo, and there are better matadors than you, even in Lima. I am half Castilian and there are no better actresses in the world. You shall not have the opportunity*—Have you got that?—*to keep me waiting again, cholo, and I shall laugh the last, for even an actress does not grow old as fast as a bull-fighter.*"

To Esteban in the shadows the picture of Camila leaning over his brother's hand and whispering into his ear was complete evidence that a new congeniality had formed such as he would never know. He seemed to shrink away into space, infinitely tiny, infinitely unwanted. He took one more glance at the tableau of love, all the paradise from which he was shut out, and turned his face to the wall.

Camila seized the note the moment it was done, pushed a coin along the table and in a last flurry of black lace, scarlet beads and excited whispers left the room. Manuel turned from the door with his candle. He sat down, put his hands over his ears, his elbows on his knees. He worshipped her. He murmured to

himself over and over again that he worshipped her, making of the sound a sort of incantation and an obstacle to thought.

He emptied his mind of everything but a singsong, and it was this vacancy that permitted him to become aware of Esteban's mood. He seemed to hear a voice that proceeded from the shadows saying: "Go and follow her, Manuel. Don't stay here. You'll be happy. There's room for us all in the world." Then the realization became even more intense and he received a mental image of Esteban going a long way off and saying good-bye many times as he went. He was filled with terror; by the light of it he saw that all the other attachments in the world were shadows, or the illusions of fever, even Madre María del Pilar, even the Perichole. He could not understand why Esteban's misery should present itself as demanding a choice between him and the Perichole, but he could understand Esteban's misery, as misery. And at once he sacrificed everything to it, if it can be said we ever sacrifice anything save what we know we can never attain, or what some secret wisdom tells us it would be uncomfortable or saddening to possess. To be sure there was nothing on which Esteban could base a complaint. It was not jealousy, for in their earlier affairs it had never occurred to either of them that their loyalty to one another had been diminished. It was merely that in the heart of one of them there was left room for an elaborate imaginative attachment and in the heart of the other there was not. Manuel could not quite understand this and, as we shall see, he nourished a dim sense of being accused unjustly. But he did understand that Esteban was suffering. In his excitement he groped for a means of holding this brother who seemed to be receding into the distance. And at once, in one unhesitating stroke of the will, he removed the Perichole from his heart.

He blew out the candle and lay down on his bed. He was trembling. He said loud with exaggerated casualness: "Well, that's the last letter I write for that woman. She can go and find

a pander somewhere else. If ever she calls here or sends for me when I'm out, tell her so. Make it plain. That's the last I have to do with her," and with that he began reciting his evening psalm aloud. But he had hardly reached *A sagitta volante in die* when he became aware that Esteban had risen and was lighting the candle.

"What's the matter?" he asked.

"I'm going out for a walk," replied Esteban somberly, fastening his belt. After a moment, he broke out with an assumption of anger: "You don't have to say . . . what you just said, for me. I don't care whether you write her letters or not. You don't have to change for me. I haven't anything to do with that."

"Go to bed, you fool. God, you're a fool, Esteban. What made you think I said that, for you? Don't you believe I mean it when I say I'm through with her? Do you think I want to write any more of her dirty letters and get paid for them like that?"

"It's all right. You love her. You don't have to change because of me."

" '*Love* her?' *Love* her? You're crazy, Esteban. How could I love her? What chance would there be for me? Do you suppose she'd give me those letters to write if there were any chance? Do you suppose she'd push a piece of money across the table every time. . . . You're crazy, Esteban, that's all."

There was a long pause. Esteban would not go to bed. He sat by the candle in the middle of the room, tapping with his hand on the edge of the table.

"Go to bed, you fool," shouted Manuel, rising on one elbow under the blanket. He was talking in their secret language and the new pain at his heart gave a greater ring of reality to his assumption of rage. "I'm all right."

"I won't. I'm going out for a walk," replied Esteban picking up his coat.

"You can't go out for a walk. It's two o'clock. It's raining. You can't go and walk about for hours like that. Look, Esteban,

I swear to you there's nothing left to all that. I don't love her. I only did for a time."

By now Esteban stood in the dark of the open door. In the unnatural voice with which we make the greatest declarations of our lives, he muttered: "I'm in your way," and turned to go.

Manuel leapt out of his bed. His head seemed to be full of a great din, a voice crying out that Esteban was going away forever, was leaving him alone forever. "In the name of God, in the name of God, Esteban, come back here."

Esteban came back and went to bed and the matter was not mentioned again for many weeks. The very next evening Manuel had an opportunity of declaring his position. A messenger arrived from the Perichole and was told harshly to inform the actress that Manuel would write no more letters for her.

One evening Manuel tore open the flesh on his knee against a piece of metal.

Neither brother had ever been ill for as much as a day in his life, and now Manuel, utterly bewildered, watched his leg swell and felt the waves of pain rise and fall in his body. Esteban sat by and stared at his face trying to imagine what great pain was. At last one midnight Manuel remembered that the sign board of a certain hairdresser in the city described the proprietor as an experienced barber and surgeon. Esteban ran through the streets to fetch him. He pounded on the door. Presently a woman leaned out of a window and announced that her husband would be back in the morning. During the fearful hours that followed, they told one another that when the doctor had seen the leg all would be well. He would do something about it, and Manuel would be out around the town in a day or two, even in a day perhaps, even less than a day.

The barber arrived and prescribed various draughts and ointments. Esteban was instructed to lay cold cloths on his brother's

leg every hour. The barber withdrew and the brothers sat down to wait for the pain to subside. But while they continued staring into one another's face waiting for the miracle of science the pain grew worse. Hour after hour Esteban approached with his dripping towel and they discovered that the moment of its application was the worst of all. With all the fortitude in the world Manuel could not prevent himself from shouting and from flinging himself about upon the bed. Night came on and still Esteban stolidly waited and watched and worked. Nine, ten, eleven. Now when the time drew near to apply the cloths (the hour struck so musically from all those towers) Manuel would plead with Esteban not to do his work. He would resort to guile and declare that he scarcely felt it. But Esteban, his heart bursting with pain and his lips a line of iron, would roll back the blanket and bind the towel fiercely in its place. Manuel gradually became delirious and under this application all the thoughts he did not permit himself in his right mind would burst magnified from his mouth.

Finally at two o'clock, out of his mind with rage and pain, and flinging himself half out of the bed until his head struck the floor, Manuel cried: "God condemn your soul to the hottest hell there is. A thousand devils torture you forever, Esteban. God condemn your soul, do you hear?" At first, the air gone out of his body, Esteban went out into the hall and leaned against the door, his mouth and eyes wide open. Still he heard from within: "Yes, Esteban, may God damn your beastly soul forever, do you hear that? For coming between me and what was mine by right. She was mine, do you hear, and what right had you. . . ." and he would go off into an elaborate description of the Perichole.

These outbursts recurred hourly. It was some time before Esteban was able to realize that his brother's mind was not then clear. After some moments of horror, in which his being a

devout believer had its part, he would return to the room and go about his duties with bent head.

Towards dawn his brother became serener. (For what human ill does not dawn seem to be an alleviation?) It was in one of these intervals that Manuel said quite calmly:

"God's son! I feel better, Esteban. Those cloths must be good after all. You'll see. I'll be up and around tomorrow. You haven't slept for days. You'll see I won't cause you any more trouble, Esteban."

"It's no trouble, you fool."

"You mustn't take me seriously when I try and stop you putting on the old cloths, Esteban."

A long pause. At last Esteban brought out, barely audible:

"I think . . . don't you think it would be fine if I sent for the Perichole? She could just come and see you for a few minutes, I mean. . . ."

"Her? You still thinking about her? I wouldn't have her here for anything. No."

But Esteban was not content yet. He dragged up a few more phrases from the very center of his being:

"Manuel, you still feel, don't you, that I came between you and the Perichole and you don't remember that I told you it was all right with me. I swear to you I'd have been glad if you'd gone away with her, or anything."

"What are you bringing that up for, Esteban? I tell you, in God's own name, I never think of that. She's nothing to me. When are you going to forget that, Esteban? I tell you I'm glad things are as they are. Look, I got to get angry when you keep going back to that."

"Manuel, I wouldn't speak of it again, only when you get angry at me about the cloths . . . you, you get angry at me about that, too. And you talk about it and you"

"Look, I'm not responsible what I say. My old leg hurts then, see."

"Then you don't damn me to hell because . . . it looks like I came between you and the Perichole?"

"Damn you to . . . ? What makes you say that? You're going crazy, Esteban; you're imagining things. You haven't had any sleep, Esteban. I've been a curse to you and you're losing your health because of me. But you'll see, I won't trouble you much more. How could I damn you to hell, Esteban, when you're all I've got? Understand, see, that when the cold cloths go on, I just lose myself, see. You know. Don't think about it twice. It's time to put them on now. I won't say a word."

"No, Manuel, I'll skip this time. It won't do you any harm, I'll just skip this time."

"I've got to get well, Esteban. I've got to get up soon, you know. Put them on. But one minute—give me the crucifix. I swear by the blood and body of Christ that if I say anything against Esteban, I don't mean it and it's just the foolish words when I'm dreaming because of the pain in my leg. God make me well again soon, amen. Put it back. There. Now I'm ready."

"Look, Manuel, it won't hurt if I skip just this once, see. It'll be good for you, sure, to not get it all stirred up just this once."

"No, I've got to get well. The doctor said it had to be done. I won't say a word, Esteban."

And it would begin all over again.

During the second night a prostitute in the next room started beating on the wall, outraged at such language. A priest in the room on the other side would come out into the hall and beat on the door. The whole floor would gather before the room in exasperation. The innkeeper came up the stairs, loudly promising his guests that the brothers would be dumped into the street the very next morning. Esteban, holding his candle, would go into the hall and permit them to rage at him for as long as they pleased; but after that he took to pressing his hand firmly over his brother's mouth during the moments of greatest stress. This

increased Manuel's personal rage at him and he would babble all through the night.

On the third night, Esteban sent for the priest and amidst the enormous shadows Manuel received the sacrament, and died.

Thereafter Esteban refused to come near the building. He would start off upon long walks, but presently drifting back, would hang about, staring at passers-by, within two streets of where his brother lay. The innkeeper failing to make any impression upon him and remembering that the boys were brought up at the Convent of Santa María Rosa de las Rosas, sent for the Abbess. Simply and soundly she directed all that was to be done. At last she went down to the street corner and spoke to Esteban. He watched her approach him, a glance mixed of longing and distrust. But when she stood near him he turned sideways and looked away.

"I want you to help me. Won't you come in and see your brother? Won't you come in and help me?"

"No."

"You won't help me!" A long pause. Suddenly as she stood there full of her helplessness there flashed through her mind an incident of many years before: the twin brothers about fifteen years old were sitting at her knee and she was telling them the story of the crucifixion. Their large grave eyes were fixed upon her lips. Suddenly Manuel had cried out loudly: "If Esteban and I had been there we would have prevented it."

"Well, then, if you won't help me, will you tell me which you are?"

"Manuel," said Esteban.

"Manuel, won't you come and sit with me up there for just a short time?"

After a long pause: "No."

"But Manuel, dear Manuel, can't you remember as children how you did so many things for me? You were willing to go

across the town on some little errand. When I was ill you made the cook let you bring me my soup?" Another woman would have said: "Do you remember how much I did for you?"

"Yes."

"I, too, Manuel have lost. I too . . . once. We know that God has taken them into His hands. . . ." But this did not do at all. Esteban turned vaguely and walked away from her. When he had gone about twenty paces he stopped and stared down a side-street, like a dog who wants to go away, but is reluctant to offend the master who calls him back.

That was all they could get out of him. When the fearful procession passed through the city, with its black hoods and masks, its candles in broad daylight, its display of heaped-up skulls, its terrifying psalms, Esteban followed it in the parallel streets, catching glimpses of it from a distance, like a savage.

All Lima was interested in this separation of the brothers. Housewives whispered together sympathetically about it as they unfurled their carpets from the balconies. The men in the wine shops, alluding to it, shook their heads and smoked in silence for a while. Travelers from the interior told of seeing Esteban as he strayed with eyes like coals along the dried-up beds of rivers or through the great ruins of the old race. A herder of llamas had come upon him standing upon a hilltop, asleep or dazed, wet with dew under the stars. Some fishermen surprised him swimming far out from shore. From time to time he would find work to do, he would become a shepherd or a carter, but after a few months would disappear and stride from province to province. But he always returned to Lima. One day he appeared at the door of the Perichole's dressing-room; he made as though to speak, gazed earnestly at her and vanished. One day a sister came running into the office of Madre María del Pilar with the news that Esteban (whom the world called Manuel) was linger-ing about the door of the convent. The Abbess hurried out into

the street. For months she had been asking herself what strategy could reconcile this half-demented boy to living among them again. She assembled as grave and calm a manner as she was able and appearing at the street door murmured "My friend" and looked at him. He gazed back at her with the same glance of longing and distrust that he had shown her before, and stood trembling. Again she whispered "My friend" and moved a step forward. Suddenly Esteban turned and breaking into a run disappeared. Madre María del Pilar rushed stumbling back to her desk and fell upon her knees, exclaiming angrily: "I have prayed for wisdom and You have given me none. You have not chosen to give me the least grace. I am a mere scrubber of floors. . . ." But during the penance she set herself for this impudence the thought came to her to send for Captain Alvarado. Three weeks later she had a ten-minute conversation with him. And the next day he started for Cuzco where, it was said, Esteban was doing some copying for the University.

There was this strange and noble figure in Peru during these years, the Captain Alvarado, the traveler. He was blackened and cured by all weathers. He stood in the Square with feet apart as though they were planted on a shifting deck. His eyes were strange, unaccustomed to the shorter range, too used to seizing the appearances of a constellation between a cloud and a cloud, and the outline of a cape in rain. His reticence was sufficiently explained for most of us by his voyages, but the Marquesa de Montemayor had other light on the matter. *"Captain Alvarado is bringing you this letter in person,"* she wrote to her daughter. *"Introduce him to some of your geographers, my treasure, though it may make them a little uncomfortable, for he is the diamond of sincerity. They will never see anyone who has travelled so far. Last night he described to me some of his voyages. Imagine him pushing his prow through a sea of weeds, stirring up a cloud of fish like grasshoppers in June; or sailing between islands of ice. Oh, he has been to China and up the rivers of Africa. But he is not merely an*

adventurer and he seems to take no pride in discovering new places; nor is he a mere merchant. One day I asked him narrowly why he lived so, and he avoided my question. I found out from my laundress what I think is the reason of his wandering: My child, he had a child; my daughter, he had a daughter. She was just old enough to cook a holiday meal, and do a little sewing for him. In those days he merely sailed between Mexico and Peru and hundreds of times she waved him farewell or welcome. We have no way of knowing whether she was more beautiful or intelligent than the thousands of other girls that lived about him, but she was his. I suppose it seems ignoble to you that a great oak of a man should go about the world like a blind man about an empty house merely because a chit of a girl has been withdrawn from it. No, no, you cannot understand this, my adored one, but I understand and grow pale. Last night he sat with me and talked of her. He laid his cheek against his hand and looking into the fire, he said: 'It sometimes seems to me that she is away upon a voyage and that I shall see her again. It seems to me that she is in England.' You will laugh at me, but I think he goes about the hemispheres to pass the time between now and his old age."

The brothers had always entertained a great respect for Captain Alvarado. They had worked for him a short time and the silence of the three of them had made a little kernel of sense in a world of boasting, self-excuse and rhetoric. So now when the great traveler came into the dark kitchen where Esteban was eating the boy drew his chair farther into the shadow, but at a distance, he was glad. The Captain gave no sign of recognizing or even of seeing him until he had finished his meal. Esteban had finished long before, but not wishing to be spoken to, waited until the Captain should have left the cave. At last the Captain walked over to him and said:

"You are Esteban or Manuel. You helped me once with some unloading. I am Captain Alvarado."

"Yes," said Esteban.

"How are you?"

Esteban muttered something.

"I am looking for some strong fellows to go on my next trip with me." Pause. "Would you like to come?" Longer pause. "England. And Russia. . . . Hard work. Good wages. . . . A long way from Peru.—Well?"

Apparently Esteban had not been listening. He sat with his eyes on the table. At last the Captain raised his voice, as to a deaf person:

"I said: Do you want to go on my next trip with me. . . ."

"Yes, I'll go," answered Esteban suddenly.

"Fine. That's fine. I want your brother, too, of course."

"No."

"What's the matter? Wouldn't he want to come?"

Esteban mumbled something, looking away. Then half rising, he said: "I got to go now. I've got to see somebody about something."

"Let me see your brother myself. Where is he?"

". . . 'dead." said Esteban.

"Oh, I didn't know. I didn't know. I'm sorry."

"Yes," said Esteban. "I got to go."

"Hmm.—Which are you? What's your name?"

"Esteban."

"When did Manuel die?"

"Oh, just a . . . just a few weeks. He hit his knee against something and . . . just a few weeks ago."

They both kept their eyes on the floor.

"How old are you, Esteban?"

"Twenty-two."

"Well, that's settled then, you're coming with me?"

"Yes."

"You may not be used to the cold."

"Yes, I'm used to it.—I've got to go now. I got to go in the city and see somebody about something."

"Well, Esteban. Come back here for supper and we'll talk about the trip. Come back and have some wine with me, see. Will you?"

"Yes, I will."

"Go with God."

"Go with God."

They had supper together and it was arranged that they were to start for Lima the next morning. The Captain got him very drunk. At first they poured and drank and poured and drank in silence. Then the Captain began to talk about ships and their courses. He asked Esteban questions about tackle and about the guide-stars. Then Esteban began to talk about other things, and to talk very loudly:

"On the ship you must give me something to do all the time. I'll do anything, anything. I'll climb up high and fix ropes; and I'll watch all night,—because, you know, I don't sleep well anyway. And, Captain Alvarado, on the ship you must pretend that you don't know me. Pretend that you hate me the most. So that you'll always give me things to do. I can't sit still and write at a table any more.—And don't tell the other men about me . . . that is, about . . ."

"I hear you went into a burning house, Esteban, and pulled someone out."

"Yes. I didn't get burned or anything. You know," cried Esteban, leaning across the table, "you're not allowed to kill yourself; you know you're not allowed. Everybody knows that. But if you jump into a burning house to save somebody, that wouldn't be killing yourself. And if you became a matador and the bull caught you that wouldn't be killing yourself. Only you mustn't put yourself in the bull's way on purpose. Did you ever notice that animals never kill themselves, even when they're sure to lose? They never jump into a river or anything, even when they're sure to lose. Some people say that horses run into bonfires. Is that true?"

"No, I don't think that's true."

"I don't think it's true. We had a dog once. Well, I mustn't think of that.—Captain Alvarado, do you know Madre María del Pilar?"

"Yes."

"I want to give her a present before I go away. Captain Alvarado, I want you to give me all my wages before I start—I won't need any money anywhere—and I want to buy her a present now. The present isn't from me only. She was . . . was . . ." Here Esteban wished to say his brother's name, but was unable to. Instead he continued in a lower voice: "She had a kind of a . . . she had a serious loss, once. She said so. I don't know who it was, and I want to give her a present. Women can't bear that kind of a thing like we can."

The Captain promised him that they would choose something in the morning. Esteban talked about it at great length. At last the Captain saw him slip under the table, and himself, rising up, went out into the square before the inn. He looked at the line of the Andes and at the streams of stars crowding forever across the sky. And there was that wraith hanging in midair and smiling at him, the wraith with the silvery voice that said for the thousandth time: "Don't be gone long. But I'll be a big girl when you get back." Then he went within and carried Esteban to his room and sat looking at him for a long while.

The next morning he was waiting at the bottom of the stairs when Esteban appeared:

"We're starting when you're ready," said the Captain.

The strange glitter had returned to the boy's eyes. He blurted out: "No, I'm not coming. I'm not coming after all."

"Aïe! Esteban! But you have promised me that you would come."

"It's impossible. I can't come with you," and he turned back up the stairs.

"Come here a moment, Esteban, just a moment."

"I can't come with you. I can't leave Peru."

"I want to tell you something."

Esteban came down to the foot of the stairs.

"How about that present for Madre María del Pilar?" asked the Captain in a low voice. Esteban was silent, looking over the mountains. "You aren't going to take that present away from her? It might mean a lot to her . . . you know."

"All right," murmured Esteban, as though much impressed.

"Yes. Besides the ocean's better than Peru. You know Lima and Cuzco and the road. You have nothing more to know about them. You see it's the ocean you want. Besides on the boat you'll have something to do every minute. I'll see to that. Go and get your things and we'll start."

Esteban was trying to make a decision. It had always been Manuel who had made the decisions and even Manuel had never been forced to make as great a one as this. Esteban went slowly upstairs. The Captain waited for him and waited so long that presently he ventured half the way up the stairs and listened. At first there was silence; then a series of noises that his imagination was able to identify at once. Esteban had scraped away the plaster about a beam and was adjusting a rope about it. The Captain stood on the stairs trembling: "Perhaps it's best," he said to himself. "Perhaps I should leave him alone. Perhaps it's the only thing possible for him." Then on hearing another sound he flung himself against the door, fell into the room and caught the boy. "Go away," cried Esteban. "Let me be. Don't come in now."

Esteban fell face downward upon the floor. "I am alone, alone, alone," he cried. The Captain stood above him, his great plain face ridged and gray with pain; it was his own old hours he was reliving. He was the awkwardest speaker in the world apart from the lore of the sea, but there are times when it requires a high courage to speak the banal. He could not be sure the figure

on the floor was listening, but he said, "We do what we can. We push on, Esteban, as best we can. It isn't for long, you know. Time keeps going by. You'll be surprised at the way time passes."

They started for Lima. When they reached the bridge of San Luis Rey, the Captain descended to the stream below in order to supervise the passage of some merchandise, but Esteban crossed by the bridge and fell with it.

Part Four

Uncle Pio

In one of her letters (the XXIXth) the Marquesa de Montemayor
tries to describe the impression that Uncle Pio *"our aged Harle-*
quin" made upon her: *"I have been sitting all morning on the*
green balcony making you a pair of slippers, my soul," she tells her
daughter. *"As the golden wire did not take up my whole attention*
I was able to follow the activity of a coterie of ants in the wall beside
me. Somewhere behind the partition they were patiently destroying
my house. Every three minutes a little workman would appear
between two boards and drop a grain of wood upon the floor below.
Then he would wave his antennae at me and back busily into his
mysterious corridor. In the meantime various brothers and sisters of
his were trotting back and forth on a certain highway, stopping to
massage one another's heads, or if the messages they bore were of first
importance, refusing angrily to massage or to be massaged. And at
once I thought of Uncle Pio. Why? Where else but with him had I
seen that very gesture with which he arrests a passing abbé or a
courtier's valet, and whispers, his lips laid against his victim's ear?
And surely enough, before noon I saw him hurry by on one of those
mysterious errands of his. As I am the idlest and silliest of women I
sent Pepita to get me a piece of nougat which I placed on the ant's

highway. Similarly I sent word to the Café Pizarro asking them to send Uncle Pio to see me if he dropped in before sunset. I shall give him that old bent salad fork with the turquoise in it, and he will bring me a copy of the new ballad that everyone is singing about the d—q—a of Ol—v—s. My child, you shall have the best of everything, and you shall have it first."

And in the next letter: *"My dear, Uncle Pio is the most delightful man in the world, your husband excepted. He is the second most delightful man in the world. His conversation is enchanting. If he weren't so disreputable I should make him my secretary. He could write all my letters for me and generations would rise up and call me witty. Alas, however, he is so moth-eaten by disease and bad company, that I shall have to leave him to his underworld. He is not only like an ant, he is like a soiled pack of cards. And I doubt whether the whole Pacific could wash him sweet and fragrant again. But what divine Spanish he speaks and what exquisite things he says in it! That's what one gets by hanging around a theater and hearing nothing but the conversation of Calderón. Alas, what is the matter with this world, my soul, that it should treat such a being so ill! His eyes are as sad as those of a cow that has been separated from its tenth calf."*

You should know first that this Uncle Pio was Camila Perichole's maid. He was also her singing-master, her coiffeur, her masseur, her reader, her errand-boy, her banker; rumor added: her father. For example, he taught her her parts. There was a whisper around town that Camila could read and write. The compliment was unfounded; Uncle Pio did her reading and writing for her. At the height of the season the company put on two or three new plays a week, and as each one contained a long and flowery part for the Perichole the mere task of memorization was not a trifle.

Peru had passed within fifty years from a frontier state to a state in renaissance. Its interest in music and the theater was

intense. Lima celebrated its feast days by hearing a Mass of Tomás Luis da Victoria in the morning and the glittering poetry of Calderón in the evening. It is true that the Limeans were given to interpolating trivial songs into the most exquisite comedies and some lachrymose effects into the austerest music; but at least they never submitted to the boredom of a misplaced veneration. If they had disliked heroic comedy the Limeans would not have hesitated to remain at home; and if they had been deaf to polyphony nothing would have prevented their going to an earlier service. When the Archbishop returned from a short trip to Spain, all Lima kept asking: "What has he brought?" The news finally spread abroad that he had returned with tomes of masses and motets by Palestrina, Morales and Vittoria, as well as thirty-five plays by Tirso de Molina and Ruiz de Alarçon and Moreto. There was a civic fête in his honor. The choir boys' school and the green room of the Comedia were swamped with the gifts of vegetables and wheat. All the world was eager to nourish the interpreters of so much beauty.

This was the theater in which Camila Perichole gradually made her reputation. So rich was the repertory and so dependable the prompter's box that few plays were given more than four times a season. The manager had the whole flowering of the 17th Century Spanish drama to draw upon, including many that are now lost to us. The Perichole had appeared in a hundred plays of Lope de Vega alone. There were many admirable actresses in Lima during these years, but none better. The citizens were too far away from the theaters of Spain to realize that she was the best in the Spanish world. They kept sighing for a glimpse of the stars of Madrid whom they had never seen and to whom they assigned vague new excellences. Only one person knew for certain that the Perichole was a great performer and that was her tutor Uncle Pio.

Uncle Pio came of a good Castilian house, illegitimately. At the age of ten he ran away to Madrid from his father's hacienda

and was pursued without diligence. He lived ever after by his wits. He possessed the six attributes of the adventurer—a memory for names and faces, with the aptitude for altering his own; the gift of tongues; inexhaustible invention; secrecy; the talent for falling into conversation with strangers; and that freedom from conscience that springs from a contempt for the dozing rich he preyed upon. From ten to fifteen he distributed handbills for merchants, held horses, and ran confidential errands. From fifteen to twenty he trained bears and snakes for travelling circuses; he cooked, and mixed punches; he hung about the entries of the more expensive taverns and whispered informations into the travelers' ears—sometimes nothing more dubious than that a certain noble house was reduced to selling its plate and could thus dispense with the commission of a silversmith. He was attached to all the theaters in town and could applaud like ten. He spread slanders at so much a slander. He sold rumors about crops and about the value of land. From twenty to thirty his services came to be recognized in very high circles—he was sent out by the government to inspirit some half-hearted rebellions in the mountains, so that the government could presently arrive and whole-heartedly crush them. His discretion was so profound that the French party used him even when they knew that the Austrian party used him also. He had long interviews with the Princesse des Ursins, but he came and went by the back stairs. During this phase he was no longer obliged to arrange gentlemen's pleasures, nor to plant little harvests of calumny.

He never did one thing for more than two weeks at a time even when enormous gains seemed likely to follow upon it. He could have become a circus manager, a theatrical director, a dealer in antiquities, an importer of Italian silks, a secretary in the Palace or the Cathedral, a dealer in provisions for the army, a speculator in houses and farms, a merchant in dissipations and pleasures. But there seemed to have been written into his personality, through some accident or early admiration of his child-

hood, a reluctance to own anything, to be tied down, to be held to a long engagement. It was this that prevented his thieving, for example. He had stolen several times, but the gains had not been sufficient to offset his dread of being locked up; he had sufficient ingenuity to escape on the field itself all the police in the world, but nothing could protect him against the tale bearing of his enemies. Similarly he had been reduced for a time to making investigations for the Inquisition, but when he had seen several of his victims led off in hoods he felt that he might be involving himself in an institution whose movements were not evenly predictable.

As he approached twenty, Uncle Pio came to see quite clearly that his life had three aims. There was first this need of independence, cast into a curious pattern, namely: the desire to be varied, secret and omniscient. He was willing to renounce the dignities of public life, if in secret he might feel that he looked down upon men from a great distance, knowing more about them than they knew themselves; and with a knowledge which occasionally passed into action and rendered him an agent in the affairs of states and persons. In the second place he wanted to be always near beautiful women, of whom he was always in the best and worst sense the worshiper. To be near them was as necessary to him as breathing. His reverence for beauty and charm was there for anyone to see and to laugh at, and the ladies of the theater and the court and the houses of pleasure loved his connoisseurship. They tormented him and insulted him and asked his advice and were singularly comforted by his absurd devotion. He suffered greatly their rages and their meannesses and their confiding tears; all he asked was to be accepted casually, to be trusted, to be allowed like a friendly and slightly foolish dog to come and go in their rooms and to write their letters for them. He was insatiably curious about their minds and their hearts. He never expected to be loved by them (borrowing for a moment another sense of that word); for that, he carried his money to the

obscurer parts of the city; he was always desperately unprepossessing, with his whisp of a moustache and his whisp of a beard and his big ridiculous sad eyes. They constituted his parish; it was from them that he acquired the name of Uncle Pio and it was when they were in trouble that he most revealed himself; when they fell from favor he lent them money, when they were ill he outlasted the flagging devotion of their lovers and the exasperation of their maids; when time or disease robbed them of their beauty, he served them still for their beauty's memory; and when they died his was the honest grief that saw them as far as possible on their journey.

In the third place he wanted to be near those that loved Spanish literature and its masterpieces, especially in the theater. He had discovered all that treasure for himself, borrowing or stealing from the libraries of his patrons, feeding himself upon it in secrecy,—behind the scenes, as it were, of his mad life. He was contemptuous of the great persons who for all their education and usage, exhibited no care nor astonishment before the miracles of word order in Calderón and Cervantes. He longed himself to make verses. He never realized that many of the satirical songs he had written for the vaudevilles passed into folk-music and have been borne everywhere along the highroads.

As the result of one of those quarrels that arise so naturally in brothels his life became too complicated and he removed to Peru. Uncle Pio in Peru was even more versatile than Uncle Pio in Europe. Here too he touched upon real estate, circuses, pleasures, insurrections and antiques. A Chinese junk had been blown from Canton to America; he dragged up the beach the bales of deep-red porcelain and sold the bowls to the collectors of virtú. He traced down the sovereign remedies of the Incas and started a smart trade in pills. Within four months he knew practically everyone in Lima. He presently added to this acquaintance the inhabitants of scores of seacoast towns, mining camps and settlements in the interior. His pretensions to omni-

science became more and more plausible. The Viceroy discovered Uncle Pio and all this richness of reference; he engaged his services in many affairs. In the decay of his judgment Don Andrés had retained one talent, he was a master of the technique of handling confidential servants. He treated Uncle Pio with great tact and some deference; he understood which errands the other should not be asked to undertake and he understood his need for variety and intermission. Uncle Pio in turn was perpetually astonished that a prince should make so little use of his position, for power, or for fantasy, or for sheer delight in the manipulation of other men's destinies; but the servant loved the master because he could quote from any of Cervantes' prefaces and because his tongue had a little Castilian salt about it still. Many a morning Uncle Pio entered the Palace through corridors where there was no one to cross but a confessor or a confidential bully and sat with the Viceroy over his morning chocolate.

But for all his activity nothing made Uncle Pio rich. One would have said that he abandoned a venture when it threatened to prosper. Although no one knew it, he owned a house. It was full of dogs that could add and multiply and the top floor was reserved for birds. But even in this kingdom he was lonely, and proud in his loneliness, as though there resided a certain superiority in such a solitude. Finally he stumbled upon an adventure that came like some strange gift from the skies and that combined the three great aims of his life: his passion for overseeing the lives of others, his worship of beautiful women, and his admiration for the treasures of Spanish literature. He discovered Camila Perichole. Her real name was Micaela Villegas. She was singing in cafés at the age of twelve and Uncle Pio had always been the very soul of cafés. Now as he sat among the guitarists and watched this awkward girl singing ballads, imitating every inflection of the more experienced singers who had preceded her, the determination entered his mind to play Pygmalion. He bought her. Instead of sleeping locked up in the wine bin, she

inherited a cot in his house. He wrote songs for her, he taught her how to listen to the quality of her tone, and bought her a new dress. At first all she noticed was that it was wonderful not to be whipped, to be offered hot soups, and to be taught something. But it was Uncle Pio who was really dazzled. His rash experiment flourished beyond all prophecy. The little twelve-year-old, silent and always a little sullen, devoured work. He set her endless exercises in acting and mimicry; he set her problems in conveying the atmosphere of a song; he took her to the theaters and made her notice all the details of a performance. But it was from Camila as a woman that he was to receive his greatest shock. The long arms and legs were finally harmonized into a body of perfect grace. The almost grotesque and hungry face became beautiful. Her whole nature became gentle and mysterious and oddly wise; and it all turned to him. She could find no fault in him and she was sturdily loyal. They loved one another deeply but without passion. He respected the slight nervous shadow that crossed her face when he came too near her. But there arose out of this denial itself the perfume of a tenderness, that ghost of passion which, in the most unexpected relationship, can make even a whole lifetime devoted to irksome duty pass like a gracious dream.

They travelled a great deal, seeking new taverns, for the highest attribute of a café singer will always be her novelty. They went to Mexico, their odd clothes wrapped up in the self-same shawl. They slept on beaches, they were whipped at Panama and shipwrecked on some tiny Pacific islands plastered with the droppings of birds. They tramped through jungles delicately picking their way among snakes and beetles. They sold themselves out as harvesters in a hard season. Nothing in the world was very surprising to them.

Then began an even harder course of training for the girl, a regimen that resembled more the preparation for an acrobat. The instruction was a little complicated by the fact that her rise

to favor was very rapid; and there was some danger that the applause she received would make her content with her work too soon. Uncle Pio never exactly beat her, but he resorted to a sarcasm that had terrors of its own.

At the close of a performance Camila would return to her dressing room to find Uncle Pio whistling nonchalantly in one corner. She would divine his attitude at once and cry angrily:

"Now what is it? Mother of God, Mother of God, what is it now?"

"Nothing, little pearl. My little Camila of Camilas, nothing."

"There was something you didn't like. Ugly fault-finding thing that you are. Come on now, what was it? Look, I'm ready."

"No, little fish. Adorable morning star, I suppose you did as well as you could."

The suggestion that she was a limited artist and that certain felicities would be forever closed to her never failed to make Camila frantic. She would burst into tears: "I wish I had never known you. You poison my whole life. You just think I did badly. It pleases you to pretend that I was bad. All right then, be quiet."

Uncle Pio went on whistling.

"The fact is I know I was weak to-night, and don't need you to tell me so. So there. Now go away. I don't want to see you around. It's hard enough to play that part without coming back and finding you this way."

Suddenly Uncle Pio would lean forward and ask with angry intensity: "Why did you take that speech to the prisoner so fast?"

More tears from the Perichole: "Oh God, let me die in peace! One day you tell me to go faster and another to go slower. Anyway I shall be crazy in a year or two and then it won't matter."

More whistling.

"Besides the audience applauded as never before. Do you hear me? *As never before*. There! Too fast or too slow is nothing

to them. They wept. I was divine. That's all I care for. Now be silent. Be silent."

He was absolutely silent.

"You may comb my hair, but if you say another word I shall never play again. You can find some other girl, that's all."

Thereupon he would comb her hair soothingly for ten minutes, pretending not to notice the sobs that were shaking her exhausted body. At last she would turn quickly and catching one of his hands would kiss it frantically: "Uncle Pio, was I so bad? Was I a disgrace to you? Was it so awful *that you left the theater?*"

After a long pause Uncle Pio would admit judiciously: "You were good in the scene on the ship."

"But I've been better, Uncle Pio. You remember the night you came back from Cuzco—?"

"You were pretty good at the close."

"Was I?"

"But my flower, my pearl, *what was the matter in the speech to the prisoner?*"

Here the Perichole would fling her face and arms upon the table amid the pomades, caught up into a tremendous fit of weeping. Only perfection would do, only perfection. And that had never come.

Then beginning in a low voice Uncle Pio would talk for an hour, analyzing the play, entering into a world of finesse in matters of voice and gesture and tempo, and often until dawn they would remain there declaiming to one another the lordly conversation of Calderón.

Whom were these two seeking to please? Not the audiences of Lima. They had long since been satisfied. We come from a world where we have known incredible standards of excellence, and we dimly remember beauties which we have not seized again; and we go back to that world. Uncle Pio and Camila Perichole were tormenting themselves in an effort to establish in Peru the standards of the theaters in some Heaven whither

Calderón had preceded them. The public for which masterpieces are intended is not on this earth.

With the passing of time Camila lost some of this absorption in her art. A certain intermittent contempt for acting made her negligent. It was due to the poverty of interest in women's rôles throughout Spanish classical drama. At a time when the play-wrights grouped about the courts of England and France (a little later, of Venice) were enriching the parts of women with studies in wit, charm, passion and hysteria, the dramatists of Spain kept their eyes on their heroes, on gentlemen torn between the con-flicting claims of honor, or, as sinners, returning at the last moment to the cross. For a number of years Uncle Pio spent himself in discovering ways to interest the Perichole in the rôles that fell to her. Upon one occasion he was able to announce to Camila that a granddaughter of Vico de Barrera had arrived in Peru. Uncle Pio had long since communicated to Camila his veneration for great poets and Camila never questioned the view that they were a little above the kings and not below the saints. So it was in great excitement that the two of them chose one of the master's plays to perform before his granddaughter. They rehearsed the poem a hundred times, now in the great joy of invention, now in dejection. On the night of the performance Camila peering out between the folds of the curtain had Uncle Pio point out to her the little middle-aged woman worn with the cares of penury and a large family; but it seemed to Camila that she was looking at all the beauty and dignity in the world. As she waited for the lines that preceded her entrance she clung to Uncle Pio in reverent silence, her heart beating loudly. Between the acts she retired to the dusty corner of the warehouse where no one would find her and sat staring into the corners. At the close of the performance Uncle Pio brought the granddaughter of Vico de Barrera into Camila's room. Camila stood among the clothes that hung upon the wall, weeping with happiness and shame. Finally she flung herself on her knees and kissed the older

woman's hands, and the older woman kissed hers, and while the audience went home and went to bed the visitor remained telling Camila the little stories that had remained in the family, of Vico's work and of his habits.

Uncle Pio was at his happiest when a new actress entered the company, for the discovery of a new talent at her side never failed to bestir the Perichole. To Uncle Pio (standing at the back of the auditorium, bent double with joy and malice) it seemed that the body of the Perichole had become an alabaster lamp in which a strong light had been placed. Without any resort to tricks or to false emphasis, she set herself to efface the newcomer. If the play were a comedy she became the very abstraction of wit, and (as was more likely) it was a drama of wronged ladies and implacable hates, the stage fairly smoldered with her emotion. Her personality became so electric that if she so much as laid her hand upon that of a fellow actor a sympathetic shudder ran through the audience. But such occasions of excellence became less and less frequent. As her technique became sounder, Camila's sincerity became less necessary. Even when she was absentminded the audience did not notice the difference and only Uncle Pio grieved.

Camila had a very beautiful face, or rather a face beautiful save in repose. In repose one was startled to discover that the nose was long and thin, the mouth tired and a little childish, the eyes unsatisfied—a rather pinched peasant girl, dragged from the cafés-chantants and quite incapable of establishing any harmony between the claims of her art, of her appetites, of her dreams, and of her crowded daily routine. Each of these was a world in itself, and the warfare between them would soon have reduced to idiocy (or triviality) a less tenacious physique. We have seen that in spite of her discontent with her parts, the Perichole knew very well the joy that might reside in acting and warmed herself from time to time at that flame. But that of love attracted

her more often, though with no greater assurance of happiness, until Jupiter himself sent her some pearls.

Don Andrés de Ribera, the Viceroy of Peru, was the remnant of a delightful man, broken by the table, the alcove, a grandee-ship and ten years of exile. As a youth he had accompanied embassies to Versailles and Rome; he had fought in the wars in Austria; he had been in Jerusalem. He was a widower and child-less of an enormous and wealthy woman; he had collected coins a little, wines, actresses, orders and maps. From the table he had received the gout; from the alcove a tendency to convulsions; from the grandeeship a pride so vast and puerile that he seldom heard anything that was said to him and talked to the ceiling in a perpetual monologue; from the exile, oceans of boredom, a boredom so persuasive that it was like pain,—he woke up with it and spent the day with it, and it sat by his bed all night watching his sleep. Camila was passing the years in the hard-working rou-tine of the theater, savored by a few untidy love-affairs, when this Olympian personage (for he had a face and port fit to play gods and heroes on the scene) suddenly transported her to the most delicious midnight suppers at the Palace. Contrary to all the traditions of the stage and state she adored her elderly admirer; she thought she was going to be happy forever. Don Andrés taught the Perichole a great many things and to her bright eager mind that was one of the sweetest ingredients of love. He taught her a little French; to be neat and clean; the modes of address. Uncle Pio had taught her how great ladies carry themselves on great occasions; he taught her how they relax. Uncle Pio and Calderón had trained her in beautiful Span-ish; Don Andrés furnished her with the smart slang of *El Buen Retiro.*

Uncle Pio was made anxious by Camila's invitation from the Palace. He would have much preferred that she continue with her little vulgarian love-affairs in the theatrical warehouse. But

when he saw that her art was gaining a new finish he was well content. He would sit in the back of the theater, rolling about in his seat for sheer joy and amusement, watching the Perichole intimate to the audience that she frequented the great world about whom the dramatists wrote. She had a new way of fingering a wine-glass, of exchanging an adieu, a new way of entering a door that told everything. To Uncle Pio nothing else mattered. What was there in the world more lovely than a beautiful woman doing justice to a Spanish masterpiece?—a performance (he asks you), packed with observation, in which the very spacing of the words revealed a comment on life and on the text— delivered by a beautiful voice—illustrated by a faultless carriage, considerable personal beauty and irresistible charm. "We are almost ready to take this marvel to Spain," he would murmur to himself. After the performance he would go around to her dressing-room and say "Very good!" But before taking his leave he would manage to ask her where, in the name of the eleven thousand virgins of Cologne, she had acquired that affected way of saying *Excelencia*.

After a time the Viceroy asked the Perichole whether it would amuse her to invite a few discreet guests to their midnight suppers, and he asked her whether she would like to meet the Archbishop. Camila was delighted. The Archbishop was delighted. On the eve of their first meeting he sent the actress an emerald pendant as big as a playing-card.

There was something in Lima that was wrapped up in yards of violet satin from which protruded a great dropsical head and two fat pearly hands; and that was its archbishop. Between the rolls of flesh that surrounded them looked out two black eyes speaking discomfort, kindliness and wit. A curious and eager soul was imprisoned in all this lard, but by dint of never refusing himself a pheasant or a goose or his daily procession of Roman wines, he was his own bitter jailer. He loved his cathedral; he loved his duties; he was very devout. Some days he regarded his

bulk ruefully; but the distress of remorse was less poignant than the distress of fasting and he was presently found deliberating over the secret messages that a certain roast sends to the certain salad that will follow it. And to punish himself he led an exemplary life in every other respect.

He had read all the literature of antiquity and forgotten all about it except a general aroma of charm and disillusion. He had been learned in the Fathers and the Councils and forgotten all about them save a floating impression of dissensions that had no application to Peru. He had read all the libertine masterpieces of Italy and France and reread them annually; even in the torments of the stone (happily dissolved by drinking the water from the springs of Santa María de Cluxambuqua), he could find nothing more nourishing than the anecdotes of Brantôme and the divine Aretino.

The Archbishop knew that most of the priests of Peru were scoundrels. It required all his delicate Epicurean education to prevent his doing something about it; he had to repeat over to himself his favorite notions: that the injustice and unhappiness in the world is a constant; that the theory of progress is a delusion; that the poor, never having known happiness, are insensible to misfortune. Like all the rich he could not bring himself to believe that the poor (look at their houses, look at their clothes) could really suffer. Like all the cultivated he believed that only the widely-read could be said to *know* that they were unhappy. On one occasion, the iniquities in his see having been called to his notice, he almost did something about it. He had just heard that it was becoming a rule in Peru for priests to exact two measures of meal for a fairly good absolution, and five measures, for a really effective one. He trembled with indignation; he roared to his secretary and bidding him bring up his writing materials, announced that he was going to dictate an overwhelming message to his shepherds. But there was no ink left in the inkwell; there was no ink left in the next room; there was no ink to be

found in the whole palace. This state of things in his household so upset the good man that he fell ill of the combined rages and learned to guard himself against indignations.

The addition of the Archbishop to the suppers was so successful that Don Andrés began to think of new names. He had grown increasingly dependent upon Uncle Pio, but waited until Camila should propose his inclusion of her own accord. And in due time Uncle Pio brought with him that courser of the seas, the Captain Alvarado. Generally the reunion had been several hours under way before Camila was able to join them after her performance at the theater. She would arrive towards one o'clock, radiant and bejewelled and very tired. The four men received her as they would a great queen. For an hour or so she would carry the conversation, but gradually reclining more and more against Don Andrés' shoulder she would follow the talk as it flitted from one humorous lined face to the other. All night they talked, secretly comforting their hearts that longed always for Spain and telling themselves that such a symposium was after the manner of the high Spanish soul. They talked about ghosts and second-sight, and about the earth before man appeared upon it and about the possibility of the planets striking against one another; about whether the soul can be seen, like a dove, fluttering away at the moment of death; they wondered whether at the second coming of Christ to Jerusalem, Peru would be long in receiving the news. They talked until the sun rose, about wars and kings, about poets and scholars, and about strange countries. Each one poured into the conversation his store of wise sad anecdotes and his dry regret about the race of men. The flood of golden light struck across the Andes and entering the great window fell upon the piles of fruit, the stained brocade upon the table, and the sweet thoughtful forehead of the Perichole as she lay sleeping against the sleeve of her protector. There would ensue a long pause, no one wishing to make the first move to go, and the glances of them all would rest upon this

strange beautiful bird who lived among them. But Uncle Pio's glance had been upon her all night, a quick glance from his black eyes, full of tenderness and anxiety, resting on the great secret and reason of his life.

But Uncle Pio never ceased watching Camila. He divided the inhabitants of this world into two groups, into those who had loved and those who had not. It was a horrible aristocracy, apparently, for those who had no capacity for love (or rather for suffering in love) could not be said to be alive and certainly would not live again after their death. They were a kind of straw population, filling the world with their meaningless laughter and tears and chatter and disappearing still lovable and vain into thin air. For this distinction he cultivated his own definition of love that was like no other and that had gathered all its bitterness and pride from his odd life. He regarded love as a sort of cruel malady through which the elect are required to pass in their late youth and from which they emerge, pale and wrung, but ready for the business of living. There was (he believed) a great repertory of errors mercifully impossible to human beings who had recovered from this illness. Unfortunately there remained to them a host of failings, but at least (from among many illustrations) they never mistook a protracted amiability for the whole conduct of life, they never again regarded any human being, from a prince to a servant, as a mechanical object. Uncle Pio never ceased watching Camila because it seemed to him that she had never undergone this initiation. In the months that followed her introduction to the Viceroy he held his breath and waited. He held his breath for years. Camila bore the Viceroy three children, yet remained the same. He knew that the first sign of her entrance into the true possession of the world would be the mastery of certain effects in her acting. There were certain passages in the plays that she would compass some day, simply, easily, and with secret joy, because they alluded to the new rich wisdom of her heart; but her treatment of such passages became

more and more cursory, not to say embarrassed. He presently saw that she had tired of Don Andrés and had returned to a series of furtive love-affairs with the actors and matadors and merchants of the town.

She became more and more impatient of acting and another parasite found its way into her mind. She wanted to be a lady. She slowly contracted a greed for respectability and began to refer to her acting as a pastime. She acquired a duenna and some footmen and went to church at the fashionable hours. She attended the prize days at the University and appeared among the donors of the great charities. She even learned to read and write a little. Any faint discrimination against her as a bohemian she challenged with fury. She led the Viceroy a horrible life with her passion for concessions and her gradual usurpation of privileges. The new vice displaced the old and she became noisily virtuous. She invented some parents and produced some cousins. She obtained an undocumented legitimatization of her children. In society she cultivated a delicate and languid magdelinism, as a great lady might, and she carried a candle in the penitential parades, side by side with ladies who had nothing to regret but an outburst of temper and a furtive glance into Descartes. Her sin had been acting and everyone knows that there were even saints who had been actors,—there was Saint Gelasius and Saint Genesius and Saint Margaret of Antioch and Saint Pelagia.

There was a fashionable watering place in the hills not far from Santa María de Cluxambuqua. Don Andrés had travelled in France and had thought to build himself a little mock Vichy; there was a pagoda, some drawing-rooms, a theater, a little arena for bull-fights and some French gardens. Camila's health had never known a shadow, but she built herself a villa in the vicinity and sipped the hateful waters at eleven o'clock. The Marquesa de Montemayor has left a brilliant picture of this *opéra bouffe* paradise with the reigning divinity parading her fierce sensitiveness along the avenues of powdered shell and receiving the

homage of all those who could not afford to offend the Viceroy. Doña María draws a portrait of this ruler, stately and weary, gambling all through the night in sums that would have raised another Escurial. And beside him she sets the portrait of his son, Camila's little Don Jaime. Don Jaime, at seven years, was a rachitic little body who seemed to have inherited not only his mother's forehead and eyes, but his father's liability to convulsions. He bore his pain with the silent bewilderment of an animal, and like an animal he was mortally ashamed when any evidences of it occurred in public. He was so beautiful that the more trivial forms of pity were hushed in his presence and his long thoughts about his difficulties had given his face a patient and startling dignity. His mother dressed him in garnet velvet, and when he was able he followed her about at a distance of several yards, extricating himself gravely from the ladies who tried to detain him in conversation. Camila was never cross to Don Jaime and she was never demonstrative. When the sun was shining the two could be seen walking along those artificial terraces in silence, Camila wondering when the felicity would begin that she had always associated with social position, Don Jaime rejoicing merely in the sunlight and anxiously estimating the approach of a cloud. They looked like figures that had strayed there from some remote country, or out of an old ballad, that had not yet learned the new language and had not yet found any friends.

Camila was about thirty when she left the stage and it required five years for her to achieve her place in society. She gradually became almost stout, though her head seemed to grow more beautiful every year. She took to overdressing and the floors of the drawing-rooms reflected a veritable tower of jewels and scarves and plumes. Her face and hands were covered with a bluish powder against which she drew an irritable mouth in scarlet and orange. The almost distraught fury of her temper was varied by the unnatural sweetness of her address in the company of the dowagers. In the earliest stages of her progress upward she

had intimated to Uncle Pio that he was not to be seen with her in public, but finally she became impatient even of his discreeter visits. She conducted the interviews with formality and evasion. Her eyes never crossed his and she angled for pretexts to quarrel with him. Still he ventured out once a month to try her patience and when the call had become impossible he would climb the stairs and finish the hour among her children.

One day he arrived at her villa in the hills and, through her maid, begged for an opportunity to talk with her. He was told that she would see him in the French gardens a little before sunset. He had come up from Lima on a strange sentimental impulse. Like all solitary persons he had invested friendship with a divine glamour: he imagined that the people he passed on the street, laughing together and embracing when they parted, the people who dined together with so many smiles,—you will scarcely believe me, but he imagined that they were extracting from all that congeniality great store of satisfaction. So that suddenly he was filled with the excitement of seeing her again, of being called "Uncle Pio," and of reviving for a moment the trust and humor of their long vagabondage.

The French gardens were at the southern end of the town. Behind them rose the higher Andes and before them there was a parapet overlooking a deep valley and overlooking wave after wave of hills that stretched toward the Pacific. It was the hour when bats fly low and the smaller animals play recklessly underfoot. A few solitaries lingered about the gardens, gazing dreamily into the sky that was being gradually emptied of its color, or leaned upon the balustrade and looked down into the valley, noting in which village a dog was barking. It was the hour when the father returns home from the fields and plays for a moment in the yard with the dog that jumps upon him, holding his muzzle closed or throwing him upon his back. The young girls look about for the first star to fix a wish upon it, and the boys grow

restless for supper. Even the busiest mother stands for a moment idle-handed, smiling at her dear and exasperating family.

Uncle Pio stood against one of the chipped marble benches and watched Camila coming towards him:

"I am late," she said. "I am sorry. What is it you wish to say to me?"

"Camila,—" he began.

"My name is Doña Micaela."

"I do not wish to offend you, Doña Micaela, but when you let me call you Camila for twenty years, I should think—"

"Oh, do as you like. Do as you like."

"Camila, promise me that you will listen to me. Promise me that you will not run away at my first sentence."

At once she burst out with unexpected passion: "Uncle Pio, listen to me. You are mad if you think you can make me return to the theater. I look back at the theater with horror. Understand that. The theater! The theater, indeed! The daily payment of insults in that filthy place. Understand that you are wasting your time."

He answered gently: "I would not have you come back if you are happy with these new friends."

"You don't like my new friends, then?" she answered quickly. "Whom do you offer me in their stead?"

"Camila, I only remember . . ."

"I will not be criticized. I don't want any advice. It will be cold in a moment, I must go back to my house. Just give me up, that's all. Just put me out of your mind."

"Dear Camila, don't be angry. Let me talk to you. Just suffer me for ten minutes."

He did not understand why she was weeping. He did not know what to say. He talked at random: "You never even come to see the theater, and they all notice it. The audiences are falling away now, too. They only put on the Old Comedy twice a week;

all the other nights there are these new farces in prose. All is dull and childish and indecent. No one can speak Spanish any more. No one can even walk correctly any more. On Corpus Christi Day they gave *Belshazzar's Feast* where you were so wonderful. Now it was shameful."

There was a pause. A beautiful procession of clouds, like a flock of sheep, was straying up from the sea, slipping up the valleys between the hills. Camila suddenly touched his knee, and her face was like her face twenty years before: "Forgive me, Uncle Pio, for being so bad. Jaime was ill this afternoon. There's nothing one can do. He lies there, so white and . . . so surprised. One must just think of other things. Uncle Pio, it would be no good if I went back to the theater. The audiences come for the prose farces. We were foolish to try and keep alive the Old Comedy. Let people read the old plays in books if they choose to. It is not worth while fighting with the crowd."

"Wonderful Camila, I was not just to you when you were on the stage. It was some foolish pride in me. I grudged you the praise that you deserved. Forgive me. You have always been a very great artist. If you come to see that you are not happy among these people you might think about going to Madrid. You would have a great triumph there. You are still young and beautiful. There will be time later to be called Doña Micaela. We shall be old soon. We shall be dead soon."

"No, I shall never see Spain. All the world is alike, Madrid or Lima."

"Oh, if we could go away to some island where the people would know you for yourself. And love you."

"You are fifty years old and you are still dreaming of such islands, Uncle Pio."

He bent his head and mumbled: "Of course I love you, Camila, as I always must and more than I can say. To have known you is enough for my whole life. You are a great lady

now. And you are rich. There is no longer any way that I can help you. But I am always ready."

"How absurd you are," she said smiling. "You said that as boys say it. You don't seem to learn as you grow older, Uncle Pio. There is no such thing as that kind of love and that kind of island. It's in the theater you find such things."

He looked shamefaced, but unconvinced.

At last she rose and said sadly: "What are we talking about! It is growing cold. I must be going in. You must be resigned. I have no heart for the theater." There was a pause. "And for the rest? . . . Oh, I do not understand. It is just circumstance. I must be what I must. Do not try to understand either. Don't think about me, Uncle Pio. Just forgive, that's all. Just try to forgive."

She stood still a moment, searching for something deeply felt to say to him. The first cloud reached the terrace; it was dark; the last stragglers were leaving the gardens. She was thinking of Don Jaime, and of Don Andrés and of himself. She could not find the words. Suddenly she bent down and kissed his fingers and went quickly away. But he sat for a long time in the gathering clouds trembling with happiness and trying to penetrate into the meaning of these things.

Suddenly the news was all over Lima. Doña Micaela Villegas, the lady that used to be Camila the Perichole, had the small-pox. Several hundred other persons had the small-pox also, but popular interest and malignity were concentrated upon the actress. A wild hope ran about the town that the beauty would be impaired that had enabled her to despise the class from which she sprang. The news escaped from the sick-room that Camila had become ludicrous in homeliness and the cup of the envious overflowed. As soon as she was able she had herself carried from the city to her villa in the hills; she ordered the sale of her elegant little palace. She returned her jewels to their givers and she sold her fine clothes. The Viceroy, the Archbishop, and the few men

at court who had been her sincerest admirers besieged her door still with messages and gifts; the messages were ignored and the gifts were returned without comment. No one but her nurse and maids had been permitted to see her since the commencement of her illness. As an answer to his repeated attempts Don Andrés received a large sum of money from her with a letter compounded of all that is possible in bitterness and pride.

Like all beautiful women who have been brought up amid continual tributes to her beauty she assumed without cynicism that it must necessarily be the basis of anyone's attachment to herself; henceforth any attention paid to her must spring from a pity full of condescension and faintly perfumed with satisfaction at so complete a reversal. This assumption that she need look for no more devotion now that her beauty had passed proceeded from the fact that she had never realized any love save love as passion. Such love, though it expends itself in generosity and thoughtfulness, though it give birth to visions and to great poetry, remains among the sharpest expressions of self-interest. Not until it has passed through a long servitude, through its own self-hatred, through mockery, through great doubts, can it take its place among the loyalties. Many who have spent a lifetime in it can tell us less of love than the child that lost a dog yesterday. As her friends continued in their efforts to draw her again into society she grew more and more angry and dispatched insulting messages to the city. It was said for a time that she was retiring into religion. But new rumors that all was fury and despair on the little farm contradicted the old. For those near to her the despair was fearful to behold. She was convinced that her life was over, her life and children's. In her hysterical pride she had given back more than she owed and the approach of poverty was added to the loneliness and the gloom of her future. There was nothing left for her to do but to draw out her days in jealous solitude in the center of the little farm that was falling into

decay. She brooded for hours upon the joy of her enemies and could be heard striding about her room with strange cries.

Uncle Pio did not allow himself to be discouraged. By dint of making himself useful to the children, by taking a hand in the management of the farm and by discreetly lending her some money he obtained his entrance into the house and even into the presence of its veiled mistress. But even then Camila, convinced in her pride that he *pitied* her, lashed him with the blade of her tongue and derived some strange comfort from heaping him with sneers. He loved her the more, understanding better than she did herself all the stages in the convalescence of her humiliated spirit. But one day an accident befell that lost him his share in her progress. He pushed open a door.

She thought she had locked it. For just one hour a foolish secret hope had come to her; she wondered whether she could make a paste of chalk and cream to spread upon her face. She who had sneered so often at the befloured grandmothers of the court wondered for a few moments whether she had learned anything on the stage that would aid her now. She thought she had locked the door and with hurried hands and beating heart she laid on the coat, the grotesque pallor, and as she gazed into the mirror and recognized the futility of her attempt she caught the image of Uncle Pio standing in the door amazed. She rose from the chair with a cry and covered her face with her hands.

"Go away. Go away out of my house forever," she screamed. "I never want to see you again." In her shame she drove him out with blasphemy and hatred, she pursued him down the corridor and hurled objects down the stairs. She gave her farmer orders that Uncle Pio was forbidden to come into the grounds. But he continued for a week trying to see her again. At last he went back to Lima; he filled in the time as best he could, but he longed to be by her as a boy of eighteen would long. At last he devised a stratagem and returned up into the hills to put it into effect.

One morning before dawn he arose and lay on the ground below her window. He imitated in the darkness the sound of weeping, and, as nearly as he could, of a young girl's weeping. He continued in this for the whole quarter of an hour. He did not let his voice rise above that degree of loudness which Italian musicians would represent by the direction *piano*, but he frequently intermitted the sound trusting that if she were asleep it would insinuate itself into her mind as well by duration as by degree. The air was cool and agreeable. The first faint streak of sapphire was appearing behind the peaks and in the east the star of morning was pulsating every moment with a more tender intention. A profound silence wrapped all the farm buildings, only an occasional breeze set all the grasses sighing. Suddenly a lamp was lit in her room and a moment later the shutter was thrown back and a head wrapped in veils leaned far out.

"Who is there?" asked the beautiful voice.

Uncle Pio remained silent.

Camila said again in a tone edged with impatience:

"Who is there? Who is there weeping?"

"Doña Micaela, my lady, I beg of you to come here to me."

"Who are you and what do you want?"

"I am a poor girl. I am Estrella. I beg of you to come and help me. Do not call your maid. I pray you, Doña Micaela, to come yourself."

Camila was silent a moment, then said abruptly: "Very well," and closed the shutter. Presently she appeared around the corner of the house. She wore a thick cloak that dragged in the dew. She stood at a distance and said: "Come over here to where I am standing,—Who are you?"

Uncle Pio rose up. "Camila, it is I,—Uncle Pio. Forgive me, but I must speak to you."

"Mother of God, when shall I be free of this dreadful person! Understand: I want to see no one. I don't want to speak to a soul. My life is over. That is all."

"Camila, by our long life together, I beg of you to grant me one thing. I shall go away and never trouble you again."

"I grant you nothing, nothing. Stay away from me."

"I promise you I shall never trouble you again if you listen to me this once." She was hurrying around to the door on the other side of the house and Uncle Pio was obliged to run beside her to make sure that she heard what he was saying. She stopped:

"What is it then? Hurry. It is cold. I am not well. I must go back to my room."

"Camila, let me take Don Jaime for a year to live with me in Lima. Let me be his teacher. Let me teach him the Castilian. Here he is left among the servants. He is learning nothing."

"No."

"Camila, what will become of him? He has a good mind and he wants to learn."

"He is sick. He is delicate. Your house is a sty. Only the country is good for him."

"But he has been much better these last few months. I promise you I shall clean out my house. I shall apply to Madre María del Pilar for a housekeeper. Here he is in your stables all day. I shall teach him all that a gentleman should know,—fencing and Latin and music. We shall read all. . . ."

"A mother cannot be separated from her child like that. It is impossible. You are crazy to have thought of it. Give up thinking of me and of everything about me. I no longer exist. I and my children will get on as best we can. Do not try to disturb me again. I do not want to see any human being."

Now it was that Uncle Pio felt obliged to use a hard measure. "Then pay me the money that you owe me," he said.

Camila stood still, confounded. To herself she said: "Life is too fearful to bear. When may I die?" After a moment she answered him, in a hoarse voice: "I have very little money. I will pay you what I can. I will pay you now. I have a few jewels here.

Then we need never see one another again." She was ashamed of her poverty. She took a few steps, then turned and said: "Now I see that you are a very hard man. But it is right that I pay you what I owe you."

"No, Camila, I only said that to enforce my request. I shall take no money from you. But lend me Don Jaime for one year. I shall love him and take every care of him. Did I harm you? Was I a bad teacher to you in those other years?"

"It is cruel of you to keep urging gratitude, gratitude, gratitude. I was grateful,—good, good! but now that I am no longer the same woman there remains nothing to be grateful for." There was a silence. Her eyes were resting on the star that seemed to be leading forth the whole sky in its wonder. A great pain lay at her heart, the pain of a world that was meaningless. Then she said: "If Jaime wishes to go with you, very well. I shall talk to him in the morning. If he wishes to go with you, you will find him at the Inn about noon. Good night. Go with God."

"Go with God."

She returned to the house. The next day the grave little boy appeared at the Inn. His fine clothes were torn and stained now and he carried a small bundle for change. His mother had given him a gold piece for spending-money and a little stone that shone in the dark to look at in his sleepless nights. They set off together in a cart, but soon Uncle Pio became aware that the jolting was not good for the boy. He carried him on his shoulder. As they drew near to the bridge of San Luis Rey, Jaime tried to conceal his shame for he knew that one of those moments was coming that separated him from other people. He was especially ashamed because Uncle Pio had just overtaken a friend of his, a sea captain. And just as they got to the bridge he spoke to an old lady who was travelling with a little girl. Uncle Pio said that when they had crossed the bridge they would sit down and rest, but it turned out not to be necessary.

Part Five

Perhaps an Intention

A new bridge of stone has been built in the place of the old, but the event has not been forgotten. It has passed into proverbial expressions. "I may see you Tuesday," says a Limean, "unless the bridge falls." "My cousin lives by the bridge of San Luis Rey," says another, and a smile goes around the company, for that also means: under the sword of Damocles. There are some poems about the accident, classics to be found in every Peruvian anthology, but the real literary monument is Brother Juniper's book.

There are a hundred ways of wondering at circumstance. Brother Juniper would never have arrived at his method had it not been for his friendship with a certain master in the University of San Martín. This student's wife had stolen away one morning on a boat for Spain, following a soldier, and had left him the care of two daughters in their cradle. He was possessed of all the bitterness that Brother Juniper lacked and derived a sort of joy from the conviction that all was wrong in the world. He whispered into the Franciscan's ear such thoughts and anecdotes as belied the notion of a guided world. For a moment a look of distress, almost of defeat, would come into the Brother's eyes; then he would begin patiently explaining why such stories

held no difficulty for a believer. "There was a queen of Naples and Sicily," the student would say, "who discovered that she was carrying an angry tumor in her side. In great dismay she commanded her subjects to fall to their prayers and ordered that all the garments in Sicily and Naples be sewn with votive crosses. She was well loved by her people and all their prayers and embroideries were sincere, but ineffectual. Now she lies in the splendor of Monreale, and a few inches above her heart may be read the words: *I shall fear no evil.*"

It was by dint of hearing a great many such sneers at faith that Brother Juniper became convinced that the world's time had come for proof, tabulated proof, of the conviction that was so bright and exciting within him. When the pestilence visited his dear village of Puerto and carried off a large number of peasants, he secretly drew up a diagram of the characteristics of fifteen victims and fifteen survivors, the statistics of their value *sub specie aeternitatis.* Each soul was rated upon a basis of ten as regards its goodness, its diligence in religious observance, and its importance to its family group. Here is a fragment of this ambitious chart:

	GOODNESS	PIETY	USEFULNESS
Alfonso G.	4	4	10
Nina	2	5	10
Manuel B.	10	10	0
Alfonso V.	−8	−10	10
Vera N.	0	10	10

The thing was more difficult than he had foreseen. Almost every soul in a difficult frontier community turned out to be indispensable economically, and the third column was all but useless. The examiner was driven to the use of minus terms when he confronted the personal character of Alfonso V., who was not, like Vera N., merely bad: he was a propagandist for bad-

ness and not merely avoided church but led others to avoid it. Vera N. was indeed bad, but she was a model worshiper and the mainstay of a full hut. From all this saddening data Brother Juniper contrived an index for each peasant. He added up the total for victims and compared it with the total for survivors, to discover that the dead were five times more worth saving. It almost looked as though the pestilence had been directed against the really valuable people in the village of Puerto. And on that afternoon Brother Juniper took a walk along the edge of the Pacific. He tore up his findings and cast them into the waves; he gazed for an hour upon the great clouds of pearl that hang forever upon the horizon of that sea, and extracted from their beauty a resignation that he did not permit his reason to examine. The discrepancy between faith and the facts is greater than is generally assumed.

But there was another story of the master of San Martín (not so subversive, this one) that probably gave to Brother Juniper the hint for his procedure after the fall of the bridge of San Luis Rey.

This master was one day walking through the Cathedral of Lima and stopped to read the epitaph of a lady. He read with an increasingly prominent lower lip that she had been for twenty years the center and joy of her home, that she had been the delight of her friends, that all who met her went away in astonishment at her goodness and beauty, and that there she lay awaiting the return of her Lord. Now on the day that he read these words, the master of San Martín had had much to fret him, and raising his eyes from the tablet he spoke aloud in his rage: "The shame of it, the persecution of it! Everyone knows that in the world we do nothing but feed our wills. Why perpetuate this legend of selflessness? Why keep this thing alive, this rumor of disinterestedness?"

And so saying he resolved to expose this conspiracy of the stone-cutters. The lady had been dead only twelve years. He

sought out her servants, her children and her friends. And every-where he went, like a perfume, her dear traits had survived her and wherever she was mentioned there arose a suffering smile and the protest that words could not describe the gracious ways of her. Even the eager youth of her grandchildren, who had never seen her, was made more difficult by the news that it was possible to be as good as that. And the man stood amazed; only at last he muttered: "Nevertheless, what I said was true. This woman was an exception, perhaps an exception."

In compiling his book about these people Brother Juniper seemed to be pursued by the fear that in omitting the slightest detail he might lose some guiding hint. The longer he worked the more he felt that he was stumbling about among great dim intimations. He was forever being cheated by details that looked as though they were significant if only he could find their setting. So he put everything down on the notion perhaps that if he (or a keener head) reread the book twenty times, the countless facts would suddenly start to move, to assemble, and to betray their secret. The Marquesa de Montemayor's cook told him that she lived almost entirely on rice, fish and a little fruit and Brother Juniper put it down on the chance that it would some day reveal a spiritual trait. Don Rubío said of her that she used to appear at his receptions without invitation in order to steal the spoons. A midwife on the edge of the town declared that Doña María called upon her with morbid ques-tions until she had been obliged to order her away from the door like a beggar. The bookseller of the town reported that she was one of the three most cultivated persons in Lima. Her farmer's wife declared that she was absent-minded, but compact of goodness. The art of biography is more difficult than is gen-erally supposed.

Brother Juniper found that there was least to be learned from those who had been most closely associated with the subjects of his inquiry. Madre María del Pilar talked to him at length about

Pepita, but she did not tell him of her own ambitions for her. The Perichole was at first difficult of approach, but presently even liked the Franciscan. Her characterization of Uncle Pio flatly contradicted the stores of unsavory testimonies that he had acquired elsewhere. Her allusions to her son were few and conceded with pain. They closed the interview abruptly. The Captain Alvarado told what he could of Esteban and of Uncle Pio. Those who know most in this realm, venture least.

I shall spare you Brother Juniper's generalizations. They are always with us. He thought he saw in the same accident the wicked visited by destruction and the good called early to Heaven. He thought he saw pride and wealth confounded as an object lesson to the world, and he thought he saw humility crowned and rewarded for the edification of the city. But Brother Juniper was not satisfied with his reasons. It was just possible that the Marquesa de Montemayor was not a monster of avarice, and Uncle Pio of self-indulgence.

The book being done fell under the eyes of some judges and was suddenly pronounced heretical. It was ordered to be burned in the Square with its author. Brother Juniper submitted to the decision that the devil had made use of him to effect a brilliant campaign in Peru. He sat in his cell that last night trying to seek in his own life the pattern that had escaped him in five others. He was not rebellious. He was willing to lay down his life for the purity of the church, but he longed for one voice somewhere to testify for him that his intention, at least, had been for faith; he thought there was no one in the world who believed him. But the next morning in all that crowd and sunlight there were many who believed, for he was much loved.

There was a little delegation from the village of Puerto, and Nina (Goodness 2, Piety 5, Usefulness 10) and others stood with drawn puzzled faces while their little friar was given to the congenial flames. Even then, even then, there remained in his heart an obstinate nerve insisting that at least St. Francis would

not utterly have condemned him, and (not daring to call upon a greater name, since he seemed so open to error in these matters) he called twice upon St. Francis and leaning upon a flame he smiled and died.

The day of the service was clear and warm. The Limeans, their black eyes wide with awe, poured through the streets into their Cathedral and stood gazing at the mound of black velvet and silver. The Archbishop enclosed in his wonderful and almost wooden vestments perspired upon his throne, lending from time to time a connoisseur's ear to the felicities of Vittoria's counterpoint. The choir had restudied the pages that, as his farewell to music, Tomás Luis had composed for his friend and patron, the Empress of Austria, and all that grief and sweetness, all that Spanish realism filtering through an Italian mode, rose and fell above the sea of mantillas. Don Andrés, under the colors and feathered hangings of his office, knelt, ill and troubled. He knew that the crowd was furtively glancing at him, expecting him to play the father who has lost his only son. He wondered whether the Perichole was present. He had never been obliged to go so long without smoking. The Captain Alvarado pushed in from the sunny square for a moment. He looked across the fields of black hair and lace at the trooping of the candles and the ropes of incense. "How false, how unreal," he said and pushed his way out. He descended to the sea and sat on the edge of his boat, gazing down into the clear water. "Happy are the drowned, Esteban," he said.

Behind the screen the Abbess sat among her girls. The night before she had torn an idol from her heart and the experience had left her pale but firm. She had accepted the fact that it was of no importance whether her work went on or not; it was enough to work. She was the nurse who tends the sick who never recover; she was the priest who perpetually renews the office before an altar to which no worshipers come. There would be no

Pepita to enlarge her work; it would relapse into the indolence and the indifference of her colleagues. It seemed to be sufficient for Heaven that for a while in Peru a disinterested love had flowered and faded. She leaned her forehead upon her hand, following the long tender curve that the soprano lifts in the Kyrie. "My affection should have had more of that color, Pepita. My whole life should have had more of that quality. I have been too busy," she added ruefully and her mind drifted into prayer.

Camila had started from the farm to attend the service. Her heart was filled with consternation and amazement. Here was another comment from the skies; that was the third time she had been spoken to. Her small-pox, Jaime's illness, and now the fall of the bridge,—oh, these were not accidents. She was as ashamed as though letters had appeared on her forehead. An order from the Palace announced that the Viceroy was sending her two daughters to a convent-school in Spain. That was right. She was alone. She gathered a few things together mechanically and started to the city for the Service. But she fell to thinking of the crowds gaping over her Uncle Pio and over her son; she thought of the vast ritual of the church, like a chasm into which the beloved falls, and of the storm of the *dies irae* where the individual is lost among the millions of the dead, features grow dim and traits fade. At a little more than half the journey, at the mud church of San Luis Rey she slipped in and knelt against a pillar to rest. She wandered through her memory, searching for the faces of her two. She waited for some emotion to appear. "But I feel nothing," she whispered to herself. "I have no heart. I am a poor meaningless woman, that's all. I am shut out. I have no heart. Look, I won't try and think of anything; let me just rest here." And scarcely had she paused when again that terrible incommunicable pain swept through her, the pain that could not speak once to Uncle Pio and tell him of her love and just once offer her courage to Jaime in his sufferings. She started up wildly: "I fail everybody," she cried. "They love me and I fail them." She

returned to the farm and carried for a year the mood of her self-despair. One day she heard by accident that the wonderful Abbess had lost two persons whom she loved in the same accident. Her sewing fell from her hand: then *she* would know, she would explain. "But no, what would she say to me! She would not even believe that such a person as I could love or could lose." Camila decided to go to Lima and look at the Abbess from a distance. "If her face tells me that she would not despise me, I will speak to her," she said.

Camila lurked about the convent church and fell humbly in love with the homely old face, though it frightened her a little. At last she called upon her.

"Mother," she said, "I . . . I . . ."

"Do I know you, my daughter?"

"I was the actress, I was the Perichole."

"Oh, yes. Oh, I have wished to know you for a long while, but they told me you did not wish to be seen. You too, I know, lost in the fall of the bridge of San. . . ."

Camila rose and swayed. There! again that access of pain, the hands of the dead she could not reach. Her lips were white. Her head brushed the Abbess's knee: "Mother, what shall I do? I am all alone. I have nothing in the world. I love them. What shall I do?"

The Abbess looked at her closely. "My daughter, it is warm here. Let us go into the garden. You can rest there." She made a sign to a girl in the cloister to bring some water. She continued talking mechanically to Camila. "I have wished to know you for a long while, señora. Even before the accident I had wished much to know you. They told me that in the *autos sacramentales* you were a very great and beautiful actress, in *Belshazzar's Feast*."

"Oh, Mother, you must not say that. I am a sinner. You must not say that."

"Here, drink this, my child. We have a beautiful garden, do you not think so? You will come and see us often and some day you will meet Sister Juana who is our gardener-in-chief. Before she entered religion she had almost never seen a garden, for she worked in the mines high up in the mountains. Now everything grows under her hand.—A year has gone by, señora, since our accident. I lost two who had been children in my orphanage, but you lost a real child of your own?"

"Yes, Mother."

"And a great friend?"

"Yes, Mother."

"Tell me. . . ."

And then the whole tide of Camila's long despair, her lonely obstinate despair since her girlhood, found its rest on that dusty friendly lap among Sister Juana's fountains and roses.

But where are sufficient books to contain the events that would not have been the same without the fall of the bridge? From such a number I choose one more.

"The Condesa d'Abuirre wishes to see you," said a lay-sister at the door of the Abbess's office.

"Well," said the Abbess, laying down her pen, "who is she?"

"She has just come from Spain. I don't know."

"Oh, it is some money, Inez, some money for my house for the blind. Quick, bid her come in."

The tall, rather languorous beauty entered the room. Doña Clara, who was generally so adequate, seemed constrained for once. "Are you busy, dear Mother, may I talk to you for a while?"

"I am quite free, my daughter. You will excuse an old woman's memory; have I known you before?"

"My mother was the Marquesa de Montemayor. . . ." Doña Clara suspected that the Abbess had not admired her mother and would not let the older woman speak until she herself had

made a long passionate defense of Doña María. The languor fell away in her self-reproach. At last the Abbess told her of Pepita and Esteban, and of Camila's visit. "All, all of us have failed. One wishes to be punished. One is willing to assume all kinds of penance, but do you know, my daughter, that in love—I scarcely dare say it—but in love our very mistakes don't seem to be able to last long?"

The Condesa showed the Abbess Doña María's last letter. Madre María dared not say aloud how great her astonishment was that such words (words that since then the whole world has murmured over with joy) could spring in the heart of Pepita's mistress. "Now learn," she commanded herself, "learn at last that anywhere you may expect grace." And she was filled with happiness like a girl at this new proof that the traits she lived for were everywhere, that the world was ready. "Will you do me a kindness, my daughter? Will you let me show you my work?"

The sun had gone down, but the Abbess led the way with a lantern down corridor after corridor. Doña Clara saw the old and the young, the sick and the blind, but most of all she saw the tired, bright old woman who was leading her. The Abbess would stop in a passageway and say suddenly: "I can't help thinking that something could be done for the deaf-and-dumb. It seems to me that some patient person could, . . . could study out a language for them. You know there are hundreds and hundreds in Peru. Do you remember whether anyone in Spain has found a way for them? Well, some day they will." Or a little later: "Do you know, I keep thinking that something can be done for the insane. I am old, you know, and I cannot go where these things are talked about, but I watch them sometimes and it seems to me . . . In Spain, now, they are gentle with them? It seems to me that there is a secret about it, just hidden from us, just around the corner. Some day back in Spain, if you hear of anything that would help us, you will write me a letter . . . if you are not too busy?"

At last after Doña Clara had seen even the kitchens, the Abbess said: "Now will you excuse me, for I must go into the room of the very sick and say a few words for them to think about when they cannot sleep. I will not ask you to come with me there, for you are not accustomed to such . . . such sounds and things. And besides I only talk to them as one talks to children." She looked up at her with her modest rueful smile. Suddenly she disappeared a moment to return with one of her helpers, one who had likewise been involved in the affair of the bridge and who had formerly been an actress. "She is leaving me," said the Abbess, "for some work across the city and when I have spoken here I must leave you both, for the flour-broker will not wait for me any longer, and our argument will take a long time."

But Doña Clara stood in the door as the Abbess talked to them, the lamp placed on the floor beside her. Madre María stood with her back against a post; the sick lay in rows gazing at the ceiling and trying to hold their breaths. She talked that night of all those out in the dark (she was thinking of Esteban alone, she was thinking of Pepita alone) who had no one to turn to, for whom the world perhaps was more than difficult, without meaning. And those who lay in their beds there felt that they were within a wall that the Abbess had built for them; within all was light and warmth, and without was the darkness they would not exchange even for a relief from pain and from dying. But even while she was talking, other thoughts were passing in the back of her mind. "Even now," she thought, "almost no one remembers Esteban and Pepita, but myself. Camila alone remembers her Uncle Pio and her son; this woman, her mother. But soon we shall die and all memory of those five will have left the earth, and we ourselves shall be loved for a while and forgotten. But the love will have been enough; all those impulses of love return to the love that made them. Even memory is not necessary for love. There is a land of the living and a land of the dead and the bridge is love, the only survival, the only meaning."

Afterword

—~~~—

Overview

Thornton Wilder wrote *The Bridge of San Luis Rey* over the period of a year, from the summer of 1926 to that of 1927, turning over the final pages to his publisher, Albert & Charles Boni, in July of 1927. The completed manuscript ran about 34,000 words, by any definition a short novel. Its brevity, in fact, caused some concern to the Boni firm, as Wilder explained in a letter to his sister: "My publisher is REVOLTED that it isn't long enough to keep up the fraud of a $2.50 book. He wants six to eight illustrations, and the Canadian and Eskimo rights."

No party to the birth of Thornton Wilder's second novel need have worried. *The Bridge of San Luis Rey* was published on November 3, 1927, in a press run estimated at the time to be 4,500 copies, priced at $2.50 each. The book was an ungainly object, designed with hideously thick paper stock, its 235 pages set with grotesquely wide margins and containing no fewer than eleven illustrations. Nevertheless, it sold out almost immediately. A little more than a month later, by December 31, 1927, 17,500 copies had been snapped up, and by June 1928—a month after

the book received the Pulitzer Prize for Fiction—sales had risen to 158,000 copies. According to a yellowing royalty statement in Wilder's legal files, "The Year of the Bridge" ended with 223,170 copies sold in a total of seventeen printings. The launch of *The Bridge* is even more remarkable when it is remembered that nearly 50,000 copies were sold in Great Britain over the same period.

These numbers will evoke no gasps from modern readers used to print runs reported in the millions for a popular best-seller. But in 1928 the commercial success of *The Bridge* was a sensational story, an adjective used to describe the event at the time. The *New York American*, the William Randolph Hearst New York City outlet, initiated the serialization of *The Bridge of San Luis Rey* in other Hearst papers beginning July 8, 1928, with unusual headlines for a novel by a highbrow author:

THE GREATEST LITERARY TREAT EVER OFFERED METROPOLITAN READERS BY A DAILY PAPER

DID THE FIVE PERUVIANS WHO WERE HURLED TO DEATH DIE BEFORE THEIR TIME?

It is an understatement to say that *The Bridge* was well received by critics on both sides of the Atlantic. The words that recur and reverberate through the notices of the day include "masterful," "masterpiece," and "triumph." When strung together, the praise was deafening, especially as fashioned into sentences by literary superstars writing in influential journals: The novel was a "star of the first magnitude" (William Lyon Phelps in *Scribner's* magazine); a "book of such aloof and untruckling beauty" (Alexander Woollcott in *The World*). English novelist and critic Arnold Bennett wrote the words in the *London Evening Standard* that are often cited by scholars as being among the first to ignite the explosion of praise for

Wilder's novel and his style. Said Bennett, "The writing has not been surpassed in the present epoch."

Language from less famous quarters also sold books: the novel was "Altogether unique," according to a review in the *Asheville Times* (North Carolina). A critic writing in the *Birkenhead News* (United Kingdom) spoke of the "bridge over which the author has passed in triumph to his rightful place among the masters." Inevitably, there were some voices of dissent, notably in the Catholic press. The *Standard* in Dublin pronounced Wilder's treatment of the Church "stupid" and the work of a man motivated by "Presbyterian malice." According to a review in *Isis* in Oxford, England, the book was disappointing in its "unexpected dullness."

A great literary success can vanish like a comet, or encounter short or long periods of neglect. But *The Bridge of San Luis Rey* has never been out of print, and over the years, in addition to its place in many anthologies, the book has appeared in numerous regular and special editions. As a paperback, for example, it was selected in 1929 to be the first book issued in Boni's pathbreaking Paper Book Series. In 1939, it was chosen as one of the first ten titles in the Pocket Book series that revolutionized publishing in this country. And from the beginning, starting with Norwegian, Hungarian, and German translations arranged in 1928, *The Bridge* has proven to be a significant perennial international presence in more than thirty languages, including Burmese and Thai.

Given its stature and popularity, an outsider might assume that *The Bridge*'s subsidiary record (as the source of works in other arts forms derived from it) would be long and even notable. But this is not true, due in considerable measure to Wilder himself. He did not believe that the nuances of the novel's language could be captured in a live dramatized form, and, therefore, denied requests for rights from many artists and writers eager to adapt *The Bridge* as a play, musical, or opera. He was not opposed to radio, and there have been several recorded

versions in this country and abroad, including a Voice of America radio broadcast to captive nations during the Cold War, and an historic recording in Germany. Nor did Wilder's ban extend to television, and he was guardedly pleased by the success—a 47-percent share of the audience—of a 1958 Du Pont "Show of the Month" production written by Ludi Clair, produced by David Susskind, and featuring a dazzling cast, including Eva Le Gallienne, Judith Anderson, Viveca Lindfors, Hume Cronyn, and Theodore Bikel in major roles. Other than a 50 percent share of the fee from the sale of rights (for which he received $15,000), the provisions of his publishing contract gave Wilder no rights in the film version sold by the Boni firm to MGM in 1928. He therefore had no direct involvement with the two films that were made from *The Bridge*—the part-sound 1929 production from MGM and a 1944 remake by an independent producer. The latter, less than memorable, is available on DVD.

What can be said in broad strokes about the sources for *The Bridge*? On the matter of tone and style, as Wilder himself explained at the time and later, no source was more important than his extensive reading in the field of classical French literature in the Princeton University Library during hours stolen from his busy schedule as French teacher and dormitory master at the Lawrenceville School in nearby Lawrenceville, New Jersey. In 1955, he explained this stratum of influence to Professor Franz H. Link, a leading student of American literature in Germany:

One comment I will make—since you have asked for it!—on the "style" of *The Bridge*—on the relatively superficial aspect of the style. During the years preceding the writing of my first two novels I had been reading intensively in the literature of the French *grand siècle*. The Marquesa de Montemayor is "after" the Marquise de Sévigné—the colors heightened in the Spanish Colonial atmosphere. Those formal portraits with which I introduce the princi-

pal characters are in the manner of Saint Simon and the memoirs of Cardinal de Retz, La Rochefoucauld, and even the portrait-making of Saint Simon and the sermons of Bossuet and Bourdaloue. Hence the "removed" tone, the classical, the faintly ironic distance from the impassioned actions is the expression—even a borrowing—from the latin thought world. Thence comes also the occasional resort to aphorism.

Other sources that Wilder himself commonly identified include a short comedic play by Prosper Mérimée, *Le Carosse du Saint-Sacrement*, which he had seen while a Yale undergraduate. This play celebrates the notorious affair between Don Andrés de Ribiera, Viceroy of Peru, and Micaela Villegas, the great actress known as La Perichole, an actual relationship that remains a centerpiece of Peruvian history and lore to this day. Wilder borrowed the name of his bridge from one of the missions founded by the Franciscan missionary Junípero Serra (1713–1784). The bridge itself was no doubt inspired by the legendary Peruvian span over the Apurímac River on the celebrated "royal road" to Cuzco. (In popular books about Peru, the tie with *The Bridge of San Luis Rey* is typically cited.) Wilder also drew on a key biblical passage, Luke 13:4, which reads, "Or those eighteen upon whom the tower of Siloam fell and killed them, do you think that they were worse offenders than all the others who dwelt in Jerusalem?"

Permeating the novel's atmosphere was the author's reading in standard sources in the history of the Spanish overseas empire and the Inquisition. Then there was Wilder's own birth history as a surviving twin brother. And in the elegant compression of the language and the book's scenic character can be seen the hand of an author with a passionate interest in drama as well as fiction.

Finally, there are two additional intriguing sources, usefully thought of as early "triggers" for *The Bridge*, and traceable to the Princeton campus, where Wilder moved in the fall of 1925

on leave of absence from Lawrenceville in order to study for a master's degree in French. There he conceived the idea for the novel. Shortly after its publication, Wilder was quoted in an interview with the Princeton undergraduate paper about the influence of the distinguished scholar from whom he took two courses in the history of French literature:

> I would like to say that the idea for [*The Bridge*] came to me while I was studying for an M.A. in French at the Princeton Graduate School. It was in a course conducted by that admirable man, Professor Louis Cons, that I received the suggestion for the first sketch in the book.

The second "trigger" is no less intriguing; after her brother's death, Isabel Wilder recalled how he once showed her "the exact spot on the campus where the idea for it came to be full-blown as he crossed a small bridge over a narrow flow of water that emptied into the lake"—a reference to Lake Carnegie.

All these sources underscore Wilder's own view in a 1928 essay about the sources of literature: "The art of literature springs from two curiosities, a curiosity about human beings pushed to such an extreme that it resembles love, and a love of a few masterpieces of literature so absorbing that it has all the richest elements of curiosity." These words, however, leave out one fundamental ingredient in the creation of literature—the author's drive to write.

The Wilder who took up residence at the Princeton Graduate School in September 1925 was only marginally interested in improving his credentials for a profession in teaching. More than anything he wanted to write, and among his possessions was the hoped-for ticket to that end—the unfinished manuscript for *The Cabala*, a novel he had been working on since 1920. In March 1925 the Boni firm, through the agency of its secretary-treasurer Lewis S. Baer, a Yale classmate and great admirer of Wilder's

writing, had informed him they wanted to publish his first novel. When he heard the good news, Wilder wrote to his family, "Let's hope this is a dawn of a new day."

By burning candles at both ends, he kept up with his graduate work, completed *The Cabala* during the fall 1925, and saw it published in April 1926, two months before he received his master's degree. *The Cabala* was a critical success and sold well for a first novel, but did not yield enough in the way of royalties to support a second year away from teaching. When the Guggenheim Foundation turned Wilder down for a grant to study theater in Germany, he faced a turning point in his life: Should he continue to teach and write around the edges and in the summers, as he was doing, or find a way to test himself more directly against his pen? He chose the latter course, in no small part because his "Peruvians," as he called them, were now buzzing in his head.

Wilder patched together the funds to support his *Bridge* year, drawing on his savings, some royalty income, and the earnings from his positions as tutor and companion, one of which took him to Europe in the fall of 1926, following a summer stay at the MacDowell Colony where he could work uninterrupted. The completed manuscript pages bore the invisible marks of hotel rooms in London, Rome, Naples, Munich, Berlin, Paris, Juan-les-Pins (a major stop), as well as economy quarters on various ocean liners. He also spent time in Briarcliff, New York; rented a room on Wall Street on the Yale campus, near his parents' home; and finished the final pages of *The Bridge* during a two-week sojourn at the YMCA in Newport, Rhode Island, in July 1927.

The story of the making of *The Bridge* is richly documented in letters to family and friends and notations in his journal. Two examples offer some sense of the excitement with which he worked on the novel: He was in Naples when he wrote, "My new book is fermenting in me like Vesuvius. On trains, in galleries, in bed . . . I receive ideas, anecdotes, phrases about my

Peruvians." He was in Paris when he heard Beethoven's Ninth Symphony and "came home and wrote the death of Manuel."

Wilder returned to Lawrenceville to teach in the fall of 1927, and was promoted to full head of one of the dormitories at the prep school. But life in the dorm soon changed dramatically. By Christmas, as Wilder wrote to Lewis Baer, the phone was ringing constantly and telegrams were arriving every twenty minutes— "Calls from producers, and don't dare use this: a report that Kipling liked it." Wilder's teaching salary that year was $3,000; from *The Bridge* alone in 1928 he earned a net taxable income of nearly $87,000 or close to a million in current dollars. As the full force of his overnight literary success hit him, Wilder toyed briefly with staying put at Lawrenceville, a place he genuinely loved and where he felt secure. But by February 1928, when he signed a contract with a major speaker's bureau to give 144 lectures over a five-year period, he had decided to step forward into what was for him the uncharted world of an acclaimed author with a growing worldwide reputation.

Students of Wilder's life will note that in 1930, however, he returned to teaching, this time at the University of Chicago in a part-time post. Nevertheless, in the classroom and in after-hours with students and colleagues, Wilder re-created a world that he needed and enjoyed—a safe, stable, stimulating base, a comfortable foundation of routine, that allowed him to roam and write, be it novels or plays. "The house *The Bridge* built" in Hamden, Connecticut, in 1929–1930, provided a different and ever more permanent anchorage when he chose to use it. Not until 1941, however, would Wilder's travels take him for the first time to Peru. On February 27, 1958, the Peruvian government honored Wilder for creating more than thirty years earlier the timeless, universal *Bridge of San Luis Rey.*

—Tappan Wilder
Chevy Chase, Maryland

Readings

The Opening Lines of The Bridge: *Two Versions*

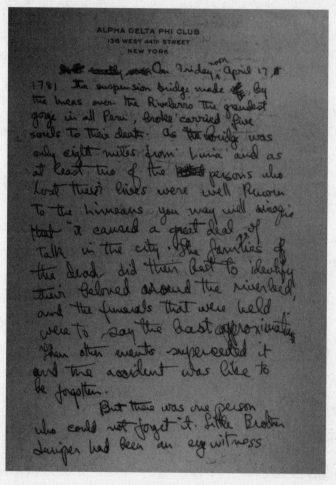

The bridge has no name in this early draft—possibly the author's first attempt—and written as early as late spring of 1926. He has used his own birth date in this version. The words reveal Thornton Wilder's knowledge of the legendary Incan span. Wilder joined the Alpha Delta Phi Fraternity at Yale and used the facilities of its national clubhouse in New York during the 1920s and early 1930s. The printed text of this letter appears on page 119.

The Bridge of San Luis Rey

Part One ～ An Act of God .

On Friday noon, July the ~~twentieth~~ twelfth , 1714 , the finest bridge in all Peru broke and precipitated five ~~persons~~ travellers into the gulf below. This bridge was on the highroad between Lima and Cuzco and hundreds of persons passed over it every day . It had been woven of osier by the Incas more than a century before and visitors to the city were always led out to see it . It was a mere ladder of thin slats swung out over the gorge, with handrails of dried vine . Horses and coaches and chairs had to go down hundreds of feet below and pass over the narrow torrent on rafts, but no one, not even the Viceroy, not even the archbishop of Lima, had descended with the baggage rather than cross by the famous bridge of San Luis Rey . St. Louis of France himself protected it , by his name and by the little mud church on the further

This is Wilder's final handwritten version and is, word for word, what would soon appear in print. In addition to showing changes of date and other details, a comparison to the earlier version reveals how the author labored to achieve the novel's "removed" tone. The printed text of this letter appears on page 119.

Alpha Delta Phi Club
136 West 44th Street
New York

On Friday noon April 17, 1781 the suspension bridge made
by the Incas over the Rivelerro the grandest gorge in all
Peru, broke carried five souls to their death. As the bridge
was only eight miles from Lima and as at least two of the
persons who lost their lives were well known to the Limeans
you may well imagine that it caused a great deal of talk in the
city. The families of the dead did their best to identify their
beloved around the riverbed, and the funerals that were held
were to say the least approximations. Then other events
superceded it and the accident was like to be forgotten.

But there was one person who could not forget it. Lit-
tle Brother Juniper had been an eyewitness . . .

The Bridge of San Luis Rey
Part One: An Act of God

On Friday noon, July the twentieth, 1714, the finest bridge
in all Peru broke and precipitated five travellers into the gulf
below. This bridge was on the highroad between Lima and
Cuzco and hundreds of persons passed over it every day. It
had been woven of osier by the Incas more than a century
before and visitors to the city were always led out to see it.
It was a mere ladder of thin slats swung out over the gorge,
with handrails of dried vine. Horses and coaches and chairs
had to go down hundreds of feet below and pass over the
narrow torrent on rafts, but no one, not even the Viceroy,
not even the Archbishop of Lima, had descended with the
baggage rather than cross by the famous bridge of San Luis
Rey. St. Louis of France himself protected it, by his name
and by the little mud church on the further . . .

Two Entries from Wilder's Journal

Wilder treated his journal as a private debating society. In these two examples, of which #40 is shown here from the original source, we see him pondering Esteban's personality and the role jealousy plays in love. Wilder did not always date entries, but, to make for efficient reference later on, he was always careful to number them.

37. Esteban's search for death (I have decided to make him much more intelligent than I first planned) is an allegory of what can be done when one has declined living. The steps he takes for release are at first merely physical. (1) rescues from burning houses (2) bullfighting. (3) provoke duels by insulting prominent tyrants etc. His motto was *Je n'existe plus.* N.B. The world seemed to be funnel-shaped and above one's life, unshakable, was the great unwinking eye of God and a voice that said: was that fair? N.B. But when he courted death by taking crazy risks on the side of good the Eye lost its reproach . . . [November? 1926]

40. In regard to Manuel-Perichole-Esteban: Behind all the different kinds of love there is one common denominator, and women recognize this when they are jealous of their husband's love of his work or his mother or even his tennis. There is a certain equivalence in all the directions in which a man may enter his will; and passion is one of the lesser "loves." [December? 1926]

After Publication

Two Letters

Scores of readers, often students, wrote to Wilder over the years seeking his position on the questions posed in *The Bridge*. In this excerpt from a letter written March 6, 1928, four months after the appearance of the novel, Wilder responds to a query from John Townley, one of his former pupils at Lawrenceville.

Thornton Wilder
Davis House
Lawrenceville, New Jersey

Dear John:

The book is not supposed to solve. A vague comfort is supposed to hover above the unanswered questions, but it is not a theorem with its Q.E.D. The book is supposed to be as puzzling and distressing as the news that five of your friends died in an automobile accident. I dare not claim that all sudden deaths are, in the last counting, triumphant. As you say, a little over half the situations seem to prove something and the rest escape, or even contradict. Chekhov said: "The business of literature is not to answer questions, but to state them fairly." I claim that human affection contains a strange unanalyzable consolation and that is all. People who are full of faith claim that the book is a vindication of this optimism; disillusioned people claim that it is a barely concealed "anatomy of despair." I am nearer the second group than the first; though some days I discover myself shouting confidentially in the first group. Where will I be thirty years from now?—with Hardy or Cardinal Newman?

Wilder writes to Chauncey Brewster Tinker, a legendary member of Yale's English Department and one of Wilder's college professors. This letter, of which a printed excerpt appears below and a few words in the author's hand here, catches the thirty-year-old author at a moment of doubt about leaving a world in which he excelled and felt at home. Davis House, the dormitory Wilder ran, housed thirty-two students. His father, Amos Parker Wilder (1862–1936), was born in Calais, Maine, and raised in Augusta.

Thornton Wilder
Davis House
Lawrenceville, New Jersey
Dec. 6, 1927

Dear Mr. Tinker:

You may imagine how exciting your letter was for me and how happy and fit-for-nothing it left me the rest of the day. It has decided me to fix on you as the judge in a new problem I have: more and more people are muttering to me that I must leave the little chicken-feed duties of the housemaster and teacher and go to Bermuda, for example, and write books as a cow gives milk. I do not know how to

answer them, but I do feel (though with intervals of mis-
giving) that this life is valuable to me and, I dare presume,
my very pleasure in my routine can make it useful to oth-
ers. Anyway no one, except you and I, seems to believe
any longer in the dignity of teaching. (though to us even
"dignity" is an understatement.) Ach, you should see the
Davis House and all the sincerity and contentment and
application that keeps coming out of 32 potential rough-
necks and Red Indians. . . .

As for your questions, oh, isn't there a lot of New En-
gland in me; all that ignoble passion to be didactic that I
have to fight with. All that bewilderment as to where
Moral Attitude begins and where it shades off into mere
Puritan Bossiness. My father is still pure Maine—1880—
and I carry all that load of notions to examine and discard
or assimilate.

No, I have never been to Peru. Why I chose to graft my
thoughts about Luke 13 upon a delightful one-act play by
Mérimée, *Le Carrosse du Saint-Sacrement*, I do not know.
The Marquesa is my beloved Mme. de Sévigné in a dis-
torting mirror. The bridge is invented, the name borrowed
from one of Junipero Serra's missions in California. . . .

It is right and fitting that you cried for a page of mine.
How many times I have cried with love or awe or pity
while you talked of the Doctor, or Cowper, or Goldsmith.

An Interview

The now celebrated author and former teacher has a visit in
France on August 18, 1928, with André Maurois, the distin-
guished French novelist and biographer. As noted, Wilder is
about to take a walking trip with the world heavyweight boxing
champion, Gene Tunney.

August 18th.—To-day we had a pleasant visit from
Thornton Wilder, the American writer, unknown until his
recent fame as the author of *The Bridge of San Luis Rey*.
An ingenious theme: the old osier bridge of San Luis Rey,
near Lima, breaks one day (about the end of the eigh-
teenth century), just when five people were crossing it.
Hurled into the ravine, they perish. An old monk who saw
the accident wonders why God sanctioned these deaths,
and for the strengthening of his faith he proposes to seek
out the causes in the lives of these five people. . . . The
sobriety of style reminded one of certain French classics,
particularly of Mérimée.

A charming man, quite young. "I'm thirty," he told
me, "like all writers of twenty-six." He holds a university
post.

"My weakness is that I am too bookish," he said. "I
know little of life. I made the characters of *The Bridge* out
of the heroes of books. My Marquesa is the Marquise de
Sévigné. In my first novel, *The Cabala*, the hero was
Keats. The method has served me well, but I don't want
to use it again. I shall not write again before I have actu-
ally observed men better."

"And on what subject?"

"It hardly matters. Don't you think that in the whole
of the world's literature there are only seven or eight great
subjects? By the time of Euripides they had all been dealt
with already, and all one can do is to pick them up again.
He took them from history, or from foreign tales. Have
you ever studied the sources of Shakespeare? I believe that
the only character he created himself was Ariel in *The
Tempest*." (I've never understood why certain critics
should stand amazed at Shakespeare's erudition or find it
extraordinary in an actor. After all, Shakespeare was not a
"humble player"; he lived at court. All his erudition is to

be found in the little books which were to his age what bookstall volumes are to ours.) "The Romans took their subjects from the Greeks, Molière from the Romans, Corneille from the Spaniards, Racine from Corneille and the Bible. . . . Ibsen seems to me the only dramatist who has really invented themes, and isn't that just his real greatness? No, there is nothing new that a writer can hope to bring except a certain way of looking at life. . . . In my own case, for instance, what I seek everywhere is the mask under which human beings conceal their unhappiness."

"So you think that all human beings are unhappy?"

"In social life, yes, all of them—in varying degrees. . . . They are solitary, they are consumed with desires which they dare not satisfy; and they wouldn't be happy if they did satisfy them, because they are too civilized. No, a modern man cannot be happy; he is a conflict, whether he likes it or not."

"Even those tanned, ruddy Englishmen with their boyish eyes?"

"Just like the rest. And the proof is that they have humour. Humour is a mask to hide unhappiness, and especially to hide the deep cynicism which life calls forth in all men. We're trying to bluff God. It is called polish. . . . Our young people in America, it seems to me, express that cynicism more honestly than most Europeans do. Freud has helped them a lot."

"But also spoilt them a lot. . . . In Freud there is a sexual obsession which simply is not true of the majority of men. . . ."

"Possibly. . . . There, again, I answer 'possibly' just to please you. Sexual life is so important."

The whole afternoon passed in pleasant conversation. He talked very well about music, especially about Bach. Then of the theatre.

"I saw *Le Misanthrope* in Paris the other day," he said, "but I was disappointed in the acting. They made Célimène into a most unattractive coquette. . . . No. . . . The terrible thing about Célimène is that she was very nice."

"I once thought of writing Célimène's diary," I told him. "It would have shown that her 'betrayals' were often, in her own eyes, merely attempts to placate Alceste and make him happy."

About five o'clock he rose. Unfortunately we shan't see him again. He is going for a walking-tour with Gene Tunney, the boxer.

"A strange companion."

"Don't think that. I'm very fond of him."

The Wilder biographer Gilbert Harrison describes the Wilder-Tunney walk in the Swiss Alps and southern France as "among the most publicized mini-events of the twenties." It was never very strenuous—a sports car donated to the champ figures prominently in the story. They are seen here (Wilder with walking stick) on the edge of Mont Blanc in September 1928.

A Lecture

Mme. de Sévigné held a place in the forefront of Wilder's pantheon of literary heroes. The portrait he fashioned of her in the figure of the Marquesa de Montemayor in *The Bridge* is an often-noted feature of the novel. On May 3, 1928, Wilder delivered the Daniel S. Lamont Memorial Lecture at Yale on "English Letters and Letter Writers." These excerpts focus on his subject and on his hero. The lecture, held at the Sampson Lyceum in New Haven, was open to town and gown and attracted an audience of several hundred. The lecture was retitled when published for the first time in 1979.

"On Reading the Great Letter Writers"

The very nature of letter writing is such that when we get together to discuss it there should never be more than a dozen persons. The great letter sequences are full of passages that you and I were never meant to see. I grant that some of the letters that I shall discuss were written with one eye on a larger audience; but many a letter by even the most conscious artists in this literature was not intended for the Complete Edition. There are letters even of Horace Walpole, the virtuoso, that he did not label *"Confidential: Please burn"* because he assumed as a matter of course that they would not be wrapped in ribbons and returned to him with the rest. Moreover, until the last fifty years, letters had always been edited, and the letter writers who might have had a lurking suspicion that their pages might be published someday never doubted that the local passages or the humdrum passages or the intimate passages would be cut out. They did not foresee the type of attention that the twentieth century would bring to such work; "morbid" they would have called it.

Moreover, there is an extraordinary aspect about the letter writers' work whereby one understands that even the consciousness of other readers does not impair or undermine the sincerity and the singlemindedness of the letters they address to the friends they really love. In the old sense, there is a "mystery" here. It is related to the mystery behind all creative literature above a certain level. Art is confession; art is the secret told. Art itself is a letter written to an ideal mind, to a dreamed-of audience. The great letter-sequences are written to close friends. But even the closest friends cannot meet the requirements of the artist, and the work passes over their shoulder to that half-divine audience that artists presuppose. All of Mme. de Sévigné's life was built about those wonderful letters. On one plane they were written to regain her daughter's affection, to attract her daughter's admiration and love. But Mme. de Sévigné knew that her daughter merely brought an amused, an indulgent, a faintly contemptuous appreciation. And time after time the letter rises beyond the understanding of the daughter and becomes an *aria* where the overloaded heart sings to itself for the sheer comfort of its felicity, sings perhaps to the daughter as she might have been. In such passages Mme. de Sévigné even defeated the purpose of the rest of the letter, even risked drawing upon herself her daughter's vexation and ill-humor. But sing she must. The audience of a work of art is never clear in a true artist's mind, but is made of souls that he has guessed at—old hero worships repersonified and loves transferred: as though the audiences at concerts and art galleries and the company of book-buyers were made up of Michelangelos and Platos and Violas and Imogens and Cardinal Newmans. Your letters and mine are messages to friends and we do them as well as we can to please the friends; but the great letters are letters to friends plus the most exacting spirits the mind can imagine.

But art is not only the desire to tell one's secret; it is the desire to tell it and to hide it at the same time. And the secret is nothing more than the whole drama of the inner life, the alternations between one's hope of self-improvement and one's self-reproach at one's failures. "Out of our quarrels with other people we make rhetoric," said William Butler Yeats; "out of our quarrels with ourselves we make literature." Self-reproach is the first and the continuing state of the soul. And it is the way we go about assuaging that reproach that makes us do anything valuable. . . .

I am supposed to be speaking about English writers, but I want to say a few more words about the greatest of all letter writers, Mme. de Sévigné. Indeed, she has almost a place in English letters, since two of our greatest loved her with a special love. Horace Walpole read and reread the volumes of her correspondence that kept making their first appearance in his time; he called her "Notre Dame des Rochers," and when he finally received the manuscript of one of her letters he treasured it above everything else he possessed. And Edward FitzGerald went so far as to prepare a little atlas and biographical dictionary and practically a concordance of her letters for his own use. The anthologists have made havoc with her reception in France. All students in that country, especially the girls, are obliged to study and imitate and comment upon a volume of her *Selected Letters*. And all the showpieces, all the stunt letters are there. But the way to enter the fair country that is her mind is to begin by not looking for the anecdotes of the court, or the flowerets of language, or the inimitable little jokes through which she sees life (for later "all these things shall be added unto you"), but to enter it as Marcel Proust said his grandmother did, by the door of the heart. For me the key to Mme. de Sévigné is

an acquaintance with her grandmother. Her grandmother was Mère Marie de Chantal, the co-worker of St. François de Sales. Mère Chantal was canonized as a Saint of the Church almost during Mme. de Sévigné's lifetime. She was one of those saints like St. Teresa who found no difficulty in living two full lifetimes in one, a Mary and a Martha. Her writings are among the minor classics of the Church. They are full of an overwhelming fixed adoration of God, and one has only to read them for a few pages to realize that it is the same blinding intensity that has been inherited by the granddaughter and fixed by some tragic accident upon a human being. And Mme. de Sévigné knew it, and the anthologies do not include those bitter and heartbroken passages in which the cards are really laid on the table:

This is my destiny [she writes to her daughter]; and the sufferings which follow upon my love for you, being offered to God constitute my penitence for an attachment which should be only for him.

Do I exaggerate?
She writes her friend Guitant:

I still am in the dark as to whether my dear daughter is coming back to Paris or not. However, I am preparing her rooms in our Carnavalet and we shall see what Providence has decreed. I ceaselessly keep this idea of Providence, Providence in my mind. All my thoughts are resigned to this sovereign will. There are my devotion. There is my scapulary. There is my rosary. There are my vigils. And if I were worthy of believing that I had a spiritual rôle to play I should say that it lay in that. But I am not

worthy: for what is one to do with a mind that sees clearly, but with a heart of ice?

One has to read thirty or forty letters to come upon such passages, but, having found them, all the rest flows with an even greater beauty. For example, I have never seen quoted in any book or article on Mme. de Sévigné a short phrase that explains the miracle of the style, and perhaps of all style:

Farewell, my blessed child; now I can go on telling you that I love you without fear of boring you, since you are willing to endure it in favor of my style: you excuse the importunity of my heart through your approval of my intelligence, isn't it just that?

Nor this terrible word:

All that is hateful in me, my daughter, proceeds from my lifetime of devotion to you.

In one of my books I made literary use of this situation with distinct allusion to Mme. de Sévigné: and I keep receiving indignant letters from lovers of the French-woman saying that I imagined it; that she, being the incarnation of grace and charm and the salon, was too sane to allow of such an interpretation.

Acknowledgments

—⚍—

The Afterword of this volume is constructed in large part from Thornton Wilder's words in unpublished letters, journals, business records, and publications not easy to come by. Readers interested in additional information about Thornton Wilder are referred to standard sources and to the Thornton Wilder Society's website: www.thorntonwildersociety.org.

Many Wilder fans deserve my thanks for helping me to accomplish this task, for which, of course, I bear full responsibility. Space permits me to extend thanks to only a few: Hugh Van Dusen, David Semanki, Barbara Whitepine, and Celeste Fellows. Four individuals deserve a special salute, and I am honored to give it: Barbara Hogenson, Russell Banks, J. D. McClatchy, and Penelope Niven.

Letters and Journals

With the exceptions noted below, quotations from Thornton Wilder's letters and his journal are taken from one of two principal sources: the unpublished letters, manuscripts, and related files in the Wilder Family Archives in the Yale Collection of American Lit-

erature at the Beinecke Rare Book and Manuscript Library, and the Wilder family's own holdings, including many of Thornton Wilder's legal and agency papers. Minor spelling errors have been silently corrected. All rights are reserved for this material. Appreciation is expressed to the family of the late Professor Franz Link, for a copy of Thornton Wilder's letter to him, and to the Lawrenceville School, for a copy of Wilder's letter to John Townley.

Publications

Excerpts from published sources are identified in the order of their appearance in the text, with permissions noted as required: Wilder's interview with André Maurois, "A Holiday Diary, 1928," appeared in André Maurois, *A Private Universe* (New York: D. Appleton & Co., 1932) and was reprinted in Jackson R. Bryer, Ed., *Conversations with Thornton Wilder* (Jackson: University Press of Mississippi, 1992), pp. 13–14. "On Reading the Great Letter Writers" was first published in Donald Gallup, Ed., *American Characteristics & Other Essays* (New York: Harper & Row, 1979; Authors Guild Backinprint edition, 2000), pp. 151–64. Reprinted by permission of Tappan Wilder.

Photographs

The Wilder-Tunney photo is courtesy of the Yale Collection of American Literature. The author's photo, taken of Thornton Wilder when he was a secondary-school teacher, is provided courtesy of the Lawrenceville School, with the special assistance of Jacqueline Haun of the Bunn Library.

THORNTON WILDER

In his quiet way, Thornton Niven Wilder was a revolutionary writer who experimented boldly with literary forms and themes, from the beginning to the end of his long career. "Every novel is different from the others," he wrote when he was seventy-five. "The theater (ditto). . . . The thing I'm writing now is again totally unlike anything that preceded it." Wilder's richly diverse settings, characters, and themes are at once specific and global. Deeply immersed in classical as well as contemporary literature, he often fused the traditional and the modern in his novels and plays, all the while exploring the cosmic in the commonplace. In a January 12, 1953, cover story, *Time* took note of Wilder's unique "interplanetary mind"—his ability to write from a vision that was at once American and universal.

A pivotal figure in the history of twentieth-century letters, Wilder was a novelist and playwright whose works continue to be widely read and produced in this new century. He is the only writer to have won the Pulitzer Prize for both Fiction and Drama. His second novel, *The Bridge of San Luis Rey*, received the Fiction award in 1928, and he won the prize twice in Drama, for *Our Town* in 1938 and *The Skin of Our Teeth* in 1943. His

other novels are *The Cabala, The Woman of Andros, Heaven's My Destination, The Ides of March, The Eighth Day*, and *Theophilus North*. His other major dramas include *The Matchmaker*, which was adapted as the internationally acclaimed musical comedy *Hello, Dolly!*, and *The Alcestiad*. Among his innovative shorter plays are *The Happy Journey to Trenton and Camden* and *The Long Christmas Dinner*, and two uniquely conceived series, *The Seven Ages of Man* and *The Seven Deadly Sins*, frequently performed by amateurs.

Wilder and his work received many honors, highlighted by the three Pulitzer Prizes, the Gold Medal for Fiction of the American Academy of Arts and Letters, the Order of Merit (Peru), the Goethe-Plakette der Stadt (Germany, 1959), the Presidential Medal of Freedom (1963), the National Book Committee's first National Medal for Literature (1965), and the National Book Award for Fiction (1967).

He was born in Madison, Wisconsin, on April 17, 1897, to Amos Parker Wilder and Isabella Niven Wilder. The family later lived in China and in California, where Wilder was graduated from Berkeley High School. After two years at Oberlin College, he went on to Yale, where received his undergraduate degree in 1920. A valuable part of his education took place during summers spent working hard on farms in California, Kentucky, Vermont, Connecticut, and Massachusetts. His father arranged these rigorous "shirtsleeve" jobs for Wilder and his older brother, Amos, as part of their initiation into the American experience.

Thornton Wilder studied archaeology and Italian as a special student at the American Academy in Rome (1920–1921), and earned a master of arts degree in French literature at Princeton in 1926.

In addition to his talents as playwright and novelist, Wilder was an accomplished teacher, essayist, translator, scholar, lecturer, librettist, and screenwriter. In 1942, he teamed with

Alfred Hitchcock to write the first draft of the screenplay for the classic thriller *Shadow of a Doubt*, receiving credit as principal writer and a special screen credit for his "contribution to the preparation" of the production. All but fluent in four languages, Wilder translated and adapted plays by such varied authors as Henrik Ibsen, Jean-Paul Sartre, and André Obey. As a scholar, he conducted significant research on James Joyce's *Finnegans Wake* and the plays of Spanish dramatist Lope de Vega.

Wilder's friends included a broad spectrum of figures on both sides of the Atlantic—Hemingway, Fitzgerald, Alexander Woollcott, Gene Tunney, Sigmund Freud, producer Max Reinhardt, Katharine Cornell, Ruth Gordon and Garson Kanin. Beginning in the mid-1930s, Wilder was especially close to Gertrude Stein and became one of her most effective interpreters and champions. Many of Wilder's friendships are documented in his prolific correspondence. Wilder believed that great letters constitute a "great branch of literature." In a lecture entitled "On Reading the Great Letter Writers," he wrote that a letter can function as a "literary exercise," the "profile of a personality," and "news of the soul," apt descriptions of thousands of letters he wrote to his own friends and family.

Wilder enjoyed acting and played major roles in several of his own plays in summer theater productions. He also possessed a lifelong love of music: reading musical scores was a hobby, and he wrote the librettos for two operas based on his work: *The Long Christmas Dinner*, with composer Paul Hindemith; and *The Alcestiad*, with composer Louise Talma. Both works premiered in Germany.

Teaching was one of Wilder's deepest passions. He began his teaching career in 1921 as an instructor in French at Lawrenceville, a private secondary school in New Jersey. Financial independence after the publication of *The Bridge of San Luis Rey* permitted him to leave the classroom in 1928, but he returned to teaching in the 1930s at the University of Chicago.

For six years, on a part-time basis, he taught courses there in classics in translation, comparative literature, and composition. In 1950–1951, he served as the Charles Eliot Norton Professor of Poetry at Harvard. Wilder's gifts for scholarship and teaching (he treated the classroom as all but a theater) made him a consummate, much-sought-after lecturer in his own country and abroad. After World War II, he held special standing, especially in Germany, as an interpreter of his own country's intellectual traditions and their influence on cultural expression.

During World War I, Wilder had served a three-month stint as an enlisted man in the Coast Artillery section of the army, stationed at Fort Adams, Rhode Island. He volunteered for service in World War II, advancing to the rank of lieutenant colonel in Army Air Force Intelligence. For his service in North Africa and Italy, he was awarded the Legion of Merit, the Bronze Star, the Chevalier Legion d'Honneur, and honorary officership in the Military Order of the British Empire (M.B.E.).

From royalties received from *The Bridge of San Luis Rey*, Wilder built a house for his family in 1930 in Hamden, Connecticut, just outside New Haven. But he typically spent as many as two hundred days a year away from Hamden, traveling to and settling in a variety of places that provided the stimulation and solitude he needed for his work. Sometimes his destination was the Arizona desert, the MacDowell Colony in New Hampshire, or Martha's Vineyard, Newport, Saratoga, Vienna, or Baden-Baden. He wrote aboard ships, and often chose to stay in "spas in off-season." He needed a certain refuge when he was deeply immersed in writing a novel or play. Wilder explained his habit to a *New Yorker* journalist in 1959: "The walks, the quiet—all the elegance is present, everything is there but the people. That's it! A spa in off-season! I make a practice of it."

But Wilder always returned to "the house *The Bridge* built," as it is still known to this day. He died there of a heart attack on December 7, 1975.

Perennial is proud to reissue the works of Thornton Wilder. Each has a new Foreword by a noted writer, as well as new documentary material edited by Tappan Wilder.

NOVELS

THE BRIDGE OF SAN LUIS REY
ISBN 0-06-008887-7 (Perennial Classics paperback)
With a new Foreword by Russell Banks

The Bridge of San Luis Rey opens in the aftermath of an inexplicable tragedy— a footbridge in Peru breaks and five people fall to their deaths. For Brother Juniper, a humble monk who witnesses the catastrophe, the question is inescapable: why those five? Through the device of Brother Juniper's drive to understand whether their deaths were caused by fate or divine intervention, Wilder's 1928 Pulitzer Prize–winning novel explores what is important and what is lasting about life and living.

"One of the greatest reading novels in this century's American writing." —Edmund Fuller

THEOPHILUS NORTH
ISBN 0-06-008892-3 (paperback)
With a new Foreword by Christopher Buckley

An exhausted 29-year-old teacher arrives in Newport, Rhode Island, in the summer of 1926. To support himself, he takes jobs in the great homes of families living along Ocean Drive—playing the roles of tutor, spy, confidante, lover, friend, and enemy in the colorful, tension-filled upstairs-and-downstairs world of Newport in the golden 1920s. Along the way, the novel raises gentle but trenchant questions about what's important, the nature and role of youth, and what wealth does to those who have it and those who do not.

"A testimony to the human race." —*New York Times Book Review*

HEAVEN'S MY DESTINATION
ISBN 0-06-008889-3 (paperback)
With a new Foreword by J. D. McClatchy

First published in 1934, *Heaven's My Destination* contains one of Wilder's most memorable characters: the heroic traveling textbook salesman George Marvin Brush. George's territory is the Midwest and, as a fervent religious convert, he is determined to lead a good Christian life. But his travels take him through smoking cars, bawdy houses, and trailer camps of Depression-era America with often hilarious results.

"A good sardonic etching of this most godless of American ages." —*Commonweal*

THE CABALA AND THE WOMAN OF ANDROS
ISBN 0-06-051857-X (paperback)
With a new Foreword

Two of Wilder's early novels are collected here: *The Cabala* (1926), a fantasy about American expatriates, and *The Woman of Andros* (1930), a novel in which Wilder creates a character that serves as his archetype of the virtue of hope.

 Perennial

THE IDES OF MARCH
ISBN 0-06-008890-7 (paperback)
With a new Foreword by Kurt Vonnegut, Jr.

First published in 1948, *The Ides of March* is a brilliant epistolary novel of Julius Caesar's Rome. Through imaginary letters and documents, Wilder brings to life a dramatic period of world history and one of its magnetic personalities.

"What distinguishes [*The Ides of March*] is a rich, shrewd, and glowing characterization of Caesar's restless mind." —*New York Times*

THE EIGHTH DAY
ISBN 0-06-008891-5 (paperback)
With a new Foreword by John Updike

First published in 1967, near the end of Wilder's life, this novel moves back and forth through the 20th century, telling the story of a talented inventor accused of murder.

PLAYS

THREE PLAYS
Our Town, The Skin of Our Teeth, and *The Matchmaker*
ISBN 0-06-051264-4 (Perennial Classics paperback)
With a new Foreword by John Guare

This omnibus volume brings together the definitive texts of three outstanding plays by one of America's most distinguished writers.

OUR TOWN: *A Play*
ISBN 0-06-051263-6 (Perennial Classics paperback)
With a new Foreword by Donald Margulies

First produced and published in 1938, this Pulitzer Prize–winning drama of life in the small village of Grover's Corners has become an American classic and is Thornton Wilder's most renowned and most frequently performed play.

"Mr. Wilder has transmuted the simple events of human life into universal reverie. . . . One of the finest achievements of the current stage." —Brooks Atkinson

THE SKIN OF OUR TEETH: *A Play*
ISBN 0-06-008893-1 (Perennial Classics paperback)
With a new Foreword by Paula Vogel

Wilder's Pulitzer Prize–winning (1943) madcap comedy of how the Antrobus family and its maid prevail over successive catastrophes has become a timeless statement about human endurance and hope . . . and the imperishable vitality of theater.

"It is not easy to think of any other American play with so good a chance of being acted a hundred years from now." —Alexander Woollcott, *Atlantic Monthly,* 1944

Available wherever books are sold, or call 1-800-331-3761 to order.

UNPLUGGED

Dedicated to my parents, who are simply the best parents of all time. I am blessed to be your daughter. Thanks for going above and beyond during the writing process.

Thanks, also, to Betsy Flikkema and the rest of the crew
at Zondervan for your great work!

The children's group of Zondervan

www.zonderkidz.com

Unplugged
Copyright © 2007 by G Studios, LLC

Requests for information should be addressed to:
Zonderkidz, Grand Rapids, Michigan 49530

Library of Congress Cataloging-in-Publication Data

Crouch, Cheryl, 1968-
 Unplugged / by Cheryl Crouch.
 p. cm. -- (The Chosen Girls)
 Summary: When her father agrees to allow the Chosen Girls to accompany him to Moscow where he has a conference, Trin, excited at the prospect of international exposure, decides this is the perfect opportunity to show Harmony and Mello how a band should be run.
 ISBN-13: 978-0-310-71269-5 (softcover)
 ISBN-10: 0-310-71269-6 (softcover)
 [1. Bands (Music)--Fiction. 2. Rock music--Fiction. 3. Interpersonal relations--Fiction. 4. Moscow (Russia)--Fiction. 5. Russia--Fiction. 6. Christian life--Fiction.] I. Title.
 PZ7.C8838Unp 2007
 [Fic]--dc22

 2006023532

Editor: Bruce Nuffer
Art direction and design: Sarah Molegraaf
Interior composition: Christine Orejuela-Winkelman

Printed in the United States of America

07 08 09 10 11 12 • 7 6 5 4 3 2 1

UNPLUGGED

By Cheryl Crouch

zonder**kidz**

ZONDERVAN.com/
AUTHORTRACKER
follow your favorite authors

You did not choose me, but I chose you and appointed you to go and bear fruit—fruit that will last. Then the Father will give you whatever you ask in my name.
—John 15:16

Sweet!

I'm glad we moved to California. I love being close to beaches and mountains. And palm trees are WAY cool ... I still feel like I'm on vacation every time I see one.

what to pack:

super suit
white boots
~~black boots~~
jeans
T-shirts for layering
layered skirt
high-top boots
coat!!!
(pink sweater)
~~green sweater~~
~~white sweater~~
necklaces
bracelets
~~pink tights~~
white long-sleeve tee
extra guitar strings
camera
~~books~~
(BIBLE!!!)
bottled water
blow-dryer

★ ★ AMERICAN ★

ROCK BAND

CHOSEN GIRLS

Live in Concert!

Saturday

4:00 p.m.

Tickets sold at the door

Chosen Girls rock RUSSIA!!!!!

I will make this trip rock! I don't want to let everyone down. I have to get our schedule for the tour in Russia.

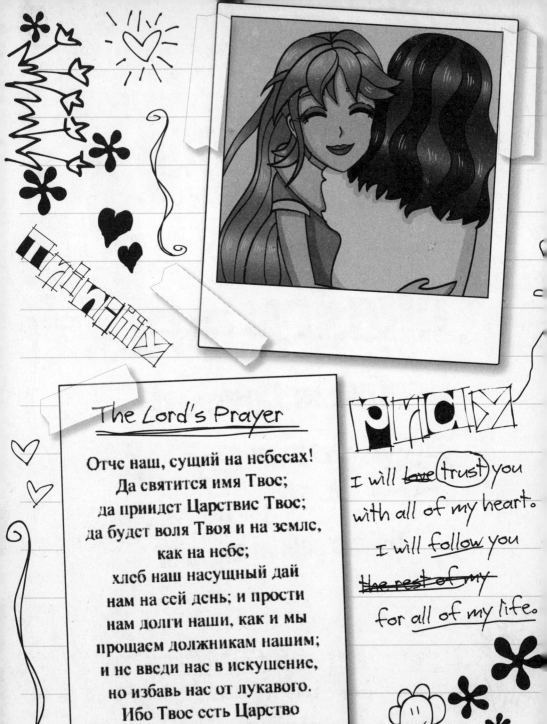

The Lord's Prayer

Отче наш, сущий на небесах!
Да святится имя Твое;
да придет Царствие Твое;
да будет воля Твоя и на земле,
как на небе;
хлеб наш насущный дай
нам на сей день; и прости
нам долги наши, как и мы
прощаем должникам нашим;
и не введи нас в искушение,
но избавь нас от лукавого.
Ибо Твое есть Царство
и сила и слава во веки.
Аминь.

pray

I will ~~love~~ (trust) you
with all of my heart.
I will follow you
~~the rest of my~~
for all of my life.

I want to be in ~~charge~~ control
but not if it (costs) me my soul
You alone know the path that's best for me
How can I ~~ever~~ give it up?

Trust you to help me ~~~~ live it up?
You made me—why's that so hard for me to see?

- [x] bake MORE cookies
- [x] get shots (OUCH!*)
- [x] pack!!! ★
- [x] (finish lyrics)
- [x] call Mello

sing*

ADMIT ONE

The Chosen Girls
7:30 pm
Theater: 3-A

I wish I could sew like Mello. It would be way <u>fabulous</u> because I could make clothes that aren't like <u>ANYONE</u> else's!

Russian Phrases to learn!

Pozhaluista = Please

Spaseebo balshoye = Thank you very much

Yzumitelno = <u>Marvelous!</u>

kak pazhivayete? = How are you?

Yielding Control to God

LOVE

Western Airlines

Depart: Los Angeles
8:05 a.m.

Arrive: New York
4:55 p.m.

Seat 64 B

0001000101101011000

Western Airlines

Depart: Los Angeles
8:05 a.m.

Arrive: New York
4:55 p.m.

Seat 64 B

0001000101101011011000 • 0010001110101011

This ticket is
nontransferable,
non-transfundable.

Plane will board
30 minutes prior
to take-off.

2 Pcs. of luggage
per passenger.

What we've earned so far:

$5 - cookie sale
$250 - jewelry sale
$625 - purses!!!

TOTAL: $~~853~~

I will trust you
with all of my heart.
I will follow you
for all of my life.
You know the ~~road~~
path ahead
so I will trust you instead
yeah, I will trust in you!

chapter • 1

...

Moving to California scared me 'cause in Dallas I knew where I fit. I survived some hard lessons in Dallas.

Like when I invited those girls from ballet to my birthday bash. Two of the coolest girls in school—my friends. Then when Ashlyn didn't show and Jade dissed everything we did at the party, I understood. They were only friends if nobody else was around.

I didn't want to start over in California. But when I got here, I met the best friends ever—Harmony and Mello. I stopped worrying about past mistakes. Soon I even quit pretending I had my act together.

Ohwow! We started our own rock band! Music videos and rock concerts. We're actually in them, instead of just watching. Sure, we had challenges, but I just knew I didn't have to worry about being embarrassed anymore.

But I was wrong.
So wrong.

• • •

"Give me one more run straight through, and then take five," said the sound engineer over the intercom.

I nodded at him through the huge glass window. The soundman, John, sat in the control room, while Mello, Harmony, and I jammed in studio four. Acoustic tiles, wood, and carpeting covered the floors, walls, and even the ceiling of the room. Our friend Lamont made faces at us behind John's back.

"Sweet! I still can't believe we're in a real recording studio," I said, ignoring Lamont as I quickly fine-tuned my electric guitar.

Mello grinned at me from behind her drum set. "I feel like we live here, after yesterday."

"But how cool is this?" Harmony asked, waving her arms at the microphones, headsets, and glass sound-isolation booths surrounding us. She jerked her head at the control room. "And Lamont looks like he's died and gone to heaven. That control room has enough equipment to launch a space shuttle."

John's voice interrupted us. "Anytime you're ready, Chosen Girls."

Mello tapped three beats and we played the intro. I smiled at Harmony, who played a solid bass line, and then nodded at Mello. We came in on the pickup note:

Oh, Chik'n Quik
Chicken on a stick
It's so yummy for your tummy
Everybody loves Chik'n Quik

Mello's alto blended perfectly with my soprano, and Harmony's bass guitar sounded awesome with my electric. Mello ended the jingle with a cymbal crash. Perfect!

"Thanks," John said. "Take a short break. Be ready to go again in five."

Harmony and I stood our guitars on their stands, and Mello grabbed a bottle of water.

"I can't wait to hear us on the radio!" Harmony said.

Mello laughed. "But … it's a chicken jingle."

Harmony rounded on her. "Most bands would be psyched to have a manager get them a gig like this. You have to start somewhere."

"But we *have* started," Mello answered. "We're on TV. We do concerts. Why do we need a chicken jingle?"

I giggled as I opened a bottle of juice. I agreed with Mello—it did seem a little lame.

"We need to break into radio," Harmony said in her I'm-trying-to-be-patient-with-you voice. "This is how we're going to do it. Plus, this job got us the hookup for our next concert," she added, digging her hand into a bag of chocolate pretzels and peanuts. "You'll see. Even Makayla and the Snob Mob will forget about our botched show in Lewisville." She flounced to the floor and popped a pretzel in her mouth.

"Makayla and the Snob Mob will always be posers, Harmony," I reminded her. "I thought you figured that out."

Lamont bounded in. "You women sound amazing." He reached for some pretzels. "You sold me. I could eat some chicken on a stick right now!"

The door burst open, and a huge man walked in. "I'm Mr. Walling," he announced in a loud bass voice. "Great studio, huh?"

Harmony put her pretzels behind her and jumped up. "The owner of Chik'n Quik?" She stepped toward him, reaching out her right hand. "I'm Harmony Gomez, manager of the Chosen Girls. I'm the one you spoke to on the phone."

"Glad to meet you, Harmony and Chosen Girls," he boomed, pumping Harmony's arm up and down. "I'm thrilled about our agreement." He seemed to fill the room with his large belly and even larger personality.

"We're ready, sir," John said, sticking his head in the door. He looked at us. "I'm going to play that last recording for Mr. Walling, so you've got a few more minutes of break." He left, and Mr. Walling followed him to the control room.

We could see them talking, but we couldn't hear them through the soundproof glass. They got still, listening. Then Mr. Walling said something. John answered him, and Mr. Walling shook his head. He frowned.

"He didn't like it," Mello whispered.

I watched the discussion, wishing I could read lips but thinking it might be good I couldn't.

"That's normal," I said. "People usually have to record like twenty times to get it right."

Mello tapped nervously on her snare. "I don't think we'll get it any better than that. We aced it."

John leaned over and pushed something, and Mr. Walling's voice filled the room. "Beautiful, just beautiful! I loved it!"

John's voice came next. "I told Mr. Walling he's got the studio for the next four hours, if he wants a few more takes. But he says there's no point."

"Do you have any songs you'd like to record?" Mr. Walling asked. "I've paid for the session, so you might as well use it. And I'd like to listen, if I may."

"Sweet!" I answered. "What first?" I looked at Mello and Harmony, not wanting to waste a second.

" 'You've Chosen Me,' " Harmony said. "Our signature song." I nodded, and Mello got us started. Something about the studio brought out the best in us. We rocked. We sang "Love Lessons" next. John had us each play individually too.

When our time ran out, Mr. Walling came in and shook our hands. "We'll see you tomorrow at the grand opening," he said.

"Yes, sir," Harmony agreed. "I put your posters all over town."

Mello asked, "What time do you want us there, Mr. Walling?"

Harmony looked sideways at her and answered, "Grand Opening at five, Chosen Girls in place by four. Right?"

"That's right," Mr. Walling agreed.

"And where is your restaurant?" I asked. Harmony frowned at me. "I just want to be sure," I explained. "After your mistake in Lewisville ..."

She glared at me, then turned to Mr. Walling and asked, "The fifteen hundred block of Hibiscus, next to the Wash-and-Run, right?"

Mr. Walling beamed at Harmony. "Just beautiful! I'll see you there." He smiled at all of us. "After what I heard today, I'm even more excited about your concert." He started for the door and added, "Don't forget to listen to the radio. The ad starts running tomorrow." His voice trailed away down the hall. "Beautiful."

John came in as we packed up. "I'll mix and balance these recordings, and you can pick up your CD next week," he told us. "I must say, for a start-up band, you record really well. It takes some groups four days to get a single."

I thanked him, and he said, "That session would usually run you $225 an hour. But don't thank me. Thank Mr. Walling."

As the door closed behind him, Harmony added, "You can also thank your awesome manager. I told you this was a good gig."

•••

Friday

We got to Chik'n Quik at three-thirty on Friday.

"I told you we didn't need to leave straight from school," Harmony griped as she hauled an amp out of Mom's Suburban.

I grabbed another amp. "Hey, better safe than sorry," I responded. "If we want to be a real band, we can't afford to be late. Or go to the wrong location."

"I know the location, Trin," Harmony huffed.

Mello stepped between us. "So Mr. Walling wants us to wear our superhero stuff?" she interrupted. "For the whole concert? Why don't we switch during 'You've Chosen Me,' like we usually do?"

"Yeah," Lamont agreed. "The superhero thing doesn't make sense without the video. It explains where your power comes from."

"I guess I can ask," Harmony answered, heading for the flatbed trailer that would be our stage. "But he wanted to know if we'd be willing to do the whole concert in costume, and I said okay. It seemed like a small thing for what he's paying us. I guess he thinks our super suits are cool."

"Way cool," I said, following her. I put the amp on the edge of the stage and waved an imaginary sword around. "Don't you wish just putting the suit on gave you superpowers?"

"I'd wear mine every day," Harmony agreed with a smile.

Lamont put the soundboard down. "Sorry, women. No power in the suits." He looked around. The stage backed up to a small lawn covered in brilliant green grass, tropical flowers, and palms. To the right, cars cruised by on Hibiscus Drive. "This is a great place for the stage. Right by the main drag. Everyone who passes will know something's going on."

Mello said, "I can't believe I'm doing this."

"It's good for you," I answered. "Little by little, you're over-coming your shyness—breaking out of your shell."

"Little by little?" she asked. "More like you went after my shell with a sledgehammer!"

We got our equipment hooked up and ran through sound checks. Then we grabbed the bags with our costumes in them. "Now, aren't you glad we're early?" I asked. "We have time to get dressed and do our hair."

Mello sighed and said, "Trin, your hair already looks great."

"Same to you, Miss Elegance," I answered with a smile.

Mr. Walling met us on the other side of the parking lot, at the door of Chik'n Quik. His bass voice rang out as he said, "Hello, Chosen Girls. Hello, Lamont! I see you found the stage. Beautiful. Come on in and look around." He held the door for us. "What do you think?"

I looked around. It looked like any other fast-food restau-rant. "I . . . uh . . . like the color of your seat covers," I offered.

"Yes, thank you," he answered. "Beautiful."

We headed for the restroom.

Mr. Walling called, "Wait. I have your costumes in the back."

I held up my bag. "No, we've got them here," I corrected. But he was gone.

He came back with a huge box. "Wait till you see these," he said, putting the box on a table. "I ordered three of them from headquarters, and I'm so pleased. You'll stop traffic—no questions asked." He opened the box and reached in.

And pulled out a chicken suit.

•••

Standing onstage, I looked through the hole cut in the beak of my suit. A few cars had already parked, and people laughed and pointed as they came toward us. More and more cars pulled in.

The chicken head I wore was thick enough to be hot, but not thick enough to block the sounds of horns honking on Hibiscus Drive. More than one guy yelled, "Hey, Chicks! Lookin' good!"

Embarrassed, I looked down at my feet. That didn't help. Red chicken claws were there where my ultracool high-heeled boots belonged.

Harmony wisely avoided eye contact. Her bright yellow beak faced straight ahead as we ran through final checks, so I could only see her white feathers and skinny yellow chicken legs.

"At least no one can recognize us." Mello's weak voice came from the direction of her drums, behind me.

I turned to look at her. "Mello, thanks to our overeager manager, signs all over town say 'Chosen Girls to perform at Grand Opening.' Everyone knows it's us."

"So what do you want me to do?" Harmony hissed. "He's paying us. He gave us a free recording session."

Mr. Walling strode across the parking lot toward us, flashing a huge smile and a double thumbs-up. He came onstage and grabbed my microphone.

"Thanks for coming out to our grand opening," he told the gathering crowd. "Please enjoy free samples of our delicious Chik'n Quik chicken on a stick while you listen to the music of the best new group in Southern California: the Chosen Girls!" He turned to us. "Open with the jingle!"

He walked offstage and we started in. I was singing, "It's so yummy for your tummy," when I first saw them in the crowd.

Makayla and the Snob Mob.

• • •

After the concert, Mom dropped us at the shed in Mello's backyard. I don't know why we call it the shed. It's more like an apartment or a studio. It's got everything—a couch, TV, plenty of room to jam. It's even decorated with real art and throw pillows that match the curtains.

We unloaded our equipment. But that wasn't all we unloaded.

"Unbelievable!" I shouted at Harmony. "You are the only person who could mess this up so royally." I put my electric down and flopped onto the couch.

"Do you think I enjoyed it?" she yelled back. She threw an armload of extension cords down. "Humiliating myself in front of Makayla and company? *Again!*"

"Forget about the Snob Mob. Half of Hopetown was there," I wailed.

"Look on the bright side," Lamont said, carrying in a drum.

Mello put a snare in the corner and glared at him. "There is no bright side, Lamont."

"But there is," he insisted. "Remember what Trin said before the concert? Based on your costumes today, I'd

say Mello isn't the only one who broke out of her shell." He slapped his thigh. "Get it? Chickens? Eggs?"

I rolled my eyes. "So *not* funny, Lamont," I told him. "Harmony, how many times do you expect us to put up with this? I'm not used to being humiliated."

"Stick around," Mello said. "You might *get* used to it."

Harmony looked at me, then at Lamont, and then at Mello. No one said anything.

Harmony blinked and took a deep breath like she didn't want to cry. Then she turned and stomped out.

Lamont followed her.

"I'm with you, Trin," Mello said. "I mean, Harmony's like a sister to me. Has been since second grade. But I can't handle any more of her messes." She sat next to me and put her head in her hands. "What we need is a manager who can actually manage." She looked at me. "I bet you'd be a good manager."

I let out a big breath and shook my head.

• • •

We needed to regroup, so we met at Java Joint later.

I apologized to Harmony for my attitude. Mello clued in and said she was sorry too. Lamont didn't make any more smart remarks, and it looked like we would be okay.

Then the Snob Mob came in. Makayla pointed to us and yelled, "Look! My favorite rock band: the Chicken Girls."

Thankfully, they got their drinks to go.

Harmony started bawling. "I'm such a loser. Why do you guys even let me hang with you? I wish ..." She stopped to

wipe her nose on her sleeve. "I wish I could just leave the country!"

I looked into her red, swollen eyes and yelled, "That's it!"

They all looked at me.

I flashed them my biggest smile and said, "It's perfect. Exactly what we need. Let's go to Russia!"

chapter • 2

...

Still Friday Night

They put their drinks down. Lamont said, "Where?"

"Russia," I repeated. "My dad told me last night that he has a conference in Moscow. It's during the next break. Wouldn't it be way fabulous to go with him? Have you guys ever been?"

They looked at me like I had sprouted an extra head.

"To Russia?" Mello asked.

"Yeah," I answered.

"No," she said.

"Nuh-uh," Lamont agreed.

"Me neither," Harmony added. "I haven't been anywhere since we moved here from Peru."

"Ohwow! Let's go!" I said.

Mello shook her head. "We can't just go to Russia," she said.

I prepared to do battle. "Why can't we?" I asked.

Mello looked at Harmony, waiting to be rescued.

Harmony tried. "Russia is, like, a foreign country," she said.

I smiled. "True that, Harmony!" I answered. "And we're free to travel abroad. We're allowed to go to foreign countries."

Mello looked irritated. "It costs money, Trin. And you have to have passports and shots and stuff."

I nodded. "We can raise the money. And it's easy to get passports. Come on! Think of the exciting experiences! We'll make memories to last a lifetime."

Harmony started to smile, and her eyes sparkled. "I've seen pictures of Red Square," she said. "It's *muy bonita*. It would be cool frijoles to get our picture made there."

I wiggled with excitement. "Raise your hand if you'd love to do a concert there. The Chosen Girls on tour in Russia!"

Harmony practically jumped off her chair. "An international tour! Sí! Let's do it!"

I looked at Lamont. "You in? We'll need you on sound."

He grinned. "Sounds good."

We all looked at Mello, who tapped nervously on the edge of the table.

"Mello?" I asked.

The corners of her mouth turned up. "I've always wanted to see St. Basil's Cathedral," she answered.

I jumped up and did a happy dance. I pulled out my cell and punched in Dad's number. When he answered I asked, "Hey, Dad, where are you?"

He was still at work.

"I'm sorry you're having to work so hard," I said. "My buds and I are at Java Joint. Can we bring you a chocolate chip mocha?"

He said sure.

I punched End and walked to the counter. "This is the kind of question you ask in person," I explained.

"And a mocha never hurts," Lamont agreed with a grin.

•••

We walked to the college campus where my dad teaches economics. I love it there — benches tucked into tiny gardens, fountains bubbling, and college students everywhere.

I said hello to Sam, who mans the guard booth, and we started uphill to the business building. The whole time we talked about Russia — what would the food taste like? How would people act?

Our voices echoed in the halls of Dad's building. No one wanted to hang out in the business department on Friday night.

Dad said hello and took a sip of his drink. "So what can I do for you fine folks?" he asked.

"Dad!" I exclaimed. "What makes you think we want anything?"

He laughed. "I don't know. Do you and your friends usually bring me something from Java Joint on Friday nights?"

I looked away. "Yeah, well ..."

Harmony spoke up. "You're a smart man, Mr. Adams. We do want something. We're hoping you can help us with a major cool idea."

Lamont caught Harmony's spirit. "See, sir," he began, "our worldviews are way too limited. There's a whole world out there, and we want to see it."

"You always say traveling is the best education a person can get," I added.

Dad smiled. "Mello, I haven't heard from you. What do you all have in mind? A trip to the beach? A weekend in the mountains?"

Mello said, "Actually, we're hoping you'll take us to Russia."

Dad's face was a riot. Total shock. *"Russia?"*

"You're going anyway," I blurted. "It will be so good for us."

Dad wiped his face with one big hand. Then he smiled. "You're right," he said. "I'd love to take you."

Mello squealed. Harmony and I screamed and jumped up and down. Lamont said, "Oh, happy day!"

"On one condition," Dad continued.

We stopped celebrating.

Dad looked each of us in the eyes, like he was measuring how serious we were. Then he said, "You raise your own money for airfare and meals."

I sighed in relief. "Well, yeah. No biggie."

Everyone looked at me, surprised. "I mean, yeah, it's big," I stammered. "But we can do it."

"It's crazy, but I really think you can," Dad agreed, nodding.

• • •

"We already have the money from the chicken jingle and the chicken concert," I said as we started walking back.

"Aha!" Lamont said. "A bright side at last."

"And raise your hand if you think a bake sale would be fun," I asked. "We could sell cookies. I've got this recipe for Simply Scrumptious Triple Chunk—"

Lamont interrupted to ask, "Do you know how many cookies you're talking about?"

"Hush, Lamont, I want to hear about the triple-chunk stuff," Harmony said. She turned to me, her eyes bright.

I ignored Harmony and answered Lamont. "I didn't say it would be our *only* fund-raiser. I said it would be our first."

"I've seen people sell stuff in front of the grocery store," Mello offered. "You know, set up a card table and a little sign—"

"Or the college campus!" I said. "College kids are always half-starved. Especially for homemade food."

We got to my house. "Come on. I bet we have enough stuff in the kitchen to make a double batch. We can start tonight, make more in the morning, and sell all afternoon. Our next $200 will be in the bag by tomorrow night."

Mello paused by the front door. "Um, my parents don't even know about the trip yet," she pointed out.

I patted her on the shoulder. "Minor detail. Bake now, explain later."

"It's getting late, Trin," Lamont said as he looked at his watch.

I handed him my cell then opened the door. "So call home. Tell them you're making cookies at my house."

"I'll help if I can lick the bowl," Harmony volunteered as they followed me inside.

"I've heard Russians love Americans," I said as I dug out the recipe. "When a friend of mine went, so many people came to see them they had to stand in the aisles and look in through windows. And they were just a church choir. Imagine what they'd do for a real live rock band!" I opened the pantry and pulled out cocoa, flour, and chocolate chips.

"Oh, yeah," Lamont said. "How about if I record the whole trip? And all your concerts."

"Sweet!" I said, setting the sugar and vanilla next to the other stuff on the counter.

Mello shook her head. "I'm not sure I'm ready for you to pick up that camera again, Lamont!"

Harmony messed with the measuring cups. "Wait. You are so getting ahead of yourselves," she huffed. "What are you thinking? We're just going to walk around in a foreign country and pull out our guitars and drums and do concerts anywhere we feel like it? As manager, I happen to know it's not that easy."

I bit my lip. Then in a calm, controlled voice I said, "I haven't worked out the details yet, Harmony. But I will. And it's going to be a trip you'll never forget. I promise."

•••

Saturday

The next morning, we set up near the college cafeteria. "This way they can buy our cookies for dessert," I explained.

Lamont popped out the legs on the card table. "I never want to see chocolate again," he complained. "How many triple chunks did we make?"

I lifted a box of cookies onto the table. "Each batch makes forty-eight cookies. We made eight batches, so that's ..."

"Three hundred eighty-four cookies," Harmony said with a moan, flopping onto a folding chair.

"No, we made three hundred fifty-four," Mello corrected.

Harmony grabbed a pen and paper. She wrote out the problem and held it up for us to see. "Three hundred *eighty-four*," she said triumphantly.

Mello grinned at her. "It was three hundred eighty-four before *you* started eating the dough. You must have eaten at least thirty cookies' worth."

Two surfer dudes wandered by.

"Want some homemade cookies?" I called.

They walked over to the table. "Do you take debit cards?" one asked.

"No, only cash," Harmony said with a smile.

"Sorry. Don't have any cash on me," he said. "You?" he asked his buddy.

"Nope. Wish I did." They left.

The campus was strangely quiet.

"Where are all the starving college kids you told us about?" Harmony asked.

I shrugged my shoulders. "I don't know. They're usually everywhere. I've never seen the campus so dead."

"First time here on a Saturday?" Lamont asked. I nodded. "Bet everyone went home for the weekend," he said.

I looked at our boxes and boxes of cookies, wondering if we should pack up and go home. But just then, four girls walked by. "Want cookies?" I asked.

"Simply Scrumptious Triple Chunk Fudge," Harmony added.

They practically ran over us. They squealed, "Cookies!" and "Chocolate!" and each bought two.

"Our first four dollars," Lamont said proudly. "Moscow, here we come!"

• • •

"Four measly dollars," Harmony complained hours later as we packed up. "I can't believe we stayed up half the night baking *and* got up early to bake *and* sat here all day and only sold eight cookies. We spent more than four dollars on ingredients."

"So, actually, we lost money," Mello pointed out.

I sighed. "We didn't quite reach our goal," I admitted.

"Reach our goal?" Lamont said. "Woman, we didn't even get on the track. We're not in the ballpark. Nowhere near the playing field—"

"I get it, Lamont," I interrupted, shoving a triple chunk in his mouth. "Be quiet and eat a cookie."

chapter • 3

...

Sunday Afternoon

I lay on my bed, staring at the boxes of Simply Scrumptious Triple Chunks stacked around my room. I sighed, got up slowly, and got a cookie out. I raised it to my mouth ... and almost gagged.

I couldn't make myself eat even one more.

I had been so sure about the bake sale. The way all of us worked together in the kitchen — way cool. We laughed the whole time, planning and dreaming about Russia. And then the whole sale flopped. *Four dollars!* Now what? Would they trust me to plan anything after this? Three hundred forty-six cookies might go stale, but I had to keep plans for the trip fresh.

I felt like those dumb boxes were laughing at me. I stuck my tongue out at them. But it ended up being the boxes of cookies that gave me my way fabulous idea.

I picked up my cell. "Harmony, emergency meeting in the shed at three o'clock. I'll call Lamont. You call Mello, OK?"

They all showed. "OK, everybody," I began. I clicked on my new PDA and found the agenda I had typed in. "We need to raise thousands of dollars, fast. For normal people, it would be impossible. But not for us!"

"Especially since we've already raised four dollars," Harmony said in her snottiest voice.

"We're about to make a lot more," I said quickly. "Get this: we sell the cookies to Lottie for fifty cents each. She can sell them at Java Joint for a buck apiece. She wins, we win."

"So if she says yes, we get … what? Almost two hundred dollars?" Mello asked. "We need thousands, Trin."

"Good point," I agreed. "But that was only phase one. Phase two: we use some of the profits to buy stuff for a car wash."

Harmony interrupted to ask, "Lamont, doesn't your mom sell stuff on the Internet?"

He nodded. "That's right."

"Do you think she'd get us a hookup to do that?"

"I bet she would."

I interrupted. "That sounds way fabulous, but there's a problem. I don't see people buying these cookies over the Internet. Why not sell them to Lottie?"

"Not cookies," Harmony said. "Something else. Like jewelry! I've got loads already made up, and it won't take long to make more."

Mello actually looked excited. She clapped her hands and said, "Excellent. It's so beautiful! We could charge lots for it!"

Harmony's face lit up. "Mello, what about those hot purses you've been making? Could you make more?"

Mello smiled. "They're way easy."

"Cool frijoles!"

I was losing control of the meeting, fast. I said, "But what about—"

Lamont interrupted. "I can set up a site for the Chosen Girls. I'll tell about the band and the trip, and show photos of the stuff you're selling. I could even sell the *You've Chosen Me* DVDs. And those new CDs, when they're ready."

Harmony jumped up and started dancing. "Oh yeah, oh yeah. Chosen Girls rock the World Wide Web."

"Let's head next door," Lamont said. "We have no time to lose."

Harmony and Mello followed him to the door without glancing at me.

I wanted to yell after them, *Excuse me. Who is in charge of this meeting? Who thought of this trip? Who invited all of you?*

Instead I mumbled, "So no one cares about all these Simply Scrumptious Triple Chunks?"

Harmony stopped and turned around. "Sí, I care. Why don't you bring a batch to Lamont's house?"

Then she was gone.

I punched the power button on my PDA, shutting off all my great ideas, and followed her.

• • •

Monday

The next afternoon I sat in the shed trying to follow Harmony's directions. I am *not* all about making jewelry.

"No, Trin, it's purple, green, blue, green, purple," she said for the fifth time.

It didn't matter, because right then I dropped one end of the string. The beads I'd been threading for the last ten minutes poured onto the carpet.

Mello looked up from the sewing machine she had carried out to the shed and giggled. "Or you could do purple, purple, blue, green, purple, green, green, blue," she said, calling out the colors around my feet.

I growled and squatted down, picking the beads out of the carpet.

"Would you rather help me with the purses, Trin?" she asked.

I would rather do my own thing, I thought. *I'm sick of helping everyone else with* their *great ideas.*

I dumped the beads in the little holder.

Harmony yelled, "Trin! Don't put them all in the same box. You have to divide them by color."

I clenched my teeth together and started sorting beads. "Sure, Mello," I mumbled. "Tell me how to make purses."

• • •

The Next Thursday

On Thursday, we sat in the school cafeteria, eating lunch at our regular table.

"Raise your hand if you think it's amazing that just one week ago tomorrow I had the big idea," I said.

Mello looked at me and said, "What idea?"

"Hello! Only the idea for the Chosen Girls to go to Russia," I answered, not believing I had to remind her.

"Oh, yeah," she said with a nod. "It's just that we've done so much since then, I forgot who first brought it up."

You and everyone else, I thought.

"We're really going. Cool frijoles!" Harmony squealed. Then she lowered her voice. "I'm excited but I'm a little nervous. What if something bad happens over there — like what if one of us gets sick? Some hospitals still don't have much medicine."

"Why don't we bring some?" Mello asked.

"My mom always packs a first-aid kit," I explained. "She's a world-class traveler. We've been all over —"

"Not for us, Trin," Mello interrupted. "For the hospitals. We could ask people to donate supplies like bandages and aspirin. Maybe even little toys for kids. Now, that would be excellent."

"Sí," Harmony said. "My mamma knows a couple of nurses. She could talk to them."

"And Dad knows every doctor in town, I bet," Mello added. "And he's friends with the manager of that toy store on Main Street."

"Nice thought, but I doubt we can pull it off," I said, shaking my head. "We'll have our instruments and soundboard and amps ..."

"But we're allowed two suitcases each, right?" Harmony asked.

"We could each fill our second suitcase with hospital supplies and toys!" Mello said.

"I don't know anyone with a toy store. Or any doctors or nurses," I complained. "No one in our family has even been sick since we moved here."

Mello patted my hand. "Don't worry, Trin. I'll fill your suitcase for you."

•••

Friday

"Do you think you can keep up with demand?" Lamont asked. "This is craziness!"

I reached for the papers he held, but he handed one to Harmony and one to Mello.

Nothing for me.

Harmony looked at her sheet. "A hundred and five necklaces?" she asked.

Mello looked up from her paper and said, "Ninety-four purses?"

Lamont nodded. "And the site hasn't been up a week!"

I looked at their shocked faces and crossed my arms. In a voice full of triumph I declared, "I told you the Internet wasn't a good idea."

"Not a good idea?" Harmony echoed. "Are you *loco*? We're making ten dollars off every necklace and every purse. Don't you see? We've made two thousand dollars in less than a week!"

"But you have to make over a hundred necklaces and purses," I reminded her.

"Sí, we're going to be very busy," she agreed, handing me a box of beads. "Get stringing."

chapter:4

...

wednesday, one week later

That next Wednesday I text-messaged the band and Lamont invitations for a Russian theme party in the shed. I didn't spill the real reason for the party: I had just gotten some great news. I hoped I could wait until Friday to tell them.

I spent the next two days printing out pictures of stuff from Russia, and posters of the Russian words for *thank you* and *you're welcome*. I even found a CD of Russian music and some Russian-language CDs.

...

Friday

I got to the shed early Friday and got everything set up—the posters on the wall and the music in the CD player. When

Harmony and Mello came, I handed them each a scarf. "We're going to tie them on our heads like babushkas," I explained, putting mine on and knotting it under my chin. I batted my eyelashes at them and smiled. "Am I stunning?"

"Just ravishing," Mello said in a sarcastic voice. She held her scarf by one corner, like it had slime on it or something. "Do we have to wear these in Russia?"

"No, Mello," I answered, trying to keep my voice sweet. "It's just for tonight. And it's supposed to be fun."

She finally grinned and put it on. "I guess it's better than turning my hair blue," she said. "I think I'll forget to take that blue stuff with me to Russia."

"No way," I said. "Blue hair is your trademark now. You aren't getting out of it, so you might as well give up."

Lamont knocked and then walked in. He looked at the three of us in our scarves and held his hand out to me.

I laughed.

He said, "What? I don't get a scarf?"

"You need one of those huge fur hats," Harmony said.

Lamont nodded and walked immediately to the hot dogs. "I'll have to get me one of those."

When everybody had their food I said, "Ohwow, do I have some news."

"I've got a scoop too," Lamont said.

"What? What is it?" Harmony asked.

Lamont looked at me and said, "You go first."

I folded my hands together and took a deep breath. "Well, I wrote the man in charge of my dad's conference. I told him all about the Chosen Girls—how we're a new band and we've won a contest and we're on TV and all. And—this is

so *sweet*—he got us a hookup with someone near Ukraine who'll set up a tour!"

I waited for them to scream with joy, but they didn't.

Mello just said, "That's good. What will we be touring out there?"

I laughed. "Not that kind of tour. I mean, I'm sure we'll tour Moscow, and we'll tour the Kremlin and all. But I'm saying this man will set up a tour for *us*—a concert tour. It's official: the Chosen Girls, on tour in Russia!"

Lamont said, "Oh, happy day! I knew you'd pull it off, Trin. And I'm pumped to be on sound."

Mello sighed and said, "I guess this means I have to take my drums. I don't see how I'm going to get them there."

"Oh, quit, Mello," Harmony told her. "This will rock. Cool frijoles, Trin!"

I beamed at them.

Then Harmony said, "So do I need to do anything special—you know—as band manager?"

My heart almost stopped. That's all I needed—Harmony messing things up on an international scale. I said, "Um, not just yet. I mean, I think I can handle it. For now, anyway. I'll … let you know." I looked around, desperate to change the subject. My eyes fell on Lamont, who sat devouring his fourth hot dog. "So, Lamont, what's your news?"

He chewed and grinned at the same time. His eyes lit up and he started nodding. Still chewing, he gave us a thumbs-up and wiggled his eyebrows up and down.

"Oh, please, Lamont," Mello griped. "Just swallow your food and tell us already!"

He kept us waiting a minute more. Finally he swallowed. "Someone really liked the website, and they offered to match

any funds we raise," he announced with a smile. "Based on what we've raised so far—if this guy comes through—we'll have enough!"

"Who would do that?" I asked. "Who would give us that much money?"

"He said to call him Mr. Smith Number One," Lamont answered.

"From the concert!" Harmony shrieked. "That concert we did at the wrong park. What a man!"

"Excellent," Mello agreed. "Maybe something good came from that disaster. I still say I've never been so embarrassed in my life. Even the chicken suits weren't that bad. When we found out hundreds of people waited at that other park ..."

"Ohwow, yes. And meanwhile, we did our whole show for—what?—eight people?" I asked.

Lamont patted Harmony's back and said, "So anyway, Mello's right. Something good has come out of it."

I noticed Harmony looked like she might cry. I guess since the whole thing had been her mistake, she was maybe a little sensitive about it. I decided to help her out. "This is great news," I said, grabbing another handful of chips. "And just in time, because we leave in a week."

Harmony looked a little more relaxed.

"I got a little something for each of you," I said, grabbing a big gift bag. I reached in, pulled out a CD, and handed it to Harmony. She got all happy ... until she looked at the cover.

"'Learn Russian in Ten Days,'" she read. "Um ... *gracias.*"

I handed Mello and Lamont theirs. "These are way fabulous. But we don't have quite ten days, so you'll need

to double up on a few lessons. Now, do you guys have any questions about traveling overseas?" I asked.

Mello made a face. "Wait. How much Russian can we really learn now? Isn't it a little late?"

"Every word you learn will be one more than you knew before," I pointed out. "People in other countries love it when you speak their language. Even if it's not perfect."

Harmony jumped up and smiled at me. "I bet you're right, Trin," she said.

I smiled back, glad to see her catch my excitement.

"And if they like us to speak it, they'll *love* for us to sing it," she said. "Let's search the Net and find a Russian song we can learn. Lamont, we need your machinery." She started for the door.

"But I had more to tell you," I sputtered.

She looked back. "Tell us while we're choosing a song to learn."

• • •

We found a website and listened to songs in Russian, but we couldn't tell for sure what they said. Then Lamont found a copy of the Lord's Prayer written out in Russian characters — *and* spelled out phonetically.

"You could sing this!" he said. "People sing the Lord's Prayer at weddings and stuff."

Harmony stood up and sang in a superhigh opera voice (it wasn't pretty): " 'Our Father in heaven, hallowed be your name.' "

Mello walked to the screen. She mimicked Harmony, but sang the Russian words. "Oht-chee nosh, soos-shee nah nyeh-byeh-sahkh dah svyah-teet-syah eem-yah Tvah-yoh."

She ran out of notes with four syllables left, so she sang them all on the same note, without taking a breath, and then died laughing. "I think we're going to need a new tune!"

Harmony looked at me. "That's your job, Trin," she said.

"The Lord's Prayer is long!" I complained. "It's going to be hard to learn. What if we mess up?"

Harmony crossed her arms and said, "Trin, the Russians will love that we're trying. Even if it's not *perfect*."

I gave her a little smirk.

Mello cleared her throat and said, "So before we figure out the music, what else did you want to tell us, Trin?"

"Well," I said, "the main thing to remember on the trip is to be flexible. Things don't always go like you expect them to when you're traveling in a foreign country. You have to be ready to go with the flow."

They nodded.

I added, "It's also good to call things 'different' instead of 'weird.' Like food, the way people act, whatever. Don't assume something's bad just because it's different from what we do here. Because believe me, it will be different."

•••

The Next Thursday

I stayed up late the night before the trip rearranging my suitcase. Since we had decided to fill our second suitcases with medical supplies and toys, I really didn't have room to spare. I finally got the perfect combos, so I could switch tops, pants, and skirts to make enough outfits to last the trip.

•••

Friday

The next morning I jumped out of bed when the alarm went off. Finally!

We grabbed Pop-Tarts and loaded our bags into the Suburban.

We had to drop off my little brother, Tucker, and then Dad wanted to stop by campus.

I asked, "What for?"

"I need to grab stamps out of my desk so I can mail these bills," he answered.

I looked at my watch. "Couldn't we do it when we get home?"

Dad said, "That depends. Do you want to have running water and electrical service when we get back? Besides, the tickets are in my desk, so I have to go to my office."

I sighed loudly.

We got there, and Dad said Mom and I could wait in the car, because he'd only be a minute. But I couldn't handle just sitting, so I followed him in. He pulled stuff out of his desk and started sticking stamps on envelopes. Then he turned on his computer.

"Dad, what are you doing?" I asked, really afraid now. "Don't start a project on the computer. We'll never catch the plane."

"I'm not starting a project. I'm setting up an automatic out-of-office reply in case anyone emails while I'm gone. That's it. It takes less than two minutes. We're not going to miss our flight."

"But, Dad, we so need to be the first ones there. I have to walk Harmony and Mello through security and stuff. They're

probably already at the airport waiting for us. They don't know what to do."

Dad typed away, ignoring me. I looked around for something I could do to speed things up. I saw the bills stacked on Dad's desk. I scooped them up and said, "I'll go stick these in the mail drop and wait in the car."

I walked to the official blue mailbox on the corner and dropped the letters in. Then I climbed in the car with Mom. True to his word, Dad came out a minute later. I sighed with relief when he started the car, and we headed toward the airport.

We were about ten minutes down the road when Mom said, "Jeff, I'd like to look at the itinerary."

Dad said, "Sure," and patted his shirt pocket. Then his pants pocket. Then his other pants pocket.

Mom said, "Very funny, Jeff. It's with the tickets, right?"

And Dad said, "Yes, it's with the tickets. And I wish I was joking. Check my briefcase."

He drove while Mom dug. Then he suddenly swung onto the shoulder of the highway and stopped the car. He stared straight ahead. I could see his hands squeezing the steering wheel so hard his knuckles turned white.

He said, "Trin, when you picked up the bills off my desk, are you sure you only got bills?"

I felt my stomach turn over. "I think so, Dad."

"This isn't a time to think so, Trin. I have to know. Is it possible that you picked up our tickets as well? Do you maybe have them in the backseat?"

I actually looked around as if they might miraculously appear, even though I knew I hadn't brought them into the Suburban. "They aren't back here, Dad," I finally said.

Dad turned to Mom. "Let's go back. Maybe they're still in my desk."

But I could tell from his voice he knew they weren't.

"What are you saying, Jeff?" Mom asked in a shaky voice. "What do you think happened to our tickets?"

Dad breathed real deeply as he exited the highway. Then he said, "I think Trin put them in the mail drop."

I swallowed. No way. I had been trying to speed things up by mailing the bills. Mailing our tickets would so not speed anything up.

"But how can we get them out?" Mom asked.

"We can't. It's against federal law to tamper with the mail. Besides, it's impossible to get something out of those mail drops." Dad pulled up to a light and signaled to go under the highway and head back to his office.

I felt hot tears start to run down my cheeks. We were going to miss the whole trip, and it was my fault.

Then Mom said, "Wait a minute! Do we even need tickets? Can't they find us by our drivers' licenses these days?"

"Not for flights to Russia, no. We have to have those tickets."

We pulled back into the parking lot at Dad's office. He went inside to look, and Mom and I ran to the mailbox.

"Ohwow, whoever invented these things must have been way smart," I said as I pushed and pulled the handle. "Dad's right. There's no way to get inside there." I kicked the bottom, hoping the whole thing might just fall over. *Ouch!*

"It's even stronger than it looks," I told Mom. "Raise your hand if you wish we had a blowtorch in the car."

"Blowtorching our tickets and other people's mail isn't the answer. I hope he finds the tickets in his office," Mom said in

a clipped voice, "or I don't know what we'll do." She wrapped her arms around herself, kinda like she wanted to give herself a hug.

I stepped toward her, but then I stopped. It was my fault she was upset. She probably didn't want a hug from me. We hadn't even left Hopetown, and I'd already ruined the whole trip.

Dad came out of the office and I thought, *Please let him be carrying tickets!*

I looked at his hands.

Nothing.

Dad said, "They have to be in the drop, and we can't get them out. All I can think is to pray that God will show us what to do."

We bowed our heads right there on the corner and Dad prayed. After he said, "Amen," he looked up and started running.

I thought, *Ohwow, now Dad's lost it. He thinks he can run to Russia.*

Then I saw why he was running. A mail carrier! On the next block!

Dad ran right up to the mail truck and started talking to the carrier. Then the little truck headed our way. Dad jogged along behind it.

The driver pulled up next to us. "So you've got a little problem, eh?" he said, jumping out of the truck. "It's a good thing it happened now. This is my route, so I can open the box."

He unlocked the box and found our tickets. He held them out but didn't release his grip as Dad latched on to them.

"Wait a minute," the mailman said, eyeing the papers with a grin. "Three tickets to Russia? I said I'd get them out, but I

didn't say I'd give them to you. Maybe I should take a little vacation."

For just a second, I thought Dad's head might implode. But the mailman burst out laughing and handed them over. We piled back into the car before we finished thanking him.

••••

By the time we fought LA traffic, parked, got our shuttle, and waited through crazy-long security lines, I thought I would have at least five heart attacks. The Dallas airport is huge, but LAX is a monster. We ran to our gate—my little carry-on wheels *click, click, click*ing on the tiles behind me.

I saw it first and yelled, "Gate 12!"

But no one stood in line. The place was empty.

They had already boarded the plane.

chapter • 5

• • •

It couldn't be. How could we send Harmony, Mello, and Lamont to Russia all alone? They'd never make it!

I noticed a smiling attendant standing by the door. Then, through the huge glass windows, I saw the plane behind her.

Our plane. It hadn't left yet.

I rushed up and handed the worker my boarding pass. I said, "Raise your hand if you thought we missed it. Thank you for still being here! Ohwow, we just had to make this flight. My friends are on the plane, and they've never been overseas. They're counting on me—I'm in charge of the whole trip!"

She reached behind me for Mom's pass and said, "Then you better get onboard. We'll be shutting the door soon."

I ran down the little tunnel, flashed a huge smile at the next attendant, went in, and looked for my seat.

Harmony and Mello yelled, "Trin! Where were you?"

I pushed my bag under my seat and said, "Ohwow, don't even ask."

That's when I noticed Lamont, with his video camera on and pointed at me. He said, "No, really, Trin. Tell us the whole story. We've got plenty of time."

My dad rescued me. He looked at a man two rows back and said, "Hey, Tom! Good to see you. It's been a couple of years." He walked back and shook the man's hand.

"Good to see *you*," Tom answered. "Thought you were going to miss the flight. This is my son, Joel."

I looked from the man to his son and stopped breathing.

Everything about Joel—wavy honey-blond hair, high cheekbones, shoulders so wide they hardly fit in the seat—was totally magazine model. He glanced up, oh-so-casually, and nodded at Dad. I wanted to do something, anything, to turn those gray-green eyes my direction.

Dad said, "I didn't realize you planned to bring your son. Let me introduce you to my wife and daughter."

Sweet!

Oh, yeah. Gray-green eyes looking at me. I felt myself drowning.

"You're going all the way to Moscow?" Harmony blurted. She stepped into the aisle, right between me and Joel. I stood behind her, a silent idiot, wiping my mouth every once in a while to check for drool.

"Where are you from?" Harmony asked.

"Bakersfield," he answered. The corners of his mouth turned up in an amazing grin. "My dad teaches economics there. That's why he's going to this conference."

"So what are you gonna do while your dad's in meetings?" Harmony asked.

He shrugged and grinned a little bigger. "Watch a lot of Russian TV?" Those gorgeous eyes finally wandered from Harmony's face. He looked at me and asked, "What will you be doing during the conference?"

"Our band is doing a tour near Ukraine," Harmony answered before I could say a word.

He looked impressed. "You have a band?"

I didn't give Harmony a chance. I said, "We're called the Chosen—"

"Please take your seats and place them in their upright, locked position. Fasten your seat belts and put your tray tables up," the intercom blasted.

"Girls," I finished, before I groaned and walked back to my seat. Then Harmony and Mello both wanted to sit by a window, so we had to do one last shuffle. We ended with Harmony by a window and Lamont beside her. I sat next to Mello in the row behind them.

While the plane taxied, I wondered why Harmony needed a window. She spent the whole time looking back through the crack between the seats, pretending to talk to us but staring at Joel.

When the plane picked up speed, she finally turned around. Mello pressed her face against the glass, and I peeked around her to watch the airport buildings whiz past.

As we lifted off, Mello reached over and grabbed my hand, squeezing it hard. I knew how she felt. The force of takeoff pressed me against my seat, and I said a little prayer. (Liftoff and landing are the only parts of flying I don't like.)

"Look! You can see the big LAX letters!" Harmony called. "And those tall pylon things outside the airport."

"But they don't look big from here. And the cars look like toys!" Mello said. Then she gasped. "The Pacific! It's beautiful!"

We stared out the windows until our world disappeared, and a blanket of bumpy white clouds replaced it. Then we stared a little longer. "Doesn't it look like you could roll on them?" Harmony asked.

"OK, time to get our heads out of the clouds," I said, reaching under my seat for my bag. "Did you all listen to the Russian-language CDs I gave you?"

They looked down and shook their heads.

"That's what I thought," I said, pulling stuff out of my little suitcase. "But don't worry. I'm all over it." I handed a player to Mello, then Harmony. "I brought all of our old portable players and copies of the CD." I gave Lamont his and put mine on my lap. I flashed them a big smile and said, "This flight is a perfect time to learn the language. And remember what I told you about jet lag. You need to try to sleep at least four hours on the plane—either this flight or the next one."

Harmony squirmed around in her seat. "Impossible! How could anyone sleep jammed into a tiny space like this?" Her eyes darted behind us, to Joel. "I feel sorry for great big guys," she said.

"That's sweet, but don't worry about me," Lamont said, flexing his nonexistent muscles. "I can sleep anywhere."

Harmony rolled her eyes, put her earphones on, and started her CD. She leaned her head back, closed her eyes, and yelled, "Thank you. *Spah-see-bah*."

The man in the seat in front of her turned around and glared. Mello, still trying to figure out her own CD, leaned up to Harmony and asked, "Why are you yelling?"

Harmony said, "What? I can't hear you! This Russian CD is too loud. No. *Nyet.* I can't hear."

I reached over the seat, pulled one of her earphones away from her ear, and said, "Turn it down, Harmony. You're blasting the whole plane."

She smiled and adjusted her volume. "I'll do that. Yes. *Dah.* I'll turn it down."

Harmony didn't make it too far past please and thank you. She fell asleep leaning against the window, and Mello fell asleep leaning on me.

I needed to make a trip up the aisle, but I couldn't stand to wake up Mello. So I waited. And practiced saying, "Where is the restroom, please?" in Russian.

By the time the plane touched down in New York, every muscle in my body hurt. My face felt greasy and my eyes were bleary, but I had a job to do. "Ohwow, I wish we had time to shop New York City! Unfortunately, we've only got 45 minutes till our next plane takes off," I announced before the little bell dinged. "We're landing at terminal 2, and we take off from terminal 6. I've studied the airport map, and I know where our gate is. As soon as you can get off the plane, follow me."

We waited by the gate until I saw Joel come out. I flashed him a smile and started leading the way across JFK— another of the biggest airports in the world. We rushed past people in bright Indian saris, embroidered African dresses, classic business suits, and baggy gangsta clothes. I found the Airtrain and we crowded on. I tried not to faint when Joel grabbed the same pole I was holding onto and grinned down at me.

"Aren't we supposed to take a *plane*?" Harmony asked as we left the terminal and rode a rail climbing higher and higher off the ground. "What are we doing on a train?"

Joel shifted his attention to Harmony and laughed. "This airport is huge. This thing gets us from one terminal to another. Then we find our gate."

"So we have to walk even more?" Harmony whined. "I wish I had a rolling bag like Trin's."

"When you travel as much as I do, you know wheels can be your best friend," I explained.

Joel looked at Harmony's backpack. "Is that all you've got? I can carry that," he offered.

Her eyes got huge. "Would you? Thanks!" she gushed.

I looked down at my bag and kicked it. "Stupid wheels," I muttered.

We got off at terminal 6, and they followed me to gate 24. I checked my watch as we walked up and smiled in relief. Then I read the sign over the desk: Flight 346 to Tokyo.

Tokyo?

I turned to the group, panicked. "They must have changed the gates! We only have 17 minutes left. What if it's in a different terminal?"

Lamont shook his head and pointed at the next gate. I squinted and read the sign: Flight 2148 to Moscow. I smiled and said, "Uh, yeah. Tricked ya!" and dashed to gate 25.

On the plane, Joel switched seats with the woman next to Lamont. The two guys totally hit it off.

"Come on tour with us, Joel," Lamont said. "Defend me from these women, I beg you!"

Joel looked at us and laughed. "I can only imagine how hard it is for you, Lamont, surrounded by gorgeous rock stars."

We giggled, but I knew my face must be bright red.

"I'd be giving up a lot. I hear Russian TV is way cool ..." Joel looked at the ceiling of the plane, like he really had to think about it. "But how often does a guy get to tour Russia with a rock band? I'm in!"

I sat back in my seat and tried not to smile too big. Over a week of looking at Joel — way fabulous.

After the flight attendants served dinner, they turned down the lights in the plane and asked everyone to close their window shades. They passed out pillows and blankets and even those little sleep masks. I put one on, and crashed.

In the middle of a great dream about Joel and me singing a duet in Russian, I heard a voice say something about landing. I forced my eyes open.

• • •

Saturday Around Noon

And woke up just in time for touchdown in Moscow. Sweet!

I couldn't wait to get off the plane. But of course I had to. I don't know why it takes everyone so long to grab a carry-on and walk off the plane. Mello, Harmony, and I stood in the aisle, waiting for people to get out of the way.

Lamont said, "You might as well sit down and relax, women. We're not going anywhere for a while."

Joel said, "He's right." He wove his fingers together, stretched his arms over his head, and yawned.

"But we're in Russia!" I told them. "We have places to see and concerts to give. I want to get out there! I want to see Red Square! I want to hug a babushka!"

Harmony shook her head. She said, "The Russian grand-mothers I've seen in pictures don't look like they want to be hugged, Trin."

I smiled. "They just need some love, Harmony," I answered.

"You probably got that right, Trin," Joel said. "A hug never hurt anyone."

I spun around to face him, but he was looking right over my head at Harmony. I felt my face flush.

"Sure," I muttered, wishing I could disappear until we finally got off the plane.

• • •

We made it through customs and dragged our gear outside, where a blast of cold air greeted us. I buttoned up my coat and announced, "First stop: Red Square."

Lamont pointed to our pile of luggage. Between our bags of clothes, our bags of medical supplies, and all the band's equipment, it looked crazy-huge. "I don't think so, Trin," he said. "We need to get rid of this stuff first."

Dad agreed. He got us (and our luggage) in taxis headed for Sergei's. Sergei is the guy with Dad's conference who got us the hookup for places to stay in Moscow. My dad is all about seeing the "real" country when he goes somewhere, so it didn't surprise me that he'd requested we stay in people's homes.

We drove past about a gazillion identical apartment build-ings until the taxis stopped at a tall one. Dad disappeared through the front door and came back with Sergei. Then he and Sergei took us to the different apartments where we'd stay the first two nights. Mom, Dad, and Lamont moved in with a family of four (up three flights of stairs). Joel and his dad stayed with an older man and his wife (only two flights up).

Mello and Harmony and I got to stay with a babushka and her little grandson. I loved them both immediately, even though they lived on the fourth floor. First chance to be flexible: no elevators, lots of luggage. At least the activity warmed us up.

The grandma looked just like a Russian babushka. I mean, I know that's what she was, but she was *so* perfect. If I looked up *babushka* in the dictionary, I might see a picture of her long hooked nose and pale blue eyes deep in a wrinkled face, with the scarf tied around her whole face. For reals.

Her grandson Alexi was maybe eight years old, with straight straw-blond hair and bright blue eyes. And he played the accordion for us. How cool is that?

Soon Sergei came to gather us all back into taxis, and we headed into Red Square. Mello fell asleep on the ride over, and I had to focus to keep my eyes open. We figured out it was the middle of the night back in California.

Ohwow, Red Square woke us up. It was bigger than I expected. I stood in the middle of the huge open part, turning slowly to see the elaborate GUM department store on one side and the pointy red wall in front of the yellow Kremlin (behind Lenin's mausoleum) on the other. And St. Basil's onion spires—each a different color, some striped, some zigzagged—made it look like a storybook castle come to life.

Mello kept saying, "We're really here. This is the real thing." And Harmony must have said "Cool frijoles" about four hundred times.

Lamont, of course, shot massive amounts of video.

We got some seriously crazy-fun pictures and bought loads of souvenirs. It took me ages to decide on a set of *matryoshka*—those famous nesting dolls that fit inside one

another. I also found a way fabulous black jewelry box with flowers painted on it, and a gorgeous scarf.

Harmony scurried around, buying stuff for every member of her huge family.

Mello didn't buy anything, but she went back three times to look at a watch one of the street vendors had for sale.

I came up beside her. "Do you like it?" I asked.

She said, "Sort of."

I whispered, "Walk away again. He'll drop his price."

She shook her head. "He says he's offering me a good deal — but only for today."

I laughed and told her that was the classic line in every country: *Only for you, only today.*

She grinned at me, put the watch down, and took a few steps.

"Wait!" the man called. "All right, for you only, a very, *very* good deal."

I winked at her as she handed him the money and strapped her new watch onto her wrist.

•••

We had set a time to meet Lamont before dinner. I stood shivering at the meeting place with Mello and Harmony. Lamont was nowhere to be found.

"We should have had a buddy system. Why did we let him go off alone?" I asked. "I hate to lose him our very first day in Russia!"

"He's probably at that Internet café we passed," Harmony said, "checking email and seeing how many hits our site has gotten since we left."

"Maybe he's with Joel. There's Joel's dad," Mello said as we watched him join my parents.

Then two men walked by. They were so bundled up in their big coats and fur hats I couldn't see their faces. One said, "Your American friends are fine," in perfect English.

My jaw dropped. "That's creepy!" I said. "What's going on? Did someone kidnap Lamont and Joel?"

Mello rolled her eyes and said, "Come on, Trin. That *was* Lamont and Joel."

The "men" turned around and laughed. Yep. Tall, lanky Lamont and honey-blond Joel looked totally different in their puffy coats and traditional fur hats.

Sergei took us to a dinner-theater place where Russian dancers and singers in traditional costumes entertained us the whole time. Ohwow, they were amazing! Especially those men who cross their arms, squat, and kick. It hurt me to watch, so sometimes I looked across the table at Joel. Nothing painful about that.

One server placed trays of cold meats and vegetables on the table. Another brought each of us a bowl of borscht—a dark red beet soup.

"What's this white stuff floating on top?" I whispered to Mello.

"Probably the same stuff that was on the tomatoes and cucumbers," she whispered back. "It tastes like sour milk."

I decided to play it safe and stabbed a cold cut with my fork. I chewed forever, but it didn't go away. "This bologna stuff is really chewy," I mumbled to Harmony.

"Trin, that's not bologna," she answered. "It's cow's tongue. Didn't you see the taste buds along the edges?"

I looked in horror at the other pieces on the tray. She was right.

I spit the rubbery meat out of my mouth. It flew across the table and missed Joel's plate by a mere inch.

He and Harmony died laughing.

"The food is *different*, isn't it, Trin?" Harmony asked.

I glared at her. "At least I didn't shoot it out my nose like you would have," I answered, wiping my mouth and cleaning up the mess on the table.

One of the Russian men stepped to the microphone and said, "We understand we are not the only performers present tonight. Among our American friends we have visiting a band called the Chosen Girls."

We looked at each other and squealed. *How did they know?*

The man said, "We would like it very much if the Chosen Girls would sing for us."

I felt my face getting hot. Sing? Here? Now?

We didn't have our guitars or Mello's drums. We hadn't slept, really, for two days. I hadn't properly fixed my hair since the plane landed, and I still felt greasy and gross.

I leaned over to Mello and said, "This isn't how I pictured our Russian debut." And this definitely didn't match my hopes for the first time I'd perform in front of Joel.

Lamont smiled at me and said, "Be flexible."

I wanted to stick my tongue out at him, but the thought of *tongue* made me gag all over again.

I looked at Mello, expecting her to bail. Instead she stood up, grabbed my hand, and led me onto the stage. She smiled out at the audience, and they clapped even louder. Then she whispered, "Let's sing 'Love Lessons.'"

"We don't have our instruments," I whispered back.

She tried to talk without moving her lips. "I don't think they care. And I don't think we have a choice. It would be rude to say no. I'd start, but I can't because you sing lead." Her lips smiled, but her eyes focused on mine with a steely look. "Now sing!"

So I sang. Mello came in on harmony, and it actually sounded pretty decent. I couldn't decide if Harmony was lucky or unlucky not to come onstage. She just plays bass and doesn't sing.

Everyone clapped and cheered when we finished, and I wondered if they thought American rock bands always sang a cappella.

• • •

When we got back to the apartment, I couldn't wait to take a bath and go to bed. I grabbed my PJs and headed for the bathroom. Our chubby little babushka met me in the dark hall and tried to explain how the hot water worked. At least I think that's what she explained.

She said something in Russian, and I said, "Huh?"

She said it again, a little louder. It didn't sound like anything on the Russian language CD. I held my hands up and shook my head to show I didn't understand.

She said it again, louder and slower. She was pretty much yelling. And she got right up next to me, looking up into my face.

I pulled out my English-Russian dictionary and tried to find whatever she kept repeating, but she flustered me so much I couldn't think. I turned pages, and she yelled. Not a mean

yell, but the kind you might use to talk to someone hard of hearing.

I finally yelled back, in English. "Look, it doesn't matter how slowly you say it, or how loudly you say it, or how close to my face you are when you say it. I don't understand you!"

Mello giggled and said, "You're forgetting again, Trin. Go with the flow!"

That night we slept on the apartment's living room floor. Our babushka laid out a bunch of blankets, and really it made a pretty soft bed. When I finally got to lie down and close my eyes, I just wanted to sleep. But Mello and Harmony got a second wind and wanted to chat.

Mello said, "How cool was that, singing onstage in Russia?"

I didn't answer.

Harmony said, "You sounded great. And they loved it! This is going to be a seriously cool frijoles trip."

"Definitely," Mello agreed. "I'm so glad we came. It's even better than I imagined."

I just snuggled into my blanket and pretended to be asleep.

chapter • 6

...

On Monday night, we left Dad behind in Moscow and took a night train headed toward the border of Ukraine. Sweet. Each compartment had little shelves that pulled down and turned into beds. Okay, so they weren't at all comfortable, and the train stopped and started all night. But what rock band doesn't have a tough ride on their first tour?

The next day a bus ride took us far from the big city. On either side of the road, barren fields stretched as far as we could see. We passed people, bundled in their big hats and coats, walking down the lonely roads or driving horse-drawn wagons. It felt like we were riding backward through time.

Finally, the bus stopped in Clinsky, where we planned to spend the next five days. We gathered our stuff and got off the bus.

Nobody.

Anywhere.

"Where's our connection, Trin?" Harmony asked.

My heart flopped around inside me. "I'm sure he'll be here soon," I answered.

Harmony said, "Did you tell him what time to meet us?"

I rolled my eyes and said, "No, Harmony, I just hoped he would guess."

Mom said, "Trin, don't joke about that. We're in a foreign country, and it is a little scary if we don't make connections."

Lamont and Joel looked around. Lamont said, "I wonder if there's a phone somewhere. Do you have his number?"

I did not have his number. I had his address, though. I thought about trying to find a taxi, but just then an old white van pulled up. The passenger door flew open and a skinny guy ran up to us. "Verily, you are Chosen Girls, yes?" he said with a huge smile.

I smiled back and held out my hand. I said, "Yes. I'm Trin. Are you Pastor Kovitch?"

He shook my hand hard, then laughed until his curly black hair flopped over his eyes. "No, indeed. I say unto you, I am merely Sasha." He started loading our luggage through the back door of the van.

"I will be happily serving as your translator," Sasha said over his shoulder. "Here is Pastor Kovitch." He pointed to an older man coming around the van.

Pastor Kovitch's smile wasn't as big as Sasha's, but it was warm. He walked up to me, shook my hand, and pounded me on the back with his other hand as he said, "Welcome."

I smiled up at him and said, "Pastor Kovitch, thank you so much for hosting us. Ohwow, we are just way excited to be here! When's our first concert?"

He smiled and said, "Welcome."

I smiled bigger and whipped out my PDA, ready to type. "Thanks! I'm Trin, and I'm in charge of the Chosen Girls on this trip. I'd love to get a copy of our schedule so I can make plans. When's our first concert?" I said again, a little louder.

He smiled and turned away from me. He shook Mello's hand and said, "Welcome."

Lamont whispered, "I don't think he speaks English, Trin. Maybe talk a little slower?"

"Or even a little louder?" said Joel with a quick grin.

I ignored them. And Mello and Harmony, who were laughing their heads off.

Sasha spoke briefly with the pastor in Russian, then told us, "Verily, Pastor Kovitch says unto you that you are among welcome. He is pleased that thou hast joined him in ministry. On this day, and at this hour, we shall go to his home."

With that, Sasha picked up the last suitcases and headed for the van. Pastor Kovitch herded us into our seats.

"Great. So when is our first concert?" I asked their backs. I guess they didn't hear me. I put my PDA back in my bag.

We drove through the streets of Clinsky, lined with little cottages trimmed in bright colors. As we bumped over the dirt roads, Sasha talked cheerfully about every sight we passed.

"Cast your eyes unto our bakery," he said, pointing to the right. "And unto your left, ye shall see the dairy."

Lamont said, "You speak English well, Sasha."

He beamed and said, "Thank you. Indeed, I thank you. I taught myself to speak English, using the King James Bible!"

We dropped off Lamont and Joel, then continued down the block, where we dropped off Mom. Sasha pulled across the street to the front of Pastor Kovitch's home, trimmed in blue.

Mrs. Kovitch stood on the porch, tall and stout, with long brown hair. Like her husband, she had a warm smile. She asked us to take off our shoes as we came in the door. I happily obeyed.

Our stuff practically filled up their whole living room. Mrs. Kovitch led us straight to a table set for dinner.

A tray of bright red tomato slices and green cucumber slices sat in the middle of the table. I noticed the soured milk stuff was in a dish on the side. Sweet.

The pastor's wife walked back and forth from the kitchen, bringing more and more food. An adorable little boy trailed behind her, holding on to a piece of her skirt. She pointed to him and said, "Andrei." I waved and smiled at him. He hugged his mama tighter, but he did grin at me a little.

Finally, Mrs. Kovitch nodded to her husband. He stood and held out his hands. Sasha stood and took one. We all crowded around the table, standing and holding hands.

The pastor bowed his head and began to pray. I didn't understand most of what he said, but I did hear "Chosen Girls."

When we sat down, Mello said, "Isn't it excellent that God can understand every language?"

I smiled. "Yeah, it is."

I noticed two loaves of bread on the table. One was dark brown, almost black. The other looked like white bread.

Every meal we'd eaten so far in Russia included both the white and the black bread. I couldn't stand the black bread—it tasted like it had been baked with cough medicine or something.

I turned to Sasha and asked, "What do you call this brown bread?"

He said, "What?"

I repeated, "What do you call the brown bread?" I pointed to the loaf.

He just gave me a blank look.

I spoke more slowly. "You have white bread," I said, pointing to the white loaf. "You have brown bread," I said, pointing to the brown loaf. "Does the brown bread have a special name?"

He didn't answer. Harmony said, "He doesn't understand, Trin. Don't worry about it."

But now I was determined. This guy was our interpreter, after all. He had to understand us. I pulled off a piece of brown bread and held it up. "What do you call this?" I asked.

Sasha's eyes lit up and he nodded and smiled.

I sighed with relief. I had gotten through.

Sasha said, "Yes, you can take showers in the morning. Just do it!"

Mello and Harmony burst out laughing.

I tried my next question. "So when is our first concert?" I asked.

Sasha said something to the pastor, and the pastor said something back.

Sasha said, "Have you all had a pleasant journey?"

I smiled and said, "Ohwow, yes. We love Russia. And we're excited about doing concerts here. Are we going to do one tomorrow?"

Sasha spoke to the pastor again. The pastor smiled, nodded, and answered him. Then Sasha turned to me and said, "I say unto you, the pastor is so pleased that you enjoy our country. He understands you have brought medical supplies for the local hospital."

Mello said, "Yes, we each have a suitcase full. And toys for children."

"After supper you can put it all in boxes so it will be ready to give," Sasha said.

"So we're doing a concert at a hospital tomorrow?" I asked, trying to get back to the important stuff.

Sasha and the pastor chatted, then finally Sasha said with a smile, "Indeed, the doctors will be most pleased with your gift."

"But what about concerts?" I asked.

Harmony said, "Come on, Trin, give up on it."

"Oh, give up yourself," I mumbled.

• • •

Sasha left after dinner, and Mrs. Kovitch led us to a tiny building in the backyard.

"*Banya*," she said and opened the door.

Steam poured out into the cold night. I stuck my head inside and saw a wooden bench on one side of the room and a kind of furnace on the other side. Mrs. Kovitch went in, picked up a ladle, and dipped water out of a big jug. Then she poured it over hot coals and more steam filled the room. She lit an oil lamp hanging on the wall.

She smiled and pointed to us, and then to a stack of towels on the bench.

"It's a sauna!" Mello said.

"They have their own sauna? Cool frijoles!" Harmony added, stepping in. "Does that sound good or what?"

We squeezed inside, and Mrs. Kovitch smiled and nodded at us before she went out and closed the door.

We pulled off the clothes we'd traveled in and wrapped up in the towels. I squeezed my eyes shut and tried to let the

heat seep all the way into my brain, but the questions just wouldn't steam away.

I so needed to know the plan. Why wouldn't they tell me about our first concert? Did Sasha and the pastor even understand my question? It seemed like they just didn't want to answer me.

Maybe there was a problem. Maybe the tour got called off, and nobody wanted to admit it. Or maybe the pastor didn't want to take responsibility for what we might do onstage.

"Trin, you no look-ah so good-ah," Mello crooned in a pathetic Russian accent. "It seems that the brown-ah bread of unknown-ah name, it no sit so good-ah in your belly."

I shut my eyes even tighter as Harmony's laughter filled the little room. "Was that supposed to sound Russian?" she asked.

I started grinning. I couldn't help it.

"Don't bother Trin," Harmony continued. "Look, she's dreaming about a certain cute guy we met on this trip. I can tell. And I don't blame her one bit."

Argh. My grin disappeared.

"And the lucky guy's name is . . ." She leaned in and whispered, "Sasha!"

My eyes flew open in surprise.

Then we all died laughing.

•••

"Hey, the trip's been great," Harmony told me as we trudged back to the house. "Thanks for setting it up."

Another surprise. I smiled and said, "No problem."

And hoped she believed me.

chapter • 7

...

"Doh-bray oo-tra, Trin."

My eyes adjusted, and I saw little Andrei smiling in my face. I smiled back, and he whispered it again. "Doh-bray oo-tra."

I whispered, "Good morning to you too, little guy." Mello and Harmony stirred under their blankets at the sound of Mrs. Kovitch's footsteps and then her voice. I couldn't understand her, but I had no doubt she said, "Get out of there right now. I told you not to wake them up!"

Andrei raised his eyebrows in an *uh-oh, I've-done-it-now* look and scampered away.

Sasha was already at the breakfast table, talking to the pastor, when we finished getting dressed.

"Verily, the pastor says unto you that you must get in the van."

I said, "Verily, are we doing a concert today?" Mello and Harmony hid their grins in their hands.

"He asks only that you get in the van," Sasha answered.

Harmony walked up. "Thank you, Sasha," she said sweetly. "Should we bring our equipment?"

Sasha spoke to the pastor again. Then he said, "Yes, please, you shall bring your equipment among you."

Mello turned to me. "Let the rocking of Russia begin!"

We changed into concert clothes, loaded the van, and picked up everyone else. Mom asked, "How are my girls?" as she climbed in. We told her about the banya. "I'll have to see if my hostess has one of those!" she said.

We drove over bumpy dirt roads, paved roads, and more dirt roads. I asked the name of the village we were heading to. Sasha talked to the pastor and then said, "Truly, it is a nearby village. We will be arriving there very soon."

I crossed my arms. What damage could come from me knowing the name of the village? Such a small thing.

We pulled up in front of an official-looking building. Pastor Kovitch spoke to Sasha, who said, "We shall unload your equipment here. Pastor Kovitch wants you shall do a concert."

Ohwow! My heart started pounding. Now that it was really here — our first concert in Russia — I felt a little crazy. "Let's go. This is it, Chosen Girls."

We hopped out of the van and started unloading equipment. We hauled stuff up the big cement steps of the building.

Pastor Kovitch tried the door.

Locked.

He said something to Sasha and took off walking around the building. I guess he hoped to find an open door. He didn't, because he came back and talked to Sasha again. Then he left.

Sasha said, "Indeed, he has gone to find the man with the key."

We sat on the steps. I watched my breath make little clouds in the cold air. Mello said, "What time does the concert start, Trin?"

"Like I know, Mello," I snapped. "Do you see them telling me anything?"

Pastor Kovitch came back alone. He said something to Sasha, who said something back in Russian. They went back and forth for a while, and neither of them sounded happy.

Finally, Sasha turned to us. "I say unto you, we are unable to unlock the building today. Indeed, you must perform your concert upon these very steps."

My frustrated huff made an extra-big cloud.

"Is there an electrical hookup?" Lamont asked.

Sasha gave him a blank look.

Lamont opened an amplifier case. He pulled out the end of a plug and pantomimed plugging it in.

Sasha nodded. "*Dah, dah* — yes. Plug. This you call plug, yes? For electric use."

Lamont sighed with relief. "Yes. You have a place we can plug in?" Again he acted out plugging in the cord.

Sasha's smile faded. "Verily I say unto you, inside this building there are many plugs. Here, though, on the steps — *nyet*. There are no plugs out here."

"So what do we have to do to get inside?" I asked. "We can't do a concert without electricity. I play electric guitar. Harmony's bass is electric. Even Mello's drums are electric! She borrowed them just for this tour because hers would take up, like, half the airplane."

Sasha stared at me. He didn't seem to get it. I walked up to the door and pulled on the handle myself, just in case.

Locked.

Beside the door, I noticed a large poster with Russian words written in red and blue ink. Sasha walked up beside me and pointed to it.

"You would like me to read this poster to you, indeed?" he asked.

I shrugged. "Does it say, 'The key is under the doormat'?"

Big-time blank look from Sasha. "No, this poster does not speak of the key. It speaks of the Chosen Girls," he answered.

Harmony said, "Cool frijoles! Read it, Sasha!"

Sasha smiled and did a little bow. "I shall. It says:

American Rock Stars

The Chosen Girls

All the way from California, America

Performing here!"

He pointed to the bottom, where someone had handwritten something. "This tells the time of today," he explained.

The words *American rock stars* got way stuck in my brain. Was the poster supposed to make me feel better or worse? We weren't going to sound much like rock stars without any juice running through our equipment.

"You see," Sasha said happily, "the people are coming!"

I didn't want to turn around, but I did. Men, women, young people, and kids gathered in at the bottom of the stairs.

"At least we know we're at the right place," I said. "And at the right time."

Harmony's eyes met mine. "Will you ever let me forget that?"

"Probably not," Lamont answered for me. "Let's figure out what you're going to do now, though."

"Right, Lamont," said Mello. "We have to fix this."

"You're our soundman," I told him. "You fix it!"

"I'm amazing, Trin," he answered. "But even I can't make your equipment work without electricity."

"We can't do anything, then. If only someone had told me where we were going, or when the concert was, I could have figured something out," I complained. "But no—everyone in Russia knew about today's concert but me and the man with the key. So we get dumped on some steps, the crowd comes, and I'm supposed to work a miracle."

"I think the miracle working is God's job," Mello said. "Why don't we pray for one right now?" She held her hands out to us.

I glanced back over my shoulder at the people standing in clumps at the bottom of the steps. Mom and Joel stood at the front of the crowd, looking worried.

I'm all for prayer, but it seemed a little late now. Still, what options did we have? I took one of Mello's hands and reached out to Harmony.

"Dear God," I prayed, "you know we want to honor you. We want to do a concert in this place that will help these people see your love. But our instruments and microphones won't work. What can we do? Please help us."

Mello prayed next. "God, this is an amazing opportunity. We're here in Russia, with people who have come to hear a concert. Help us be flexible. Help us honor *you*."

Harmony said, "We need you, God. Help us to know what to do."

"You are bigger than sound systems and instruments, God," Lamont prayed. "Let your love shine through these girls today. Amen."

When we looked up, Sasha stood there with a huge smile on his face, a guitar in one hand and a balalaika in the other. Pastor Kovitch stood behind him with a bongo drum or something.

They held them out to us.

So this was our answer to prayer?

Harmony took the guitar—of course. Mello took the bongo. That left me with the balalaika, a three-stringed, triangle-shaped Russian guitar.

I messed around with it, and a couple of people clapped. Ha!

I told Sasha, "Look, this isn't going to work. Make an announcement and explain what happened. Tell them to come back tomorrow—or whenever we can get inside and get plugged in."

Harmony played a few chords and adjusted the strings. "Shut your mouth and tune, Trin," she said.

I plucked the balalaika again and decided it sounded all right. As I worked out the fingering, I heard Pastor Kovitch's voice. He stood at the top of the steps, making an announcement.

Harmony whispered, "Sasha, what is he saying?"

"He says indeed we are unable to get into the building, thus you cannot plug in your equipment," he said.

I sighed with relief, glad he had decided to call it off.

The crowd clapped and cheered. Harmony, Mello, and I looked at each other. Harmony whispered, "Sasha, what is he saying now?"

Sasha translated, "He says that you are such talented performers that you will entertain them anyway. And at this time, he welcomes the Chosen Girls."

Mello looked at me and shrugged. Then she sat on a step and put that bongo drum between her knees. She said, "You've Chosen Me," and tapped out four beats. Harmony joined in, improvising on the guitar while Mello got a serious rhythm going on the drum. They sounded way fabulous. But I knew they couldn't do much without me, since I play lead guitar and sing the main part.

I was crazy-frustrated with the way this concert was going, but I did the only thing I could do. I hauled the balalaika to the middle of the "stage," and took charge. I sang my heart out and did the best I could on the new instrument, playing only the first two strings freestyle.

Mello started doing the echo part, and something weird happened. Standing outside, with just our voices and the acoustic instruments, "You've Chosen Me" sounded like a whole different song. It seemed almost Russian.

I could tell the people felt it too. They really cheered for us. We even did our Lord's Prayer song in their language. The words had to be close to right, because, ohwow, it was a huge hit.

In between songs, I explained their meaning, and Sasha translated for us. I hoped he got it right without telling them to go home and bathe or anything.

During the fourth song, I noticed the crowd shifting and moving around. I thought, *Oh, no! We're losing them. They're getting bored.* But that wasn't it at all. I heard a loud *moo*, and in came the cows. For real—a small herd of cattle plodding right through the middle of our audience. The babushka herding them along looked up and waved at us as she shooed them past.

I wanted to laugh or cry, but since I couldn't decide which, I just kept singing. We finally made it to the last song.

After the concert, Pastor Kovitch stood up to speak, and Sasha led us to a row of boxes. "Verily I say unto you, the pastor asks that you give these out."

"What are they?" Joel asked, joining us.

"These are Bibles. Many people in this village do not own a Bible," he explained.

We took our places behind the boxes, and as soon as the pastor said, "Amen," the people started pushing and shoving to get the Bibles. We handed them out as quickly as we could—even Mom came and helped.

"Why are they so pushy?" Mello asked.

"Their country has been through some tough times," Lamont answered. "Lots of times, these people have probably waited for something that was gone before they ever got to the front of the line."

"And not having a Bible . . . ," Harmony added. "Can you imagine? I think I have three. I don't even know how many are in my house."

I smiled at a little girl as I handed her a Bible. I wanted to tell her what a difference it could make. I wanted her to know God loved her—that he had chosen her. But she left and an older man stood in her place. I handed him one too, and then gave one to a woman my mom's age. I thought about the awesome privilege of giving people the very words of God, and I almost started crying.

When everyone had a Bible, Sasha led us down the street to a house. Inside, a group of older ladies stood smiling at us from behind a table piled with food.

"Ohwow! That looks so good!" I said to them. I didn't even care that they couldn't understand me. "I didn't know how hungry I was!"

They smiled even bigger, and I thought maybe they could understand—at least my smile.

We sat down to a lunch of more tomatoes and cucumbers and potatoes and bread.

I tried to scrape the Russian sour cream off a cucumber with a fork. "So how weird is it that they put sour cream on everything but the potato?" I whispered.

"And watch out for the gelatin," Lamont said. "It's not really Jell-O. I think it's congealed chicken broth."

"Chicken Jell-O!" I answered. "Ew. Where's a good old McDonald's when you need one? How do people eat this every day?"

Lamont said, "Maybe we could suggest chicken Jell-O to Mr. Walling. It could be a new side dish at Chik'n Quik."

We didn't laugh.

"Hey, uh, good job today, women," he said, changing the subject. "But didn't you feel like that concert got a little long?"

I snapped my head up. "No. We sang the same number of songs we always do. Why?"

He tore off a piece of white bread and handed the loaf to Joel.

"That's for sure, Lamont," Joel said. "At one point I thought, 'They're going to sing until the cows come home!'"

I flipped my hair at their obvious setup, while they cracked up. Mello turned to Harmony and explained. "That's an American saying from when everyone farmed. It means

somebody just won't quit till the end of the day, when the cows come home."

Harmony said, "I know that, Mello. Just because I'm from another country doesn't mean I'm stupid."

Mello's eyes got all teary. "I'm sorry, Harmony," she said. "I don't think you're stupid."

Harmony looked at me. "Trin, you said we should remember things in a new country are different—not weird."

I blinked. Where did this come from? "Yeah, I said that."

"But you are totally making fun of the food," she said. "You have no idea what kind of sacrifices these people have made so we can eat like this."

I looked down at my plate. "Ohwow, Harmony, you're right. I've been way rude."

"Sí, you have," Harmony said. "Since we first talked about this trip, you've been Miss Foreign Relations. But guess what? I am *from* a foreign country, and yeah, things are different. People don't have money here. They're giving up food from their own tables to feed us. Show some respect."

I felt like crawling under the table. Even Lamont clenched his teeth. But Harmony wasn't finished.

"You prayed for people to see our love and they did," she said. "Maybe you ought to think about seeing their love too."

Nobody spoke another word till Sasha came to load us all back into the van, but I ate every bite of the chicken Jell-O.

chapter • 8

...

We drove along for a while before Sasha said, "You have heard of Chernobyl?"

"That's where the nuclear power plant blew up, right?" Lamont asked. "Wasn't that back in the 1980s?"

"Dah, 1986. It was a terrible thing for our country," Sasha answered. "Many people had to run to save their lives."

Joel asked, "Is there still radiation around?"

Sasha nodded. "Indeed, there is a place near Chernobyl that is still called the dead zone."

I felt a shiver run up my spine.

"In the dead zone, radiation is so strong that some say no one may live there for at least another six hundred years," Sasha explained. "Maybe nine hundred. The houses, schools, and businesses are still there. But they are all empty."

"Like ghost towns," Harmony said in an awed whisper.

I looked out the front of the van and noticed some kind of warning sign blocking the road. Pastor Kovitch pulled the van over and parked.

"We have arrived," Sasha said. "You may get out now."

I didn't see a concert hall or any people. "Where are we?" I asked.

Sasha looked surprised. "Why, we are at the dead zone," he answered.

"I don't get it. Are we here on purpose?" Mello asked as we climbed out of the van.

"I think this is Sasha's idea of a cool tourist site," Lamont said.

Ahead, we saw houses and other buildings. Sasha climbed over the barrier and walked toward them. We followed him.

"That must have been a school," Mello said, pointing to a rectangular brick building with a swing set beside it. The wind blew the swings back and forth. I imagined the children who used to swing there, and I shivered again.

Harmony pointed to a different building with a large sign on the front. "I bet that was a store."

"Dah," Sasha said. "The sign says Bicycles for Sale."

"It feels weird to be in the middle of a town like this and not hear cars and people," Joel commented. "It's so quiet."

"It's too quiet," Harmony agreed. "Sasha, is it okay for us to be here? I mean, the people had to leave because of the radiation, right? Is this safe?"

Sasha nodded gravely. "You be here for one hour, you run, you jump, you laugh. But if you remain here for one day . . ." He looked around before turning back to us to say, "You must be dead."

"Well, I've seen enough!" Lamont said abruptly. He turned back to the van.

We followed him quickly.

"That was weird," Mello said as we got in and found our seats.

Lamont said, "I think the Chosen Girls should have a new motto after this."

"What?" Harmony asked.

He smiled. "The Chosen Girls: Radiating God's Love."

I rolled my eyes.

"I've got another one," Harmony said. "The Chosen Girls: Glowing for Jesus."

As we drove back to the pastor's home, I realized he didn't live far from the dead zone. With Sasha's help, I asked Pastor Kovitch about it before dinner. "Is there a lot of radiation around here too?"

Sasha listened to the pastor's answer then told me, "Yes, it is higher than normal here. That is why we have plenty of food to eat. People in the rest of Russia don't want to eat food that we grow here, near Chernobyl."

"But aren't you worried about it?" I asked.

Pastor Kovitch shook his head. Sasha translated. "Not so much for me." Then tears started running down the pastor's face. He pointed to his little boy, who sat on the floor stacking up blocks, and Sasha translated, "It is my son who will suffer, because he is growing up with the radiation. And it is very possible that his children will have deformities or diseases because of it."

I couldn't imagine. "Why do you stay here? Why don't you move?"

The pastor smiled at me and said through Sasha, "The people here need a pastor. Many of them can't move away — this is where their homes and families are. They need someone to teach them about God."

I felt tears running down my own face as my heart filled with a new love for this man who was so devoted to God's call.

••••

That night, Lamont and Joel came over to hang with Mello, Harmony, and me.

"It's harder than I thought — being in another country," Mello said.

Harmony nodded. "Sí, it's frustrating not being able to talk to people. How can we make a difference if they can't even understand us?"

"You should have listened to your language CDs," I reminded her. "I told you over and over before we left the States, but you wouldn't believe me. Now you see how important it is."

She said, "Oh, whatever. I don't hear you chatting it up in Russian, Trin."

Joel said, "No way could a beginner explain the gospel in Russian, Trin. Think about it."

"That's right," Lamont agreed. "No matter how many times we listened to your CDs. What we need is a way to communicate without words. Like a pantomime."

Harmony almost jumped off the couch. "Cool frijoles! Lamont, you're a genius."

"Definitely. What an excellent idea," Mello agreed.

"You mean like mimes with white gunk on their faces?"
I asked, holding up my hands and pretending to touch the
walls of an invisible box closing in around me. "How can we
help anybody by pretending to be in a box?"

"You can act out any kind of story, Trin — try thinking
outside the box," Lamont answered.

"Yeah," Harmony said, "like, try thinking something might
be a good idea even if you aren't the person who thought
of it."

"Ohwow! That was rude," I said. "I do not think I'm the only
person with good ideas."

"Tell me one time you liked an idea you didn't think of,"
Harmony insisted.

"Well," I said. "Just give me a second."

"Exactly!" she said.

"This isn't helping," Joel said. "What could you do a panto-
mime about?"

"Did you bring your superhero suits?" Lamont asked.

"Sí," Harmony answered.

"And your swords and shields?"

Mello said, "Uh-huh."

"How about a skit about the power of prayer?" Lamont
suggested.

Mello nodded. "Excellent. Maybe we could kind of act
out the scenes from the "You've Chosen Me" video, where
each of us is being attacked by P. Ride, Jealous E, and Rival
Ree."

I glared at Lamont and said, "It's a toss-up on who should
play the part of the demons, but I have a couple of ideas."

• • •

Thursday

I didn't want to admit it, but the skit turned out way cool. The next day we went to an orphanage — the perfect place to try it out.

"It's a good thing I reminded everyone to bring the white suits so we'd have the stuff for the skit," I told Harmony. "There must be a hundred little kids here."

She said, "Sī. We got lucky this time. You really should try to find out where we're going each day, Trin, so we can be prepared."

I growled and went to get my guitar.

We set up on a makeshift stage and performed an all-out concert for the kids, who clapped harder than any of our other audiences. Sometimes I had to sing looking up at the ceiling because I wanted to cry looking at those beautiful faces. I wished I could take them all home, so they could grow up in a family.

About halfway through, we sang "You've Chosen Me." Then Sasha came up onstage to explain what the song meant. When he stepped down, we started the skit. Harmony and I acted out a fight. It wasn't too hard to pretend on that part. Then Lamont came slithering toward Mello in a red costume we had thrown together. The kids squealed and shrieked and tried to warn her, but he attacked with his laser eyes. No real lasers, just Lamont pointing his fingers. Mello went crazy — stomping and snorting around, sticking her nose in the air and making fun of me. She did a great job exaggerating what jealousy looks like. I couldn't believe shy Mello could turn it on like that. The kids loved it.

Next, Harmony came onstage and she and I had it out. Then Lamont got her. Harmony made Mello's craziness look totally calm. She acted out rivalry, running over to me and pointing back at Mello, then going to Mello and pretending to whisper things about me. The kids giggled, and I knew they understood what she was doing. No doubt kids everywhere—even Russia—act that way.

Lamont got me last. I acted out pride. I stuck my nose in the air and looked down at the other two, and walked around them shaking my finger at them. I pointed to myself to show them they needed to be more like me.

We turned away from each other and stomped off to separate parts of the stage. Then, one at a time, we let our shoulders droop and made sad faces to show we didn't like the way we were acting.

Mello dropped to her knees in prayer, Harmony walked over and knelt beside her, and I came and knelt beside Harmony. Lamont switched off the spotlight long enough for us to quickly peel away our normal concert clothes to reveal our superhero suits underneath.

We leaped up, dressed in white from head to toe, as Lamont flipped on the strobe lights. We grabbed our swords and shields and stood poised for battle.

Lamont tried to creep up to Harmony. She did a karate roundhouse kick and pointed her sword at him. She held it like it had so much power coming out of it she could hardly stand up, and Lamont shook like he was being electrocuted. He fell back and the kids cheered madly.

He lay there for a while, shaking and kicking. Then he started slithering toward Mello. She raised her sword and pretended to jab at him. He started shaking again, and did a

slow-death scene worthy of an Academy Award. The children went way crazy.

When he raised his head again, he looked at me, then at the kids, then back at me, like, "Should I try it?" The kids shouted, "Nyet! Nyet!"

He didn't take their advice. He took a few huge breaths and dragged himself to me on his elbows. I had no mercy. I twirled around and then brought my sword down, pointed at his back. This time he shook and twitched for ages. He slowed down, until he finally stopped and lay still. When the kids began to cheer, he did one last twitch.

Harmony and Mello and I sheathed our swords and grabbed each other's hands. We each put a foot on Lamont's back to symbolize our triumph, and we raised our hands and eyes to God in praise.

The children stood up and clapped and yelled. It was way fabulous.

We finished out the concert in our superhero suits. Afterward, we gave away the toys. The kids loved them. I guess they don't have as many toys as most kids in the States. We also signed autographs for the kids and took pictures with them. I figured if I couldn't take the kids home, at least I could take their pictures with me. And as I looked into their eyes and drank in their smiles, I knew they would always have a place in my heart.

I asked Sasha if we were going to go to any more orphanages. He said, "Indeed, I do not believe we will today." And when I asked where we were going next, he just walked away.

Back in the van, Harmony said, "I love those kids! I want them all!"

"Me too," Mello agreed.

"What's next, Trin?" Lamont asked. "Do we have another concert today?"

I couldn't tell if he was serious or if he just wanted to torture me into admitting I didn't have a clue.

chapter • 9

...

The van pulled up in front of a tall building, and I dashed to get to Sasha the moment he got out.

"Are we doing a concert here?"

"Nyet," he answered.

"What are we doing, then?" I asked, determined to get a handle on this thing, language barrier or not.

"Verily, you are going to give the supplies you brought," he answered.

I looked up at the building. "Is this a hospital?"

"Indeed, it is."

Sweet! I had information. I opened the door of the van and stuck my head in.

"OK, everybody, listen up," I said. "This is a hospital, and we're going to take in the medical supplies we brought."

"Are we doing a concert?" Mello asked.

A question I could answer! "No concert," I said with a smile.

"But we're dressed in our superhero suits," Harmony pointed out.

Why hadn't I realized that?

"I'm not going into a hospital dressed like this," Mello complained.

I looked down at my white outfit. "Of course not. We're going to put our other clothes back on over these." I climbed in and grabbed my clothes. We grunted and groaned as we struggled to get our stuff on in the crowded van.

Finally dressed, we got out. Lamont and Sasha had already lined up the boxes of supplies on the sidewalk.

I said, "Each of you grab a box." We followed Pastor Kovitch inside. He shook hands with some important-looking people, and soon we were surrounded by doctors and nurses who talked loudly and looked through the boxes we held.

One nurse picked up a bottle of aspirin and held it high, calling out words in Russian. Everyone murmured happily. They reminded me of little kids at Christmas.

A doctor finally took my box from me. He looked at me with tears running down his face and said, "Spah-see-bah!"

I swallowed a lump in my throat and said, "You're welcome." I couldn't even remember how to say it in Russian. I felt overwhelmed. I couldn't imagine what it would be like to run a hospital without basic stuff like aspirin.

I remembered that I hadn't liked the idea of bringing medical supplies—or toys—when Harmony and Mello suggested it. I hadn't wanted to mess with it. Now I just wished I had brought more.

One of the important-looking men called for everyone's attention. He spoke in a loud voice. When he finished, everyone looked at us and cheered.

Sasha explained, "He said you are a group called Chosen Girls, rock stars from America, traveling in Russia doing concerts. He said you thought of us before you ever left your country and gathered up these supplies for our hospital. He said you are more than rock stars. You are heroes!"

I looked down, embarrassed. I could see the legs of my superhero suit sticking out below my cropped pants. If they could see my cruddy attitude, they'd know why I didn't much feel like a hero.

We went back to our village. After we changed clothes, Mrs. Kovitch signaled that the three of us should follow her. She took little Andrei by the hand and walked out the door.

Harmony said, "Where are we going, Trin?"

"Why are you asking me?" I snapped, walking out behind the pastor's wife. "Why does everyone always ask me?"

Mello followed and said, "Because you act like you know everything."

I rolled my eyes. "Whatever."

"Whatever?" Mello echoed. "You want so bad to be in charge. You've been in charge of everything your whole life, haven't you? You took control of Harmony and me the week you moved to California."

I said, "What? I took control of you?"

"Who started the band? Who entered us in the contest?"

"So I suggested we might enter a contest, and you think—"

Mello stomped along behind Mrs. Kovitch and Andrei. "Suggested. Right. Just like you *suggested* coming to Russia."

"Are you saying you wish we didn't have a band?" I asked.

"That's not what I'm saying," Mello answered.

"So you wish we hadn't come to Russia?" I continued.

Mello shook her head. "I love it here. I'm definitely glad we came."

I stopped walking and put my hands on my hips. "I don't get you, Mello. If you're glad about Chosen Girls and you're glad about the trip, what are you griping about?"

Mello ignored me and turned to Harmony. "If you take away the control freak's control, what do you have?"

Harmony said, "Come on, Mello. Quit."

"Just a freak!" Mello said, answering her own riddle and whirling toward me. "Am I right, Trin? You can't stand it here because it's the first time in your life you aren't in control."

"You're just jealous," I snapped back. "You're always in the background. You say you like it there. But really, I think you want to be like me. You wish you could get things done. Well, I'm sorry, but I'm not letting you—or Pastor Kovitch—ruin this trip."

I turned away from her and followed Mrs. Kovitch down the street again. "Talk about a person who thinks she knows everything," I muttered. Mrs. Kovitch and her son went inside a little shop and we went in after them.

Harmony pointed to a large photograph on the wall—a picture of an ice-cream sundae. "Look, Mello! Look, Trin!" she said happily. "This is an ice-cream shop. No fighting in here, *amigas*. Just ice cream and happy times, OK?"

I sat in silence and watched little Andrei eat his ice cream. He got a drop of it on the end of his nose, and he giggled and giggled. I laughed too. But then I started thinking about him growing up with all that radiation, and my eyes got teary. Then I thought at least he had a family—not like the kids at the orphanage.

I couldn't stop the tears. They just kept running down my face. I used my napkin and tried to turn away so no one would see me.

Mrs. Kovitch looked worried. I'm sure she wondered what my deal was — she takes me out for ice cream and I cry the whole time.

Mello thought it was her fault. "I'm sorry, Trin," she said. "I should have kept my mouth shut about the control thing."

"It's not that," I said. "He got ice cream on his nose and it made me think about radiation and that made me think about the orphans and—" I stopped long enough to start sobbing. "It's all just . . . so . . . sad!" I put my arms on the table and buried my head in them. I could feel Harmony and Mello patting my shaking shoulders. I felt like an idiot. An absolute, double-scoop, deluxe idiot.

Then I felt little Andrei's arms reaching around my neck. I turned and gathered him up, and held him while I cried. He used his chubby little fingers to wipe the tears off my face, which of course made me cry all over again.

By the time I pulled myself together, my ice cream had melted. I scooped up the strawberry-flavored milk with my spoon and slurped it. Then I managed a weak smile and a *spah-see-ba* for Mrs. Kovitch.

Harmony echoed my thanks, and I didn't even care that Mello wouldn't meet my eyes.

chapter • 10

...

The next day we drove up in front of a huge brick auditorium with people filing inside.

"Look! The doors are open!" Harmony said. "We'll be able to plug in!"

Mello looked terrified. "So many people! I bet that place could hold thousands."

I whipped out a compact and checked my hair in the little mirror. "OK, this is going to be the concert we were meant to give," I said. I handed the mirror to Harmony. "I'm in charge and nothing is going to go wrong. You primp while I go over the details. Same format as the orphanage. We'll do the skit after 'You've Chosen Me.' I'm way glad we'll have juice this time." I turned to Lamont. "You're sure the electrical converters are good to go?"

"No problem," he answered. "We have some of the biggest ones they make."

"Mello, you don't have the blue hair stuff in the van, do you?"

"No," she said. "But I just sprayed it this morning."

"I think it could use more," I told her. "You feeling okay about the electric drum set?"

"Definitely. I'm getting used to it. But I did like that bongo the other day," she answered. "It felt very back-to-nature to beat something with my hands."

Lamont said, "OK, Nature Woman, remind me to never put a real drum in your hands again."

"Harmony, don't forget we switched the Russian song to *G.*"

"Sí," Harmony answered. "Cool frijoles! I'm ready to rock."

I opened the van door. "Everybody is responsible for their own equipment," I reminded them. "It looks like we could be on any time now. Grab your stuff and let's go!"

I ran around and opened the back of the van. I reached for my guitar, but Sasha said, "Nyet. You shall not be needing to carry your equipment."

"It's okay, Sasha, we're used to it," I explained. "Besides, Joel and Lamont will help. This is a performance, right?"

"Nyet. Well, dah," he said. "Verily, I say unto you, it is a performance, but—"

I rolled my eyes. "We don't have time to verily right now, Sasha. I'm trying to run this band, and you aren't helping me any. We're obviously late for this concert, so we've got to hurry! Harmony, grab your guitar and an amp. Mello, grab your drums and an amp. Lamont and Joel, get everything else."

I took my stuff and started running for the building. I could hear the others coming behind me.

People walking into the building stopped to stare at us. I figured it must be way obvious we were the American band

they were coming to see. Between my pink hair, Mello's blue hair, and our wildest clothes, we for sure didn't blend into the crowd.

All the Russians wore browns or blacks and totally subdued styles. We even passed a group of girls in black dresses. Lamont said, "They sure get dressed up for rock concerts over here."

I called over my shoulder, "I guess it's a big deal. I wish we had time to sign autographs!"

Harmony said, "We'll have time afterward. Let's get set up."

We headed into the building and straight down the aisles, past hundreds of people who were already seated.

"Gorgeous auditorium," Mello huffed as we jogged up the steps and onto the stage.

"I'm not really in the mood to appreciate the architecture," I snapped. "I hate this. Why couldn't they get us here in time to set up?"

"Nothing like tuning up in front of hundreds of people," Harmony agreed.

Lamont helped me plug in my amp and guitar with the converters. Joel, of course, helped Harmony. I strummed a chord and smiled as the sound filled the building. It would be great to finally do a real concert in a real concert hall.

I looked around while I tuned. I noticed Pastor Kovitch in a heated discussion with a man in a suit. The man pointed to us and said something. He didn't look at all happy.

I said, "Look, the pastor is getting in trouble for bringing us so late. But we're going to be so awesome that everyone forgets about it. Got it?"

"Definitely," Mello agreed as she warmed up on her drums with a roll on the snare and a few cymbal crashes.

Harmony played a bass pattern and said, "There's Sasha."

Sasha joined the discussion with Pastor Kovitch. Then he headed toward us, practically running.

"Lamont, Joel, get off the stage," I said. "It looks like Sasha is coming to introduce us."

Lamont smiled. "We finished just in time," he said.

Sasha dashed up the steps.

I flashed him my biggest smile. "Bet you never saw a band set up this fast, did you? We're ready."

His face turned red. He nodded, took a big breath, and nodded again. "Verily, I say unto you, you set up very fast, but—"

"So introduce us," I said. "We're ready to rock, and those people out there look like they're ready for a concert."

"They are ready," Sasha said, stopping to lick his lips, "for a choral youth competition."

"A choir contest?" Harmony asked. "We're a rock band. What are we doing at a choir contest?"

"Unfortunately," Sasha answered, "I am utterly unable to answer that question. I tried to tell you not to bring your equipment, but you did not listen unto me." He drilled little holes into my eyeballs.

"You mean, the Chosen Girls aren't performing here?" Mello asked. That familiar look of panic and embarrassment covered her face.

Sasha smiled and nodded, obviously relieved. "Indeed! The Chosen Girls are part of the audience today." He pointed to the hundreds—maybe thousands—of people in the auditorium. "The Chosen Girls shall sit and enjoy the Russian choirs." He looked at the man in the suit, who now waited, arms crossed, in the wings. A group of about twenty Russian

young people stood behind him — the girls in long black dresses, the boys in white dress shirts and black pants. "You shall remove your equipment now, yes?" Sasha finished.

I wanted to run backstage and hide, or take the next plane home to America. But instead we quickly, quietly cleared the stage and took our seats.

I scrunched down in my seat beside Mom as the first performers filed onto the stage.

"Don't they look cultured, standing straight and tall in those long black dresses? They are so classy," Mom whispered. I looked down at my pink lace-up shirt and cropped pants, and tucked my high-heeled boots under my seat.

"Aren't they amazing?" Mom said while we clapped for the fourth choir. "That's true talent! They must study classical music for years to sing like that."

She might as well have said, *Not like your band, Trin, that just gets together in some garage shed and makes stuff up.*

The sad song the next choir sang matched my mood. My big attempt to run the band went way beyond disaster, and Mom picked the worst possible place to tell me I'm not truly talented or classy.

"Why do all their songs sound sad?" Mello whispered. "Everything is in a minor key."

"I don't know," I whispered back. "Maybe because life stunk here for so long. Or maybe they're sad for us, since we just embarrassed ourselves so completely."

While the man in the suit announced the winners, Lamont leaned over. "Maybe the Chosen Girls will win for shortest performance. Are you still sticking around to sign autographs?" he asked.

I stuck my tongue out at him.

•••

Pastor Kovitch's church choir won the whole thing. He came around, beaming and shaking hands. He looked so happy I guess he forgave us for almost bombing the entire competition. And the choir members kept coming up, shaking our hands and trying to talk to us. You'd have thought we really did do a concert instead of just humiliating ourselves.

We finally got out our Russian-English dictionaries and attempted some conversations. Of course, Sasha got in the mix too. I mostly talked to Natalia, a tall girl with long blonde hair. She said she loved my hair and my clothes, so I felt a little better. I told her congrats on winning the contest, and she smiled a huge smile.

I saw Mom watching Natalia and me. I wondered if she wished she could switch us out—leave me in Russia and take quiet, classy, award-winning Natalia home.

I decided I wouldn't blame her if she did.

chapter • 11

...

I couldn't decide who I was most mad at—myself for rushing onto a stage we didn't belong on, the pastor for not revealing one plan ever, or Sasha for just verily getting "unto" my last nerve. Mello and Harmony obviously didn't feel my pain.

"You're amazing, Trin," Harmony began as soon as we got back to the pastor's house. "I didn't *think* I could ever be more embarrassed than the day I took us to the wrong park, and then I *knew* I'd never be more embarrassed than when we did a concert in chicken suits. But you managed to show me up."

"You got that right," Mello agreed. "Setting up for a concert in front of a thousand people waiting for a classical music competition!" She looked in the hall mirror and added, "And I'm dressed like this! And my hair is blue!"

"Would you get over your blue hair?" I sputtered.

Harmony crossed her arms. "It was bad, Trin. Seriously. I mean, I know I don't have much room to talk. I've made my share of mistakes. But, wow! That was a big one."

I sat down and started unlacing my boots. "Raise your hand if you think it must be fun to be you," I said. "Just along for the ride, enjoying the countryside. You don't have the pressure of coordinating this trip, Harmony. You either, Mello. All you two have to do is go where you're told. So why don't you get off my back? I'm doing the best I can."

"In what way?" Mello asked, sitting on the floor to pull off her own boots. "Not to be rude, but how exactly are you coordinating this trip? You don't have a clue what we're doing."

"Sí," Harmony agreed. "I don't think you know any more than we do."

I jumped up off the couch. "Ohwow. That's it." I stomped out of the room.

"Where are you going?" Harmony called.

I looked back at her. "To find the pastor."

Pastor Kovitch sat at the table in the kitchen, reading a newspaper.

I said, "Excuse me. May I speak to you, please?"

He looked up and smiled. He said, "Welcome."

I groaned. How could I find out what I needed to know? I pulled my little English-Russian dictionary out of my pocket. I tried to find *plan*. I couldn't find it. I did find *I learn*, so I said that: "Ee-zoo-chah-yoo." Then I flipped the pages until I found *tomorrow*: "zhav-tra." That was as close as I could get to saying, "I want to learn what we're doing tomorrow."

He smiled and said, "Hah-ra-shoh."

That means *good*.

Maybe he thought I meant I would learn something tomorrow. Like not to run up onto the stage when I wasn't supposed to.

Argh!

I looked around the kitchen. Mrs. Kovitch stood at the sink peeling potatoes, with little Andrei at her feet. I asked, "Sasha?"

The pastor spilled out a stream of Russian. At the end of it he pointed to me and said, "*Mhat.* Mama?"

I said, "Is Sasha at the house my mom's staying at? Is that what you're saying? Can I go get him so he can translate?"

The pastor smiled and shook his head. He said something to his wife and she turned around and shrugged. I tried again. I pointed to myself and said, "Mhat." Then I pointed in the direction of the house she was in. "Sasha." And I pointed toward that house again.

"Dah!" the pastor and his wife both said. "Dah, dah!"

I smiled and said, "I'll go get him. I'll be right back."

I ran down the street and found the right house. I knocked on the door and asked for Sasha. I couldn't believe how relieved I felt to see him. "Sasha, can you come translate, please? I'm trying to speak to the pastor," I explained.

"Indeed!" he answered. "I say unto you, I will be pleased to help you on this day."

• • •

Back in the Kovitch kitchen I whipped out my PDA, flipped it on, and said, "I want to know what we are doing tomorrow, please."

Sasha looked like the question hurt him. He spoke to the pastor, who also didn't look excited about it. After the pastor

answered, Sasha said, "Verily, I say unto you, tomorrow should be a good day for you and your friends."

I clenched my fists and took a deep breath before I said, "Sasha, that's not what I want to hear and you know it. Tell me exactly what we are doing tomorrow. I want the names of the villages we're going to and the times we'll be at each one. And I want to know if we're doing concerts or greeting orphans or listening to Russian choirs. Now!"

Sasha didn't even repeat my questions to the pastor. He said, "Indeed, the pastor will not answer these questions."

I felt tears running down my face. "But why not? Why is everything a secret? Why can't he tell me what's going on? Ohwow, it's making me crazy!"

The pastor said something to Sasha, and they started a whole big conversation in Russian. Mrs. Kovitch got into it too. I think maybe she felt sorry for me. I hoped she would tell her husband to give it up and let me in on the details.

Finally, Sasha turned back to me. "Verily I say unto you, the Americans are sometimes different from the Russians, dah?"

"Well, now, there's something we can agree on, Sasha," I said.

"In your country, it is important to be on time I think, and to have a plan," he continued.

I nodded. "Of course," I agreed.

Sasha nodded. "Pastor Kovitch has plans, yes, but the Lord may change those plans, dah?" he explained. "In Russia, many, *many* times things do not go as we plan them to. We do not like to disappoint our guests from America if these plans must change. So Pastor asks, please, that you trust him. He has made good plans for you. You trust him, and he will trust the Lord, dah?"

I sank down onto a kitchen chair. So that was it. I was defeated.

Sasha patted my shoulder. "I think it is very difficult for you to trust others, dah? Perhaps you like very much to be in control of things?"

I put my face in my hands and mumbled, "Dah."

After supper, Mrs. Kovitch led us back out to the banya. When we were all wrapped in our towels and the steamy mist, I told Mello and Harmony the bad news.

"I'm sorry. I'm a failure. I absolutely demanded Pastor Kovitch tell me tomorrow's plans, but he wouldn't." I wiped a washcloth across my sweaty face. "You're both right. I don't have clue one about what we're doing."

Harmony gave my shoulder a squeeze. "That doesn't make you a failure, Trin," she said.

I looked at her in surprise. "Of course it does. Raise your hand if you think a leader needs to know what's going on in order to lead."

Mello shook her head and said, "Sometimes a leader just needs to know who to follow. Maybe on this trip, we should just trust Pastor Kovitch to show us what to do."

"That's exactly what he said," I told her. "That he wants us to trust him, as he trusts the Lord."

"Is that so bad?" Harmony asked.

"Yes, it is! I don't know what we're doing tomorrow!" I shouted.

Harmony said, "OK, Trin, what if I told you I had the scoop?"

"No way."

"Just listen," she continued. "We're going to Dharstvenyee at 9:00 a.m. to do a concert in a concert hall. At noon, we'll

do another concert in Kahkboda, and the people there will serve us lunch afterward. Then at 3:00 p.m. we'll do one last concert at a church in Skhabyanoy. Do you feel better now?"

"Ohwow, yes. But how did you find all that out? Did you listen to Pastor and Sasha through the wall or something?" I asked.

"Wait," Harmony continued. "Now tell me how to get to that first village — the one that starts with a *d*."

I laughed at her. "Yeah, right."

"OK," she said, "how about the other two? Do you know where they are?"

"No. Do you?" I asked.

"Nope," she answered. "So how does knowing the plan really help us? If the van broke down or the pastor got sick, it's not like we'd know how to get there."

"Your point is?" I asked.

"I get it," Mello interrupted. "Even if you know the plan, you aren't in control, Trin. None of us are. Not even when it's stored in a PDA. We just don't know enough to take charge. That's why the pastor is asking us to trust him."

"But it's so hard!" I complained. "I'd rather do it myself."

"Remember what happened when you did?" Harmony reminded me. "Disaster at the choir contest."

"Do you see what this is?" Mello asked. "This is a total life lesson, happening right here in the Russian banya."

Harmony made a face at her and said, "What?"

"This isn't just about control during the Russia trip. This is about who will control our whole lives. Get it? We're just as clueless bumbling through life as we are about getting around in Russia," she said. "Over here, the pastor knows the

language and the places, and we can trust him to make the plans for us."

"I get it!" Harmony blurted out. "In life, God is the one who has it all figured out. We can run around trying to be in charge—"

"And make stupid mistakes," I added.

"Or we can trust God with the plans," Harmony finished.

"Ohwow. You're right, Mello. This is way deep."

"This is totally like the verse I found last week," Harmony said. "I tried to memorize it. It's Jeremiah, for sure, but I'm not sure about the numbers. I'm thinking 29:11. 'For I know the plans I have for you ... plans to ...'" She stopped. "What's the rest? Something about help."

I smiled and finished the verse for her. "Plans to prosper you and not to harm you, plans to give you hope and a future."

Harmony looked surprised. "You know that verse?"

I looked up at the ceiling of the banya and took a big breath. "I know it, yeah. Living it is something else."

We sat quietly for a few minutes, watching the steam rise.

"Hey," I asked, "does that mean we aren't really going to Dobraykatooey or wherever it was?"

"Sí," Harmony answered. "I made all that up to teach you a lesson."

"I should beat you up," I said.

Harmony laughed. "Try it. You're forgetting I'm a blue belt in karate."

"It doesn't matter. I can't move," I said.

"No kidding," Mello agreed. "The banya is working wonders. I'm so relaxed I'm about to pass out. We should probably go back in the house."

"Can we pray first?" I asked quietly.

"*Bueno* idea," Harmony said, reaching for my hand. She bowed her head and prayed, "God, this trip has been cool frijoles. But it's also been hard. We don't know the language and we don't know what to expect from one minute to the next. Help us trust Pastor Kovitch and follow his lead. Help us relax and enjoy the days we have left. And help us trust you."

Mello added, "God, you are so good to let us come here. It's been just excellent. But we do need your help. It's stressful! Guide Pastor Kovitch as he makes plans for us. Help us follow his lead, and help us follow you."

I felt tears running down my face. At first when I opened my mouth, my voice didn't work. I cleared my throat and said, "God, my friends are right. It's hard for me to trust Pastor Kovitch. I want to be in control. But I can't. Help me let go." I took a deep breath. "Not just of the trip. I want you to take control of everything—my whole life. Amen."

Harmony and Mello threw their sweaty arms around me.

Mello said, "There has to be a song in this."

"I wish I had your talent for putting my feelings into words," I told her. "I'd love to be able to describe how I feel right now."

Mello closed her eyes and leaned against the wall for a minute.

"If only I knew what you help me to know," she said, "I would have been here a long time ago ..." Just in those first few words, I knew Mello's heart was totally about our next big song.

Harmony interrupted, "Wait, wait ... listen: Make me worthy of this journey. Pick me up so I can see where I been ain't where I'm going." And I knew we had a chorus and the bridge.

The three of us worked together until we had verses and a tune.

"We have got to go in and try this with instruments!" Harmony said.

I looked around the banya before we left. I wanted to remember it clearly—the place where I gave it all to God.

"So anyway, what do you think we'll do tomorrow?" Harmony asked as we opened the door and the cold air blasted over us.

I looked at her in amazement. Hadn't we just had an hour talk about that? I jabbed her with my elbow and said, "You are so, so lucky you are a blue belt."

chapter • 12

• • •

The next morning Sasha told all of us to load everything we brought to Russia into the van, and he took off driving. We finally stopped in front of a big building that looked like a school. A bus parked beside us.

Harmony said, "Look! It's the Russian choir!"

"Maybe they're doing the concert today," Mello said.

We climbed out of the van and I went to find Natalia. She laughed when she saw me and gave me a big hug. I pulled out my Russian-English dictionary and we started trying to talk.

Then Sasha walked up and said, "Verily, I say unto you, you should get your equipment set up."

"So the Chosen Girls are doing the concert?" I asked.

Sasha smiled. "Indeed, the Chosen Girls will do a concert with the Russian choir."

I wanted to panic. Our rock band and their classical choir? How would that work?

I told Natalia I had to go, and I went to the van to get my stuff. Harmony, Mello, Lamont, and Joel were there too. I said, "Hey, did you hear the news? We're doing this concert with the Russian choir."

Harmony said, "I don't see that working very well. We don't speak Russian. How can we do songs with them? Or do they do songs, then we do songs?"

"Or do we go first?" Mello asked. "And then they wrap it up?"

"Don't freak," I reminded them. "God's in charge. Let's talk to him about it, OK?"

We all grabbed hands. I prayed, "God, this day belongs to you, and we belong to you. We choose to trust you to make this concert what you want it to be. Amen." I said, "Let's set up and see what happens."

Once we were onstage and tuned up, Sasha came over with the choir director. "This is Nickolai Petrohvna. He leads the choir, and he wants very much we shall plan together today's concert."

I smiled at Nickolai. "Sweet. Let's plan."

Sasha said, "I am not sure why you say, 'sweet.'"

"*Har-ah-shor*," I corrected. "Good."

Sasha nodded and said, "Nickolai likes for the choir to sing first, maybe four songs."

We nodded.

"Then the Chosen Girls sing maybe three, and do the drama about prayer?"

We nodded again.

"And then he likes the choir to sing together with the Chosen Girls, the song you sing in Russian—the Lord's Prayer."

Harmony blurted, "Cool frijoles!"

Sasha asked, "What is this *frijoles*?"

"It means *beans* in Spanish," Mello said with a giggle.

"So you want cold beans?" Sasha asked. "I will check on that. I think we will not eat, though, until after the concert."

Harmony shot a look at Mello. "Don't confuse the poor guy," she said. Then she turned to Sasha. "*Cool frijoles* means *good*—har-ah-shor."

He smiled and said, "Oh, it becomes clear to me. So everyone is happy with the plan?"

We told him we were.

Sasha nodded and in his serious voice said, "Sweet. Sweet, cold beans!"

• • •

We stayed backstage while the choir sang. Their music, of course, was way fabulous.

I had mixed feelings about being in the same concert as Natalia's group. I thought about my mom in the audience, wishing her daughter sang and dressed like the choir members. I whispered to Mello, "They make me feel kind of shallow or untalented or something."

Mello looked totally surprised. "No way! Are you forgetting God called you? He made you the way you are, Trin—from the songs he gives you down to the way you dress."

After the choir, Pastor Kovitch spoke to the audience for a while. Then he introduced us, and the crowd clapped so loud you'd have thought we were U2 or something.

During the first song, I kept looking at Natalia in the front row. I tried to stand up straight and tall, and sing in a little more professional voice. I toned down my guitar a lot too.

Harmony stared me down, but I just smiled at her and kept singing. After the song, she ran over to me while everyone clapped for us. "Please, Trin, the Chosen Girls are a rock band, not a classical choir. You're ruining everything."

Then she ran back to her place.

The next song was "You've Chosen Me." It's based partly on my life verse, John 15:16. I think about the verse every time we sing the song. The verse says, "You did not choose me, but I chose you and appointed you to go and bear fruit—fruit that will last. Then the Father will give you whatever you ask in my name."

When I moved to California, it helped so much to know God chose me. Maybe now God was using Natalia and the whole Russia trip to remind me that he chose me—*me*: loud, bossy, bold, pink-haired, rock-star Trin.

If I could trust him with my future, why couldn't I trust him to make me who he wanted me to be?

I smiled as I sang to him. I let my body move to the music, I let my voice soar, and I let it rip on my guitar. After the song I looked at Harmony. She gave me a thumbs-up. I felt like God was giving me a big thumbs-up too.

For our third song, we sang the new one we'd made up in the banya. We called it "Top of the World," and writing it had ripped all the way into my soul. The second verse was totally my own work and I loved how it summed up our whole Russia experience:

Doesn't it seem strange
How quickly things can change
When you're ready to open your heart.
I just can't keep it down.
Gotta shout it out.

Find more ways to give praise to you, God.
Help me to spread your word
Till every soul has heard,
'Cuz I wanna be here.
Yeah, I wanna come through
And I wanna reach out,
And I wanna be true.

I couldn't help smiling through the whole song.

Next we did the drama about the power of prayer. The adults surprised me by loving it as much as the kids at the orphanage had.

When the time came for the closing song, the choir filed back up onto the stage and stood on either side of us. We sang the Lord's Prayer in English the first time, then the choir sang it in Russian. We closed by singing it in Russian together. I couldn't believe how fabulous it sounded. I got chill bumps all over — singing in Russian with a Russian choir. Way cool.

After the concert, we gave away New Testaments again — hundreds of them. I hoped the people would actually go home and read them. I felt that same urge to tell them what a difference God can make. Could they understand enough from our concert?

When the last person in line had a Bible, Sasha hurried us back into the van. This time we followed the bus to another village. On the way, Sasha turned around and said, "Surely you can do the same thing once again, dah? Another concert with the choir?"

"Dah," I answered. "That will be sweet."

•••

The second concert went even better, maybe because I didn't compare myself to Natalia. And afterward some old people fed us. Ohwow, loads of food.

As I dug into my second helping of potatoes, Mello whispered, "Remember what Pastor Kovitch said about the food? That there's so much of it because of the radiation?"

I almost choked. Instead I swallowed, smiled, and said, "Another chance to trust God, huh?"

Harmony giggled and I looked at her. "Hey, this day is going just like you said it would, Harmony. Two concerts and a lunch. If we do another concert after this, I'll never believe you were making all that up."

Right then Sasha walked up. "Verily I say unto you, we have today one more event. You must make yourself ready to go."

Harmony laughed so hard, tea shot out her nose. Hot tea. When she could talk again she said, "It's a fluke, I promise. I really didn't know what we were doing. I still don't."

• • •

Mello and Harmony fell asleep after lunch as the van bumped along the dirt roads. When we stopped, it looked like we were in the middle of nowhere.

"Sasha, are we back in the dead zone?" I asked as I climbed out.

He smiled. "Indeed, no, this is a place of much beauty," he answered.

The choir bus pulled in next to our van, and Natalia climbed out. She grabbed my hand and pulled me over a grassy hill, with everyone else following. On the other side, a huge banner said, in English, "Thank you, Chosen Girls!"

"Verily I say unto you," Sasha began, "the pastor wants we shall all gather beside the lake." He pointed to an area where a few people stood, waiting.

Joel said, "Hey! What's my dad doing here?"

"Look, Trin!" Harmony yelled. "There's your dad too!" Mom practically ran to him. They kissed, and then put their arms around each other. I snuck up behind Dad to give him a hug, but when I got close enough to hear Mom, I froze.

"You won't believe what Trin did on this trip," Mom said. *Uh-oh*, I thought. *Here comes the choir contest story.* "She made friends with a beautiful Russian girl named Natalia."

Oh. Not the contest, I thought, completely freaking out. *Mom's going to tell him all about Miss Perfect Natalia.* I shouldn't torture myself, but I couldn't help it. I plopped on a nearby blanket with a sigh, willing myself not to listen but unable to avoid it.

"She amazed me," Mom bubbled. "How could she reach out to someone she couldn't even communicate with? But you know our Trin. She had her little dictionary and gave it her best shot. I wish you could have seen her!"

I stared at my knees. Was she talking about me? *I amazed her?*

"And onstage!" Mom went on. "Such a presence. I would have died to get up in front of maybe a thousand people in another country. But Trin just sings as if it's only her and God. It's beautiful. Jeff, I thought my heart would burst through my chest."

"She's quite a girl." That deep voice belonged to Joel's dad. "You've done a fine job raising her." I had to look up. And I blinked to make sure I was actually awake.

"Oh, thanks. But I certainly can't take the credit," Mom answered. "Trin's nothing like me. I wish I had her exuberance . . . her charm. I'm a wallflower, myself."

"A very charming wallflower," Dad said, leaning down to kiss Mom on the forehead.

I stood up, wiped away a tear, and cleared my throat. "Enough smooching," I said. I pushed my way between Mom and Dad, looked up at Dad, and said, "It's so good to see you!"

"You too, Trin," Dad said as Pastor Kovitch clapped his hands together three times. Everyone got quiet and sat on blankets, logs, or large rocks. Joel, surprisingly, sat down right next to me.

Pastor Kovitch spoke to the crowd as Sasha repeated his speech in English.

Sasha translated, "When my friend told me an American rock band was coming, I felt nervous. I didn't know what kind of people they would be or what kind of message they would share. But I am so pleased that God led me to invite the Chosen Girls to Clinsky.

"This band has been a real help to our ministry. They brought medical supplies, which are a blessing to our local hospital. Some of the doctors and nurses who did not believe in God were very touched by this act of kindness from Christians.

"They brought toys to our orphans. When those children play with their new toys, they will remember the Chosen Girls. They will remember their music and the power of prayer.

"They drew people in — by the thousands — who would never have come to church to hear me preach. They shared

the good news, and allowed us to share the good news as well."

The crowd burst into applause, and I didn't notice the tears streaming down my face until Joel grinned and wiped them away with his thumb.

"And most importantly," Sasha translated, "they handed out Bibles. The Word of God is living and active. It will change the lives of those who read it."

"I would like to read a letter a young woman brought by our church this morning." Pastor Kovitch pulled a sheet of paper out of an envelope and held it up for everyone to see. Then he read the letter aloud.

Sasha translated,

> Pastor Kovitch,
>
> I want to tell you what happened to me yesterday. I was out of hope and miserable when I wandered by the city hall. I heard rock music, and I remembered the American band was playing.
>
> I love rock music, so I went inside. There weren't any empty seats, so I stood in the aisle.
>
> The Americans onstage looked so happy. They didn't look like the rock stars I've seen on TV. I wondered what made them different.
>
> I watched the lead singer—the girl with pink hair. She seemed very confident. And I knew enough English to know she was singing about God choosing her. I thought maybe that was what made her happy.

At the end of the concert, I took a Bible. I started reading in Matthew, and I couldn't stop. I stayed awake most the night, reading.

That's how I learned God has chosen me too. He sent his Son to die in my place, so I can belong to him.

I found the address of the church in the front of the Bible, and I am going to bring you this letter. And on Sunday, I will come to church to learn more about the God who loves me.

I wish you would please tell the Chosen Girls thank you for coming to Russia. Because of them, I now have hope.

Pastor Kovitch folded up the letter and put it back in the envelope. Then he pulled out a stack of envelopes and—while Sasha translated for us—said, "The letter I read is one of eighteen I have received since the Chosen Girls have been here. I'm sure there will be many more in the days to come." He looked right at us and said in Russian, "Spah-see-bah."

Our whole little group of Americans stood together later, talking about what an amazing good-bye party the Russians surprised us with.

"Thanks for letting Joel sit by you," Lamont whispered.

I looked at him in shock.

"Don't pretend you haven't noticed!" Lamont said. "He's tried to get near you this whole week."

"Me?" I asked. "Me?"

Mello interrupted us. "Um, what's Pastor Kovitch doing?"

We looked at him. He bent over and put his hand down, then stood up and held it out. Then he did it again. And again.

"He's finally cracked," Harmony whispered. "I think you put him over the edge, Trin."

"Me?" I asked. "Maybe the whole tour. The pressure of lining up all those concerts. Or maybe—ohwow—I bet it's the radiation! It finally got to be too much!" I looked at him and said, "I wonder if this can be reversed? What if we could get him to the States?"

Mrs. Kovitch looked at her husband, but she didn't look worried. She just smiled and held one fist up in front of her mouth. Then she started moving her lips, but no sound came out. She swayed back and forth.

"*No es bueno!*" Harmony cried. "They've both gone *loco*. I guess we can be glad this didn't happen days ago."

"But we can't just leave them like this," I said. "They have a child to take care of. Ohwow, does 9-1-1 work in Russia?"

Mello shook her head and smiled.

I looked at her in shock. "What are you smiling about? There is nothing happy about two wonderful people losing their mental abilities because they've chosen to serve God in a radiation-infested part of Russia."

"No, but there is something happy about two Russians thanking us for handing out Bibles and singing," Mello answered.

I looked back at Pastor Kovitch bending over, reaching down, and holding his hand out.

Then I looked at his wife holding her fist by her lips, mouthing words and swaying back and forth.

They smiled at us and said, "Spah-see-bah!"

Oh. I guess pantomime was *their* way of overcoming the language barrier too.

"Well, that's a relief!" I said. I smiled at them and said, "Pah-zhahl-oos-tah."

Sasha came over to say good-bye, and I freaked. I didn't have a good-bye gift. I ran back to the van, found my suitcase and dug around in it. I didn't have much left. Then my eyes fell on my Bible. It's a New International Version. Way easier than King James.

I pulled it out and flipped through it. I'd underlined all my favorite verses in it. Some of them had notes and dates in the margins — times God showed me something big. The most recent ones were from this trip. I bit my lip. Did I really want to let it go? I took a big breath and knew it was right.

I walked back over the hill and handed Sasha my favorite Bible.

"Hey, Sasha, I love the way you say 'verily' and 'unto you,' but if you want a Bible that sounds more like the way Americans talk, you might try this one."

He looked at the cover and read, "New International Version. I say unto you, Trin, I shall try to find one of these. I have noticed that the Chosen Girls do not speak in the same way I do, and I want to improve my English. Thank you for your suggestion, but I do not have a gift unto you." He tried to hand it back.

I shook my head and pushed it back into his hands. "Your English is fine, Sasha, and your gift was driving us everywhere and telling us what everyone said. But this is my Bible, and I've marked my favorite parts. I want you to have it, to remember me by."

His eyes got misty. He opened the Bible and looked through it. "Spah-see-bah," he finally whispered. Then he looked up and smiled and said "Ohwow, this is sweet, dah?"

I smiled back and said, "Verily."

When Sasha told us to get back in the van, I totally lost it. I hugged Natalia and cried my head off. I felt like an idiot—I had only known her for a few days. She kept saying, "Heaven," and pointing to the sky, then to me and her. That made me cry even harder—the sadness of knowing how long it would be until I'd see her again, and the sweetness of knowing I absolutely would see her again. And the next time, we would be able to understand each other, forever!

I got in the van and sat on something lumpy.

"Wait!" I yelled at Pastor Kovitch, who had already started the van. "I forgot!"

It was my pink nubby sweater—the one Natalia loved. I ran to the bus and banged on the windows, asking for her.

She finally came out, and I handed her the sweater. She started crying and talking to me in Russian. I think she felt bad about not having a gift for me. I shook my head and tried to tell her it didn't matter.

Then she smiled real big and put her hands behind her neck. She undid the cross necklace she had on, and reclasped it on me.

One last hug, and I ran back to the van. As we drove away, I put my hand to my chest and wrapped it around the crucifix that dangled there.

In Russia I learned about letting go ... but the cross? That's the one thing I'll always hang on to.

Chosen Girls

PRAYER
changes things.

g STUDIOS

SOLO ACT

zonderkidz

Created by Beth Michael
Written by Cheryl Crouch

chapter • 1

• • •

Thursday

My life used to be simple. All I needed: a good book and my fluffy fleece blanket.

Then everything changed with the Trinvasion. Since Trin Adams moved here and took over our lives, my best friend Harmony and I have never been the same.

Sure, I'm glad Trin talked us into being a rock band. I'm a real drummer now. But I don't like being out front, even though I can do it. Thankfully, I won't have to worry about that for a while.

Now summer's here, school's over, and my only scheduled gig is going to Surf & Sand City, where Harmony and I spend a week every year—huge cliffs overlooking the ocean, tons of cute boys, and time to read and do a whole bunch of nothing.

But best of all, no band, no work, and no Trin . . .

• • •

I had just rolled into my softest fleece throw and shuffled to my bookshelf to choose a book when my cell phone rang "La Bamba."

"Harmony?"

"Hello, Mello!" Harmony's voice blasted out at me. "Are you packed?"

"Packing."

"I knew it. Are you ready for some serious fun-o-rama?"

"I'm ready for some rest-o-rama, Harmony — picking out a novel as we speak."

I could practically hear her rolling her eyes.

"You've got to be the only teenager in Southern California who thinks a retreat at Surf & Sand City is about resting," she accused.

"You can do whatever you want," I answered. "You'll know where to find me."

"On your favorite cliff, reading a book," she said in her most disgusted voice.

I closed my eyes and pictured it. I could almost smell the ocean and feel the breeze. "Definitely."

"I can't believe we leave tomorrow. One o'clock, just like last year?"

"Definitely."

"And you signed us up to room together, right?"

"Definitely."

"Hasta mañana!"

I punched the End button on my phone. Before I even put it down, it rang again. But it wasn't "La Bamba."

"Hello?"

"May I please speak to Mello McMann?"

"This is she," I answered.

"Hello, this is David Karuthers. You know that I'm coordinating this year's retreat. Today I'm pulling together last-minute details at the office. Are you coming to choir practice tonight?" he asked in his bouncy voice.

"Yes," I answered, trying to figure out what choir had to do with anything.

"Do you think your friend Harmony could come with you? And maybe you could come early? I'd like to speak to the two of you about the trip."

I paused before I answered. Was this about last year's retreat? The speaker's shoes hot-glued to the ceiling? Or the toothpaste on the pillows? Or maybe the water-balloon launcher?

If so, he needed to talk to Harmony, not me. Maybe it wasn't the best idea to invite her to join my youth group on this trip every year.

I said, "I think so. I'll call Harmony."

"Great. Meet me at the youth center at six thirty."

• • •

"If I was going to get in trouble for that stuff, don't you think it would have happened last year?" Harmony whispered as we walked up the church sidewalk.

I shrugged. "Maybe they found out something new. Maybe someone just now complained. How should I know?"

"So why do you have to be here? All you did last year was read."

I threw an arm around Harmony's shoulder. "I guess I'm guilty by association," I said with a groan.

We found Mr. Karuthers inside the youth center. He didn't look mad at all. He smiled real wide, bounced over to some chairs, and pulled three of them into a triangle.

"Here, girls, have a seat," he said. "Thanks for coming."

I looked at Harmony, and she raised her eyebrows. So far, so good.

"Mello, Harmony, I want this retreat to be a special time for everyone who attends. I know it's a good time to relax, but I think it should be more than that."

Harmony shot me a look. I felt like saying, "I don't think he's talking about pranks and water-balloon fights."

"Last night I went down the list of students who will be attending," he continued. "When I got to your names, I knew I had the answer I've been looking for!"

My heart started beating out a warning. I didn't want to be anyone's answer to anything. I wanted to hide on my cliff and read.

He smiled at us and asked, "How would the Chosen Girls like to do an outreach concert on the beach Saturday night?"

"Cool frijoles!" Harmony said, probably as much from relief about not being in trouble as from excitement about the concert.

I tried to process. One concert wouldn't be such a big deal. I would only lose one evening of downtime. But I would have to bring my drums. And Trin.

It wasn't what I had planned on.

Mr. Karuthers talked on and on about how all the campers could pass out flyers Friday. Loads of people would come. He said the concert would be a great opportunity for people to hear the positive message our band loved to share.

I started simmering inside. *I don't care if those people hear our message, Mr. Karuthers. I want to read my book, not do a concert.*

But I smiled and said, "Definitely, Mr. Karuthers. We'll check with Trin, but I'm sure she'll say yes. Can our sound-man come too?"

• • •

Lamont agreed immediately, offering to help with more than sound. He'd always wanted to go to Surf & Sand City. And Trin definitely said yes. Actually, she screamed, "Ohwow! Yes! Sweet! I can't wait! What should I pack?"

I knew Trin had been feeling left out since Harmony and I had planned to go without her. I finished packing and spent the rest of the night chatting online.

Trin: *ohwow — it's right on the beach?*

Harmony: *sí. muy bonita. bring sunscreen.*

Trin: *sand volleyball?*

Me: *n surfing lessons, horses, mountain biking*

Harmony: *LOL! like mello ever did any of that b4!!! but u will luv it, trin — just wait til u c the cabins. way cute*

Trin: *i can't wait. i just have 2 learn 2 surf!*

Lamont: *i haven't been on a board in months*

Me: *thx for the warning — we'll stay out of ur way*

Trin: *how many pairs of shoes r u bringing?*

Me: *2*

Lamont: *what does THAT matter?*

Harmony: *be quiet, Lamont. i packed 5*

Trin: *i think i can make it with 8*

Lamont: *we're only there a week. why do u need 8 pairs of shoes?*

Trin: *didn't some1 tell u 2 b quiet?*

I could see Harmony was psyched about Trin's going. Now she'd have someone to hang with. I should have been happy for her, since I just wanted to kick back. But instead I felt irritated.

• • •

Friday morning we met early at the shed behind my house. Harmony and I had used the shed as a playhouse for years, but now it serves as a studio. We needed to run through the songs and make sure we were all cool with the plan. Lamont joined us, since he lives right next door.

I did some rolls on the snare to warm up. Harmony got out her bass, and Trin started tuning her electric. I asked what song we should start with.

Trin looked past me, smiled her hugest smile, and said, "I can just imagine pounding to the edge of a cliff on the back of a black stallion, overlooking the Pacific Ocean—"

"Just don't run over Mello. She'll be sitting on that cliff, reading," Harmony said.

I shook my head. "If we don't get started, I'll never get to chill. We'll be practicing the whole time."

"Should I bring the camera?" Lamont asked. "I can tape the concert."

"A concert on the beach!" Harmony said. "It might be our biggest one yet. Sí, tape it!"

"But in order to do a concert, we'll have to know what song we're opening with," I reminded them. "Which brings us back to why we're here this—"

"Are we changing to superhero suits halfway through?" Harmony interrupted.

"Wait! I forgot to pack mine!" Trin said, already walking across the room. "And my white boots. Ohwow, I better go right now." She packed her guitar into the case. "And I forgot bracelets! I so am not good with last-minute packing."

"You definitely should do the super suits," Lamont said. "That's your trademark. It's what makes the Chosen Girls stand out. Either super suits or chicken suits."

Harmony whirled to face him. "The chicken disaster is over. Do not mention the chicken suits, the chicken concert, or the chicken jingle unless you want me to practice my newest karate move on you."

Lamont shut his mouth, but he started humming the tune for *Chik'n Quik / Chicken on a stick / It's so yummy for your tummy /Everybody loves Chik'n Quik.*

Harmony put her guitar on the couch and raised her arms to fighting position.

"You didn't say I couldn't hum!" Lamont cried, crossing his arms in front of his face in self-defense.

"What about our practice?" I asked Trin. "We didn't even run through one song."

"We'll have to do it when we get there," she said as she ran out the door. "See you at one!"

Harmony put her arms down, and Lamont sighed in mock relief. She grabbed her bass, put it in the case, and fastened the latches. "Know what? I forgot my new bracelets too!" she said. "And I think I should take my purple flip-flops." She moved toward the door.

"Harmony," I whined. "I don't want to spend the whole time we're there practicing for the concert."

She looked back at me. "Don't worry, Mello. We'll be fine," she said. Then she left too.

I looked at Lamont. "Please don't tell me you need to pack bracelets or flip-flops," I begged him.

He shrugged. "Nope. But I do need to get my camera and the charger and—"

"Fine!" I said. "Just go."

He walked toward the door and said, "Mello, the concert will be great. The Chosen Girls can do this with their eyes closed. What's wrong with you?"

I shook my head. I did know one thing—now that the Chosen Girls were officially involved, this retreat would be anything but downtime.

Double-Booked

Book Two • Softcover • ISBN O-310-71268-8

In *Double-Booked*, Harmony finds that a three-way friendship is challenging, with Trinity befriending a snobby clique and Melody all negative. Through a series of mistakes, Harmony unwittingly unites the two against her and learns that innocent comments hurt more than you think. Ultimately, the Chosen Girls are united again in time to sing for a crowd that really needs to hear what they have to say.

Solo Act

Book Four • Softcover • ISBN O-310-71270-X

Melody needs some downtime—and the summer youth retreat will really hit the spot! But a last-minute crisis at camp means an opportunity for the band to lead worship every morning, plus headline the camp's big beach concert and go to camp for free. Too busy and unhappy, Melody makes some selfish choices that result in the girls getting lost, sunburned, in trouble, and embarrassed. Can she pull out of the downward spiral before she ruins camp—and the band—completely?

zonderkidz

Overload

Book Seven • Softcover • ISBN 0-310-71273-4

Melody discovers a latent talent for
leadership that she never knew she had.
When she begins a grief recovery group
for kids like her, she loses her focus
on the work God is doing through the
Chosen Girls.

Reality Tour

Book Eight • Softcover • ISBN 0-310-71274-2

When the Chosen Girls go on their
first multi-city tour in a borrowed RV,
Harmony's messiness almost spoils their
final show. What's worse, she almost
blows her opportunity to witness to her
cousin Lucinda.

zonder**kidz**

zonder**kidz**.

We want to hear from you. Please send your comments
about this book to us in care of zreview@zondervan.com. Thank you.

Grand Rapids, MI 49530
www.zonderkidz.com

ZONDERVAN.com/
AUTHORTRACKER
follow your favorite authors